SOLOTRAMP

by

Eleanor Addy Binnings

Contents

SOLOTRAMP

Eleanor Addy Binnings

Voices of Experience, Denver CO

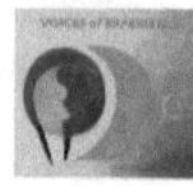

ISBN: 979-8-9876787-0-1

Imprint: Independently published

Cover design by: Eleanor Addy Binnings

Printed in the United States of America

PROLOGUE

Standing by the bedroom wall, her hands wrapped in white rope behind the board, the flash of Wally's camera blinded Micky. She closed her eyes and imagined the light fixture on the ceiling crashing down on his head.

Instead of going to the park last night to watch the public fireworks display, Wally had handed Micky a sparkler and lit it, saying, "Hold this to the sky and pray for the Lutheran Church. They just voted to allow women to be pastors."

They spent half of today in church and then dinner with Wally's friends who liked to talk about books she'd never heard of. Afterward, she waited in his red GTO in the shopping center while he went in to check on the recovering animals in his vet clinic. Wally was a veterinary surgeon. That night he tied her to the bloodwood plank again.

When he finished taking pictures, he untied her, pushed the bloodwood under the bed, and set the alarm clock to six for her to get up and make his breakfast.

He pulled his sex book out of his nightstand drawer and showed Micky a picture of a girl getting spanked. "You know this is what has to happen when a wife doesn't serve her husband. Because if she's not properly disciplined, she's on her way to hell. Her husband is obligated to save her." He tapped her forehead with his finger. "God's will."

Wally's wrong, she thought. People can get a divorce if their marriage doesn't work. Daddy didn't like Mama being an astrologer, so he got a divorce and built a cabin in the mountains.

Micky hadn't seen Mama since the night she ran away from home, more than two years ago. The last time she saw Daddy was eight years ago on her tenth birthday. She touched the star sapphire that Daddy had given her and wished on it for Wally to be done for the night.

"I've got a surgery in the morning," he said, answering her silent wish.

"Who is it?"

"That Great Pyrenees pup—patellar luxation."

"His knees, right?"

"Good. You're learning, Michaela." He knelt beside the bed. "Let's say our prayers."

Still in her garter belt and black stockings, she knelt. "Now I lay me down to sleep," he prayed. "Father, you know my worries and care for my troubles. I lay these situations at your feet. I will always be faithful. Amen."

"Amen," she said and got into bed next to him. "Good night," he said and gave her a kiss on her forehead in the same place he'd tapped.

She lay beside him close to the edge, keeping as much space between them as possible. Staring at the shiny points on the light fixture hanging from the middle of the ceiling, she imagined the bloodwood plank sliding out from under the bed and flying back to

Brazil like a magic carpet. Imagined the girl in Wally's book standing up and swinging her arm back and slapping the man spanking her with all her might.

Beside her Wally snored and made clicking sounds in his throat.

She prayed: *Please forgive me for feeling not only angry but doubtful of You. If You took my memory, it might be easier for me to be good.*

She counted past a thousand, trying to get to sleep, breathing in Wally's English Leather cologne that he sprayed all over himself on weekends.

She could hear fireworks go off in the distance.

Then God commanded her—a white blaze of light in her mind: *GO* blazing in white letters over a blue arrow pointing to the door.

Wally lay on his back, his eyes twitching, his snore like a growl, the click in his throat.

She lifted the sheet and slipped out of bed, edged down the dark hall to the laundry room. She felt around for the basket of clean clothes she'd brought in from the line yesterday but hadn't folded yet. Not bothering to take off the garter belt and stockings, she shook out her granny dress she found in the basket. Never mind it needed ironing, she yanked it over her head and sprinted into the living room and snatched her purse off the rosewood end table by the comfy lounge chair where she read her library books. In the kitchen, she opened the cupboard to get the Quaker Oats box where she stashed money. The coins jangled; she listened for Wally.

As silently as possible, she opened the screen door to the high-pitched choir of the crickets and slid her black-nyloned feet into the sneakers she'd gotten all muddy from watering her garden. The latch on the gate creaked. She froze and listened: Crickets chirping. Rumble of thunder. Distant siren. She closed the gate behind her and ran to the street and jumped into the Falcon Wally bought her two weeks ago—tossing onto the seat her patent leather black purse filled with a rat-tail comb, three pens, two pencils, driver's permit, Chapstick, Kleenex, library card, thirty dollars and eighty-seven cents from the Quaker oats carton—and the wad of clean clothes she'd grabbed from the basket. Raindrops splashed onto the windshield as she jammed the key into the ignition.

If she drove north, she would wind up in Wyoming—un-good memories.

If south, Pueblo—un-good memories.

She couldn't go to the neighborhood where she'd lived with Chaz and Floss before she met Wally. She might find someone she knew, but it would be the first place Wally would hunt her. She kept looking in the rear-view mirror dreading he was following—silly because all she could see were anonymous headlights.

She drove west, feeling trapped in the great outdoors, raindrops falling like enormous glistening tears on the windshield.

A glaring zigzag of lightning struck right in front of the car—and BOOM! She knew where to go: Of course! Into the mountains to Daddy's cabin.

Lightning lit up the Tastee Freez where Daddy used to buy giant ice cream cones for her and big brother Ty. The giant color TV sign flashed color by color until all colors lit. Fat raindrops dropped past the floodlights by the shopping mall; the wet street gleamed with neon signs shining rainbows into the puddles.

A sudden qualm—Daddy might not own the cabin anymore. But where else could she go? She had no one. Not back to Mama and her creepy boyfriend. Daddy disappeared eight years ago; her brother Ty was in the Army (most likely in Vietnam); Chaz was dead.

She had never spoken to Wally about the Golconda cabin. She'd be safe from him there. How had she let herself marry him? No, she wasn't going to provoke herself—just sing and drive. She turned on the radio but heard only static. The Falcon seemed intuitive about heading to the mountains, and for the first time in forever, she believed she made a good decision—going to a place she loved. The qualm faded, and she drove resolutely.

At first the road ran flat with a ridge of hills to the west. As she entered the mountains, the night grew darker. Steep, twisty, a drop-off on the right side of the road. She gripped the wheel and determined not to think of anything that could freak her out. She'd only been driving for a month.

She sang, "I Say a Little Prayer" over and over, like she did at Wally's house when he wasn't there because that song always made her think of Chaz. Never mind Chaz didn't believe in prayers, she liked to sing him one. Maybe now in heaven, he would like prayer. Or if he went to hell, maybe prayer could lift him out. If she didn't pretend she was forgetting him, Wally would smack her. Now driving, she could sing to Chaz freely.

The rain stopped. Now the lightning was behind, and she rolled down the window. The tires whirred on the road, and she burst into singing "Ain't No Mountain High Enough." She missed Chaz's voice singing with her. The dark clouds broke up. Still so dark, no moon. After many miles, she came upon a tall sign for a gas station she'd never seen before—the first light in miles and brand new, not open. "In the Summertime" caught in her throat because a new gas station meant she might be on the wrong road. But she kept driving and peering into the night for something familiar, and then whew, finally a sign said *Golconda 6 Miles*.

Strange. Beautiful. The stars took over the sky. She turned on a familiar gravelly road that would surely lead to the lane that led to the cabin. She jounced over the rocks and ridges, and there was Daddy's cabin, a dark spot on the hillside under the stars.

A wild thought passed through her mind that Daddy would be there, but the clearing was vacant, outlined by the mountains. The white sparkle of the sky shimmered. She listened to the rush of Gangue Creek tumbling over stones in the crevice across the meadow. Gazing at the glistening Milky Way just outside the windshield, a drape of peace surrounded her. She stretched out on the front seat of the Falcon.

When she woke at sunrise, flaming red clouds clustered at the top of Fire Peak. The chilly morning air felt fresh. In daylight, the cabin looked vacant, yet the qualm rose again that the cabin belonged to someone besides Daddy. At least no cars around. She went up to the porch and peeked in the window. It looked the same as it used to!!!

Everything was how she remembered. The knotty pine walls, the old furniture that had Daddy cussing when he brought the load here in an old truck he'd borrowed. The scratched wooden buffet that held unmatched dishes, the iron bedstead with the squeaky springs, the black and white striped mattress where Daddy would spread his sleeping bag. The chest filled with raggedy towels. The old green sofa with the same plushy, velvety texture the upholstery had eight years ago when she had her tenth birthday here. Everything the same as if Daddy had never disappeared and any second would come through the door and tell her to clean the fish he and Ty had caught.

To her enormous relief, when she tried the door, it swung open.

PART ONE

Journal of Michaela Isabel Abel

JULY 6, 1970—SUNRISE MONDAY

No one else will read this notebook. I'll write my secrets, and when I get them out of my mind, I will bury my diary of memories at the top of the Fire Peak trail beside the bristlecone pine.

For the first time since I've lived with Wally, I am home.

Writing freely in this notebook with no eyes scanning the page over my shoulder.

Singing at the top of my lungs.

Walking on the ground, not on eggshells.

I may not have a clue what I'm doing or what will happen, but I am free of Wally.

I'm home!

I don't want to be tied up. I never want a husband to take pictures of me dressed in nothing and tie me to a board again. I never knew marriage was about this! I don't want to ever be married again.

I want time to go on, never pressing me, just folding me up and carrying me along. I want the sun going down tonight to come up again in the morning and turn Fire Peak pink.

I want there to be nothing to hurt me, nothing to make me feel bad. Please, God. Let me lose my memories of troubles that make me anxious.

I want to figure out a way to fix it so I never go back to Denver.

I think I would kill myself if I had to keep living with Wally.

Thank you, God, for sending me here to the place I love most. Thank you for making my mind see your blue arrow with GO in sparkling white stars pointed at the door.

Thank you, God.

Guessing it's close to 6 a.m.

Wally won't be awake yet and noticing I'm gone. Every day at seven he takes his twenty-minute shower & another twenty minutes to wave his Liberace hairdo, using half a can of Adorn hairspray in front of the bathroom mirror. Once I stood by the door watching him spray a cloud over his waves and joked that he should give Governor Love hairdo directions. He set down the Adorn can and smacked me across the face. "You need to respect your elders."

"Or elders hit you?"

And he smacked me again, knocking me into the wall.

I've learned to keep silent most of the time. Every time I see a picture of Governor Love, I remember what it feels like to slam into the wall and crouch on the floor looking up at Wally.

When he comes out to the kitchen and I have not set out his breakfast, he'll likely think I'm in the back yard watering my garden. The cherry tomatoes are turning red, and I intended to pick them for dinner tonight. Now he can pick them himself. Tomatoes—my goodbye gift to the man who got me ripping up everything I write into tiny pieces because he comes up behind me and pretends to adjust the light while he tries to read what I am writing.

Thursday night while I took a bath, he rearranged my drawers. I found the letter I started writing to Ty balled up in the trash basket under the sink in the kitchen. I held out the crumpled paper, and Wally said, "What's that? Why did you throw it away?" He took it and unballed it and read: "Dear Ty—The sky is yellowish today. Yellow haze. It looks like the sky is poisoned." He balled it back up. "Good lord, Michaela. The word is smog."

He's the boss of everything.

I polished his seven-foot 2x3 bloodwood to glossy red with Daddy Van's lavender beeswax wood polish while he kept saying, "Rub harder right there" as if I needed instructions on how to rub a board! He bought his bloodwood imported from Brazil at the woodcraft shop for a small fortune of twenty-five dollars, said it was rare.

The woodcraft shop could create a new sign to hang in their window: *Bloodwood. Perfect for tying up your wife.*

Do lots of men tie up their wives? Daddy never did! Do all the men in Wally's church take pictures of their wives like he does? I had to sit in the reception area of his dentist's office one night while they developed the pictures of me in the dental lab. No matter what, Wally makes me do what Wally wants. He doesn't care what I want.

Wally made me make metal polish out of lemon juice and salt, and I polished all the copper bottoms of his saucepans (and my gold wedding band that is now in the knife drawer in his kitchen). Wally complained about the copper bottoms and made me do them all over again. I can't imagine why polishing stuff is more important that learning about music or making sculptures.

When we'd gotten into the car at the grocery store on Saturday before lighting up the sparklers, Wally accused me of flirting with the clerk. I snapped, "I'm not a flirt!" and he growled, "Shut up, Michaela, or you will go to hell." His face flushed like bright red sunburn. "Remember: jealousy arouses a husband's fury, and he will show no mercy when he takes revenge."

"You don't have to be jealous." I suddenly felt sorry for him because the clerk was cute, and no matter how long Wally spends doing his hair, he will never be handsome.

At first, Wally was my angel. He swooshed me up and rescued me. I didn't say no to marrying him because you can't say no to an angel. My seventh-grade teacher often told us that if a stranger to your family does you a favor, they're an angel God has sent to help.

I stopped thinking of Wally as my angel when he said losing my baby shows I'm an irresponsible drug addict. Twice. The first time pot; the second, speed, and that was before I got pregnant! I tried one puff of pot during my trip to Wyoming—which Wally knows nothing about—but I made the mistake of telling him I tried speed once with Chaz. So he believes I'm addicted. Wally says those drugs ruin your body forever because they affect the genes, and he won't listen to the logic that if I was addicted, I would be taking the drugs—or at a minimum, longing for them. I am anti-speed!

I've seen Chaz shoot it in the crook of his arm. When I tried it with him, I just sniffed white powder. Chaz used to be energy on high, but I didn't like that up and jittery feeling, like I couldn't stop: I redid the bookcase. I cleaned out the refrigerator. I talked all the time—like Chaz. I can't remember what I said—I just remember this force pushing words out of my mouth—all night!

Although I constantly nagged Chaz to quit speed, he still loved me, but sometimes I think he loved speed more.

Wally told me he loved me twice on our wedding day and one time during sex. But I can't grasp why he would want me with him. We don't get along for even one day—never mind I do try to please him. I don't want to start sparks with him. When he asks if I love him, I say, "Yes, of course. You are my husband." My husband. My obligation.

But why is it my obligation to let him take pictures of me? Most husbands don't do this to their wives, do they? Despite my wild experiences as a runaway, I never imagined husbands tied their wives to boards and then photographed them.

Thank you, God for that glowing blue arrow under the blazing white Go. You pointed me to the door. Now I have no obligations, except to You.

Chaz and I met this guy who lived in a cardboard box near the confluence of Cherry Creek and the Platte River. He looked like Freddie the Freeloader. He said he was a solotramp and a sculptor who needed to escape to the San Luis Valley and make a garden of rock sculptures and live natural for the rest of his life. We started calling just about everyone who was on their own and tramping in the direction toward their destiny solotramps. We decided to go to the San Luis Valley in five years and see his garden. We liked the word. Chaz and I wrote a song called 'Solotramp.'

I never told Wally about 'Solotramp' and definitely never sang it—he says my voice is annoying to hear. I don't want him to picture what Chaz and I did together. He's already made up his mind what our relationship was like, and what I say never matters. When Wally makes up his mind, he never changes.

I changed my name for him!

In the hospital, everyone called me Mrs. White, and I didn't realize at first they were talking to me. When I get divorced, I will not keep White for my name the way Mama kept Abel for her name after she and Daddy got divorced.

Her name used to be Adams. She says she likes Abel because it comes first in the alphabet. There are seven names ahead of Abel in the Denver phone book.

Aaron, Aban, Abayta, Abbe, Abbeta, Abby, Abeca, then us. After us is Aber. Daddy's name hasn't been in the Denver phone book since 1963. I started playing detective and searched for Daddy in the library's phone books of all the major cities they had. I didn't find Michael Isaac Abel at all, but I did find a couple Michael Abels in different cities and wrote down their addresses and sent them letters. No answer. Isabel is the only Abel in Denver.

My middle name is Isabel after Mama, and my first name is after Daddy, Michael = Michaela. But most everybody except Wally calls me Kaela or Mick or Micky.

Now I'm getting hungry, but no stores in Golconda are likely to be open this early. I hope the old-fashioned grocery store is still in business on Night Street. With thirty dollars from my oatmeal carton, I'm not at risk of immediate starvation. I don't know what I'll do when my money runs out, but no point in worrying now. You cannot predict what will happen when you run away.

You pray it won't be worse than what you ran from.

What does Wally do with the pictures after he develops the film with his dentist? I'm afraid he wants to put the pictures of me together in a book like the sex book he keeps in his nightstand drawer. I hope he won't send them to that magazine he keeps a stack of under the bed.

He said he ties me up because I'm like a wild animal and must be tamed. He said God says people who act like wild animals are destructive. I never told him I went to Christian school and that I know of a passage in Galatians that talks about how people who act like wild animals hurt each other and give into their worst desires. I guess that's what he was referring to, but I don't want that conversation with him.

What is my worst desire?

Killing myself.

Being tied up makes me want to end it. I never thought such a thing when I was with Chaz. It wasn't easy, Chaz taking speed all the time. But the future with Wally—please, no.

I want God and Jesus to like me. So I try to put my desires aside. I am rarely snappish out loud although words are fighting to come out of my mouth to tell Wally off, and I keep my hands down when they are ready to smack him back. Anything is an excuse for him to "discipline" me (as he calls it). Whack with the back of his hand. I admit that I am like a wild animal in that they will run for their lives, which is exactly what I am doing right now.

Wally says he married me to save me. At first to save me from being an unwed mother and then to save me from being bummed about everything (meaning Chaz and the baby); now he says worshipping at his church and learning to garden and working at his vet office and giving him what he wants help save me for heaven. But he won't let me join the church choir never mind my most favorite thing in the world is singing. He claims the choir director is a sneaky man and a hypocrite. The choir director looks to be about Wally's age but could pass for Cary Grant.

Wally insists I learn to make pies to take to the church potluck suppers. He says as a young bride, I am required to develop a repertoire of recipes. (Like my repertoire of books I've read and songs I've learned to sing?) I don't mind mastering flaky piecrust, but so far mine is mealy. Open a can of cherry or apple pie filling or cook up a box of pudding—that part of making a pie is easy.

I try to make my cooking taste good, but Wally harps: "The biscuits are heavy." "The gravy's lumpy."

I like my biscuits smooth and buttery drenched in honey—and the gravy?—we're talking about two or three tiny pinhead balls! He always keeps an eye out for my mistakes.

He started setting the alarm for me to wake at six so the fried potatoes for breakfast can cook longer. The only time he doesn't carp about my cooking is when I fry up a pound of sausage and mix in six eggs and a can of cream of onion soup and dump the mixture on some Bisquick dough I spread out in a pan and blob liberally with Velveeta cheese and bake for a half hour at 375.

Wally gobbles up the mess. Six eggs! He calls it real Texas.

I make this delight every Thursday morning because that's the day his cleaning lady comes, and she gets the sausage grease spatters cleaned up. She's been cleaning for Wally for three years from when this house was brand new. When she arrives at one p.m. on the dot, I let her in, and she walks past me toward the kitchen as if she doesn't see me—she's never spoken to me!—so weird—so I holler bye to her and take off to the movies. Wally's house—the littlest house on the block, a ranch with a one-car garage—not a long walk to the Continental. The last movie I saw was *Butch Cassidy*. Now I am kinda hiding out like he did (except I have not robbed anyone). The Cooper Theater is not easy walking distance, but it has the biggest screen in the whole world, and I am not exaggerating. The first movie I saw at the Cooper with Daddy and Ty was about the Grimm fairy tales. In Cinerama!—the gigantic orange curtain opened up to a gigantic curved screen. And the music blew me away.

Thursday is the only day I'm allowed to go to the movies, and Wally expects me to tell him all about it. *2001 Space Odyssey* is going to be starting, and I made the mistake of telling Wally I wanted to see it. I told him the preview was about outer space and how I knew the music because I used to play my mother's 78, and he jumped up and pointed his finger at me like he had to punctuate every word: "You SHOULDN'T have been ALLOWED to LISTEN." Point, bend, point. "That music celebrates anti-God." Point, point, point.

Did you ever decide to not like music you liked? I don't say.

"Ape to man, man to star child. Strauss and Kubrick are evolutionists."

I didn't know what he was talking about then, and I'm still not exactly sure.

When the preview of *2001 Space Odyssey* came on, the music made me immediately picture "Also sprach Zarathrustra" under Victor on the red record label on Mama's 78. I played it a lot. I even made up a dramatic dance to it!

Of course, Wally tapped me on my forehead. "Evolution is wrong because God created the universe just like it is." Tap, tap, tap.

"The music doesn't have words," I said and wiped my forehead with the back of my hand.

"Ev o lu tion," he said breaking the syllables into little knives at the end of his tapping finger.

I'd never heard of evolution.

Is that like when Mama said she's more evolved than most people? How does music without words say that? Why did he get so riled up?

I mistakenly told him I remembered another Strauss record of Mama's. That record is an opera. On the album cover under the title *Salome*, a girl is leaning back, her eyes closed, a reddish glow like a fire around her. A man's face looks up at her from her lap.

"Huh. Salome ordered John the Baptist's head. That is his severed head in her lap."

Uck! I'd never realized that the man on the record jacket didn't have a body! I thought it was love!

When Wally told me this, I couldn't believe Salome did such a thing because I learned at Sunday school Salome anointed Jesus when he came off the cross. She was his aunt. She went into Jesus' cave. Salome means peace. She wouldn't want to cut off John the Baptist's head!

Then Wally brought up the fact I'd once foolishly mentioned to him—that Mama is an astrologer. "Your mother is not a Christian, so I'm not surprised she was brainwashing you with *Zarathustra*." He opened his Bible to Mark and read to me about the damsel who danced for Herod who said he'd give her anything, and her mother told her she should get John the Baptist's head. "The dancing girl is Salome."

Wally told me all about a Salome play that tells how wicked she was when she tried to seduce John the Baptist, and when she failed, she was happy to have his head cut off. Not the same story I read in Mark in the Bible! It's the dancing girl's mom who wants his head. The dancing girl does not seduce anyone. She's a girl, not a woman.

I read every verse in Mark in Wally's Bible, and I didn't see the name Salome. Herod said that he already killed John the Baptist once, but when he rose from the dead, Herod put him in prison. So Herod has his head cut off again and gives it to the dancing girl, and she gives the head to her mother. (What a gross mom!) It doesn't say why Herod would do something like that for her other than she danced quite magically. He told her he'd give her half his kingdom! Why would having John's head cut off be better than having half the kingdom? Some people are so confusing!

If John the Baptist was raised from the dead before, why couldn't he do it again? Is there some sort of unspoken limit?

That's an example of our conversations!

Since I don't like to ask Wally questions because he lectures and lectures and taps me on the forehead, I looked up Zarathustra the next day I went to the library (I'm allowed to go the library on Friday and Tuesday for one hour.) I had never thought about what *Also sprach Zarathrustra* on Mama's record cover meant— just a title of foreign words. I found out: Friedrich Nietzsche wrote a book in German called in English

Thus Spoke Zarathrustra, and then Strauss wrote the music to celebrate the book. The book tells the story of a Persian prophet who lived way before Jesus, but Nietzsche's book was not written super long ago like the Bible. I did not check out the translated book because Wally would have smacked me, for sure, if I did. On the second page of the Prologue, Zarathustra says God is dead. And then he starts talking about how people will evolve into Superman but have to be true to the earth. I will read it someday.

So—there are two Salomes in the Bible—if the one holding John the Baptist's head was actually named Salome. The one who anointed Jesus wasn't necessarily his aunt, but she actually does have her name in the Bible. Wally's Salome was bad; my Salome was good.

But he was wrong that Herod or Mark ever said her name, and no matter what the play says, his Salome is really just a talented girl whose mom is worse than Mama.

Now I'm curious about the beginning of everything. If I had a Bible up here, I'd read the Book of Mark again. I miss reading! No books here. No library in Golconda.

I do not get how Zarathustra relates to Wally's Salome—and cannot imagine how Zarathrustra relates to *2001*! Now nobody will stop me from seeing that movie!

My hand is tired of writing. I'm going to see if I can find the trail Ty and I created that leads to the top of Fire Peak.

At the bottom, our trail is overgrown with clover. Now I'm sitting near the top with my notebook in my lap, leaning back against a boulder. Here is the bristlecone pine with two trunks—twisty dead branches on one and on the other trunk, green bursts of long needles with baby cones in the center.

I see our initials that Ty carved into the dead-looking one. TEA—MIA. The top looks like a long stick.

The first summer, building the cabin, Daddy sawed, Ty hammered nails, and I filled cups with Duffy's root beer and fed them potato chips I dipped into sour cream. It was fun to poke chips in their mouths because their hands were dirty. We slept outside on the ground in a tent. The next summer Daddy's cabin was finished, and Ty and I made the trail by moving rocks and scraping the dirt with our shoes. We set up piles of pine cones and rocks every so often to mark our trail. We ended right here at the bristlecone.

Ty told me this kind of tree is the oldest living thing. That's why it's so twisted up, but nothing can hurt it.

Small compared to other conifers. A hundred years from now, someone will come up our trail, and we'll be dead, but our initials will still be here, and the live part of the tree will still be deep green.

For school, I wrote a report on the bristlecone, but since I said it was older than Jesus, I received after-school detention for a week in the Penitence Room. Mama laughed and said,

"What are you being penitent for? Stating a fact?"

Today looking at our initials carved on the tree, a chill runs through me. I miss Ty.

I just quit trying to draw the gorgeous pale yellow columbines because their spurs are hard to capture—golden tails under the petals. I love to draw as much as I love to sing, but I hope I am better at singing because I'm a very bad artist.

Wally won't let me sing in the choir at his church. He said, "Just because you were in a choir doesn't mean you have any singing talent. Choirs in schools are the sad consequence of required music classes."

He sounds like music classes are a bad thing. I never had a music class, but in church choir, I kind of figured out the notes on the page after a while. Madge the choir director was a soprano and played the organ, too, and answered my questions. Chaz was never in choir though he had an amazing voice. Our funnest thing to do was to sing together and create our own songs.

I often wish I'd told Chaz all the truths about me. I never told him about Wyoming, but I should have.

I didn't tell Wally either, but I avoid telling Wally anything and everything about myself if I can help it. Before the wedding, he wanted to know if my parents would come. That's when I told him Mama was an astrologer, but Daddy didn't like that, so they got divorced. I didn't want Wally to know Daddy's missing, but I didn't lie to him when I said I didn't want my parents to know I was pregnant before I was married. So he just took me to Texas to get married, and he even bought me a beautiful wedding dress in an empire style to cover the baby. I was eight months pregnant.

Before we got married, Wally was sweet to me.

Then I became his wife, and Wally changed. It didn't matter that I was so pregnant; he insisted on sex the first night. Then the baby was stillborn. It crossed my mind that the consummation caused it. I try to push that thought away because she's dead & neither of us can change that.

He says it's my fault everything with Chaz spun into a disaster. Wally wasn't there. How would he know?

I constantly nagged Chaz about speed, mainly because he couldn't sleep when he took it. I was not thrilled with his idea of becoming a shaman after he read *Don Juan*, but Wally and Nathan told him he had shaman qualities and should really go to Central or South America as soon as he finished his conscientious objector service.

In those days I didn't know how biblical Wally was. I didn't see that side of him before we got married. We all thought he was that cool bone doctor with the cool car. I was shocked to find out he is a veterinary surgeon.

Wally told his friends Mary Ann and Billy about Chaz taking the yagé. "Michaela's roommate took it and went crazy and his heart rate went up so fast, he died."

"Dangerous," Mary Ann said.

"Yes. Combined with methamphetamines, extremely dangerous. But the right dosage is another story. Have you read Burroughs' account of going to the Amazon and trying this brew that provides the most "derangement of the senses" as he puts it?" Wally added in his smarty pants voice. "A hallucinogen."

Mary Ann and Billy looked interested. "What's the name of the book?" They were his friends he was always talking about books with.

"*The Yagé Letters*. A collection of letters between him and Allen Ginsberg. You know."

"Obscene! You really read it?" Billy asked.

"That's how I found out about yagé ."

I said, "I never heard of it," and Wally frowned at me. "Young people will try every drug on the planet."

I could correct Wally, but why get slapped for talking back?

"Just imagine what my wife's fate would be if I didn't rescue her from those drug addicts."

"Burroughs killed his wife, didn't he?" Billy asked.

"Shot her, yes.

"Congratulations on your marriage," Mary Ann said to me.

Wally filled her glass with Johnnie Walker. "As Ginsberg wrote: 'The weight of the world is love.' It was the right thing to do." He filled his glass and told me to go get a bowl of peanuts from the kitchen.

Even so, how can I not love Wally in some way? He didn't have to pick me and Floss up on the freeway that day. He didn't have to do the surgery on my knee. He didn't have to give me a home and a wedding. He didn't have to lie to his parents, to his sister and brother saying Chaz's baby was his. He didn't have to take me to a grief counselor. He didn't have to let me earn seven dollars a week to spend on myself however I choose. He didn't have to give me a garden. He didn't have to teach me to drive. He didn't have to give me the Falcon.

Wally has done all these things. I am kicking the gift horse.

I am not fair. He rescued me when I asked God for an angel.

A super hard thing to think about is the probability that Chaz and Floss lied to me. I am certain they told me their parents lived in Chicago. But within two hours of Floss's call to tell them Chaz was flipping out, their parents arrived in a station wagon with a Colorado license plate.

I used to picture their large house Chaz and Floss said they'd escaped from: the gated driveway, the maid answering the door, the swimming pool and the shooting range in the basement, the lake like an ocean nearby, their dad carrying a briefcase and always in a hurry, their mom snappish and bossy.

So confusing! How could the parents get to our place so fast if Chaz and Floss weren't lying to me?

Possibility: their parents were visiting someone in Colorado. Somehow Floss's collect call to Chicago got to someone who then phoned them at who they were visiting in Colorado and told them to go to our address. That's what I want the truth to be.

The moment they arrived, everybody partying at our place fled across the hall to Nathan's. Chaz's mother made a quick disaster when she swept through our apartment dividing up our things and stashing everything she thought belonged to Chaz or Floss in paper bags. I jumped up and grabbed back *Where the Red Fern Grows* and my goofy purple-haired troll doll Chaz gave me the night he showed me our tickets to the Pop Festival. He didn't look up when his mom shoved the envelope with our tickets into her purse.

His spirit had evaporated. I couldn't understand a word he mumbled, and he seemed unaware I was stroking his back and whispering to him everything would be okay. Floss acted like a mess, too. She ripped out of the bags whatever their mom packed and threw everything on the floor.

She screamed at them, "It's your fault he's like this!"

What had she expected? That Mom and Dad would come in and fix him real quick and we could go on as usual? She was a runaway, too! When she gave up Chaz, she gave up herself!

No one paid attention to me—I could have been watching a movie enacted in my apartment.

I confronted Floss as her dad was dragging her out the door. "Chicago? Chicago? They're from Chicago?" She gave me a weird look and yelled, "Let me go!" But her dad dragged her to the station wagon and pushed her in.

Everyone was gone.

Except the baby moving inside me.

I said aloud: "God, please. I need an angel."
A second later Wally knocked on the door.

And he helped me. He took me to his house and let
me stay with him when I was evicted. He got me an
obstetrician and paid for the hospital. Right now he is
probably worried about me because he doesn't know
where I am.

But I am so glad I never told him about this cabin
nor one word ever about Golconda.

Two sides to Gemini Wally. (At least two sides.)
And the weight is to the negative.
I was right to never confide in him. No reason to.
His own version is what stands.
Two sides of my heart:

        the grateful side, the answer to my
prayer.
        the let-me-out-of-here side. Enough is
enough.

I want to be erased from his mind. I left the
wedding ring in the kitchen in the drawer next to the
knife he used to cut the rope.
If he loves me, he needs to learn the rule of love: If
you love someone, they'll disappear.
Everyone I love goes missing.

Chaz and I used to make clouds disperse with our minds—we'd stare at the same small cloud and imagine it coming apart—well, not imagining so much as commanding. We'd feel so powerful when it broke up or disappeared into another cloud.

We had so much fun together.

Missing someone feels like being ferociously hungry all the time.

I have missed Chaz every day.

My mind fills

with you.

And I'm beyond sad

once again.

Oh oh oh!

How could you die?

How could you?

I wonder if my little song is more about Chaz or more about our baby. No one knows of her except Wally and Floss, but Floss is gone, too. Her face at the window as they drove off behind the ambulance—red, crying.

Golconda

I parked across the street from the grocery store in front of the real estate office. The window used to show cowboy shirts with pointy designs on the shoulders hung on branches suspended on chains, and leather belts draped over pine stumps. My favorite belt: swirly designs with a silver horse's head buckle. Ty's: claw buckle, eagles engraved into the black leather. Now Ty and the western store are gone.

Another change: The grocery store now displays merchandise on metal shelves under fluorescent lights instead of the wooden shelves and light bulbs hanging from the ceiling.

Not changed: The grocer's eyes still a vivid blue, his gray beard goes down to the middle of his chest, and he wears red suspenders and a blue bowtie.

The last time we came in (8 years ago!), he gave me and Ty a pair of dice. While Daddy bought hot dogs and chips, Ty and I discovered Lydia Pinkham's potion, and its label left us wondering what can false unicorn be? (I looked it up and learned about a white flower that resembles a unicorn horn but does not grow around here.) When we got back to the cabin, Daddy taught us how to play Even or Odd. We had a shiny purple metal cup that we covered the dice with while we put up quartz rocks for our bets.

I bought two loaves of bread, carrots, apples, peanut butter, apple juice, and t.p. for a dollar ninety-six. More expensive than in Denver. The steering wheel in my Falcon burned my hands, so I held on with a tissue. I drove down Night Street past the Opera House Café. I felt tempted to park in front and go in for a grilled cheese sandwich and ice cream like we used to do with Daddy, but: be frugal, Micky.

I wonder if the fat, laughing lady still runs the café and whether the teenage girl with the black ponytail down to her waist still waitresses. Rosie.

Rosie used to give me and Ty bubble gum when we were hanging out on the boulders playing our Rocks game. Sometimes when we were singing out there, I'd see her standing at the back door of the café—I like to think she liked to listen to us since Ty has a good voice. Of course, Rosie isn't a teenager any more because it was my tenth birthday the last time I came to Golconda.

Ty's birthday is Wednesday. He's a Cancer. Mama said that means he's a Crab. Despite Cancer being a Water sign, he has a lot of Fire in his chart, Sagittarius rising and moon in Leo. Like Daddy, his Mercury is in Air sign Gemini. But Mama said Daddy's fast Mercury is ahead of the sun, which is why he talks so much.

Daddy would stay inside the café talking to people forever. Sooner or (usually) later, we'd drive back to the cabin to cook up hot dogs or fish from Gangue Creek to eat on the porch under the stars. After we ate, beside the campfire, Ty and I would sing all the songs we could think of while Daddy hummed. In the morning we'd set up the cans and shoot 'em down. Daddy said I have a steady hand.

No refrigerator in the cabin, but plenty of pots and pans and dishes and silverware. The silverware belonged to Mama's mama, and through the black tarnish I can read LIA engraved in cursive letters. I used to dig in the dirt with the spoons. They're heavy and don't bend. The dishes are stacked in the green-painted buffet that used to belong to Mama's mama, too, like the sofa I'm sitting on. Plush green velvet, but if you whack it with your hand, a cloud of dust. Mama always said she hates to clean house because her mama followed her around with a duster, meaning anything she cleaned wasn't clean enough. I guess the holes are from mice gnawing.

We drove all the way to Clovis for the grandmothers' funerals. On their way home from a bingo game, our grandmothers got in an accident with a semi-truck. Mama's mother got decapitated, so they closed her casket, and I never saw her. Daddy's mother's coffin was open, an older lady sleeping in her church clothes is what she looked like. On the drive back to Denver, Daddy puffed on his cigar and Mama puffed on her cigarettes, and they talked about spending their inheritance on land in Golconda.

Mama said, "What do you want to do? Hide up there? I'll look up the astrology."

Daddy screeched to a stop at the edge of the highway and told us to get out. We stood by the car in the dark. "Look at the sky." Daddy pointed. "Look at the stars." I stared up to the sky—the sliver moon, the white belt of stars.

"If those stars predict the future, Isabel, how come you didn't predict our mothers' accident?"

"Why would I predict such a thing?"

"If you can't tell the future, then why waste your time on stupid astrology?"

Mama blew out a stream of smoke. "I wish we flew to Clovis instead of enduring this long, boring drive."

"Since you hardly ever leave the house, I can't imagine you getting on a plane."

"Introverts fly, too. I want to go to the moon." The moon—a curved sliver above the distant mountains surrounded by millions of stars. "I love moonlight," Mama said.

"No moonlight on the moon," Ty announced, and Daddy laughed, and we all got back in the car.

"What if our mothers are ghosts now riding back to Denver with us?" Mama patted the seat. "What if they're right between us?"

I never heard of ghosts before, but I could tell they scared Ty. He leaned into the front seat.

"No such thing as ghosts. Right?"

"Right," Daddy said. "No such thing."

"You can't be sure," Mama said.

"How come?" I asked.

"You need to stay away from all the heebie jeebie bullcrap. I swear, Isabel," Daddy shouted and sped up the car. "You'll believe anything."

"How about you?" Mama rolled down her window a little and flicked out her burning cigarette butt. "You believe in God."

"That's not the same."

"How can you be so sure?"

Daddy lit his cigar again. Smoke from his cigar and her new cigarette wafted into the backseat. People always smoke when they disagree.

Next thing, Ty got switched from the public school to the Christian school where I started kindergarten.

Daddy said he had to protect us from Mama's heebie jeebies.

Did Mama do something heebie jeebie to make Daddy disappear? Ty and I continually asked her where he went.

"Timbuktu? Hawaii? Antarctica? A good father would write his kids letters from all those places," she said. "A good father would stay in touch."

Did that mean she knew where he was or didn't know? Was he traveling around the world?

I never heard back from the letters I sent to the Michael Abels. Maybe Mama opened a letter from Daddy and never gave it to me. Why wouldn't any daddy answer a letter that asked if he was a little girl's father?

Two ways to take the divorce: Sad. Daddy didn't live with us anymore. Glad. Visiting him at his apartment and coming up to the cabin equaled two new places to explore. The first step of disappearing was when he moved into his own apartment on Acoma and bought me and Ty sleeping bags for when we visited him.

****

When I was little, Ty would help me pour milk on bowls of Cheerios and read me stories from library books. Ty had a little kid voice for Pippi Longstocking and a loud growly voice for Paul Bunyon. One day not long after Daddy moved out, Ty and I gobbled up our cereal and ran down to the church because a bus was there to take the Sunday School kids from all the True Churches to a picnic. Ty had his permission slip, but I forgot mine, so I had to race back home to get it before the bus took off.

Mama wasn't at her astrology and not in the kitchen, so I flung open her bedroom door.

Mama and That Man naked in her bed with the covers around their feet, his hairy butt sticking out. Mama pulled up the sheet to her chin and said my permission slip was on the windowsill in the kitchen. I spun down the hall, swiped it up, and flew out the front door and back to church where the bus waited for me. Tina saved me a seat, and off we drove to the park with a lake for the picnic.

Tina and I won Jesus pictures for the sack race, and we played Red Rover and tried out badminton and volleyball and hula hoops. People fished in the blue lake under poufy clouds that reflected in the water. We cooked burgers and s'mores, and I found a dead, stinky fish behind a tree.

On the way home, Tina and I sang with the other kids on the bus.

A-B-C-D-E-F-G,

Jesus died for you and me

H-I-J-K-L-M-N,

Jesus died for sinful childREN, AMEN!

She and I used to do everything together back then, more at her house because they didn't want Tina to be exposed to Mama's astrology. Her father was the pastor, so they lived right next to the church. I got to watch television at Tina's, and we'd make our dolls play the stories, like *Lassie*. Mama wouldn't buy a TV.

After we got off the bus, when I walked home with Ty, I told him what I saw in Mama's bed when I went back for my permission slip that was under the geranium on the windowsill in the kitchen.

"You are a god dammed liar," he said.

"No, I am not! His butt is hairy. Isn't that weird, Ty?"

Dozens of grasshoppers were hopping all over our front stoop. He picked one up and threw it at me. "Mom wouldn't do that. You're a liar."

The grasshopper caught in my shirt and lost a couple legs when I tore it off and threw it back at him.

I followed him through the swinging doors into the kitchen where Mama was trimming dead leaves off the geranium with red flowers. "You know what, Mom?" Ty said. "Micky said you were in bed naked with your lawyer."

Mama spun around with the shears in her hand looking like the fierce bulldog down the street that always barked at us. "Did you say that? Did you tell your brother that?" She was right in my face.

I said yes, proud of myself and sure Mama would tell Ty I was not a liar.

Instead, she slapped me. "Don't you ever lie again," she said. "You go to your room right now."

"We woulda known if he spent the night, Mick," Ty said in the meanest voice possible.

My face stinging, I cried all the way to my room—and kept crying even after my face stopped hurting because she was so unfair to call me a liar. She did not come to me to apologize for her mistake. I fell asleep on my bed. I must have been exhausted from the picnic because I woke the next morning to my ceiling light still on, still dressed in the same clothes I'd worn to the picnic.

The next weekend with Daddy, I told him Mama slapped me for telling Ty I saw her in bed naked with her new friend. At first he said, "I don't believe it," so I was afraid he was going to call me a liar, too. But he said, "Oh, I believe you, hon. I don't believe your mother could be so stupid."

Ty was at Christian Soldiers camp, and Daddy and I spent the weekend together at his apartment near downtown—bare of furniture except for the pull-out couch where he slept and two sleeping bags on the floor for me and Ty. That day, I put my sleeping bag on top of Ty's, so it was softer.

Because he didn't have a table and chairs, we sat on the floor with our plates, and he taught me Blackjack. From his cigar box full of pennies, we each took a handful for our bets. Daddy brought me home on Sunday afternoon, but instead of just dropping me off, he led the way into the house and stamped through calling, "Isabel!" I followed him out back. He yelled at her, "Don't you have a brain in your head?"

Mama pulled clothespins out of her clothespin apron and clipped a wet blouse to the line. He yelled, "You're sleeping around and letting the kids see?" and she stooped down and pulled out Ty's jeans from the wicker basket on the ground and didn't look at him. Taking clothespins out of her apron pocket, she snapped the blue jeans to a different line. He stopped yelling and stood there with his arms crossed. She didn't look at him until she finished clipping my blue pajama top. She turned and gave him that fierce bulldog face. "Good Lord, Mikey. Look at her chart. She's prone to fantasy with all those 12th house planets. Isn't she always playing make-believe?"

"A six-year-old kid is going to fantasize you in bed with somebody? Come on, Isabel." He was not yelling although the neighbors likely could still hear his loud voice.

Mama whispered: "Micky's got her Moon in Scorpio."

He punched her. She fell on the ground under the sheets hanging on the line. I started to run to her, but Daddy dropped to his knees and said, "I'm sorry. I'm sorry," and waved me off.

He swooped her up and carried her into the house.

I stayed outside and played in my fairy tale forest in the sumac. I am breaking a Commandment to say this, but I was sort of glad he punched her. She called me a liar. In my fairy tale forest, the queen always punishes the transgressor.

When Ty came home from Christian Soldiers' camp, he asked Mama how she got her black eye. "Your father's jealous," she said. "He punched me because I have a boyfriend. But we're divorced. I have a right."

"Dad hit you?"

"Oh honey, I'm all right. Kind of sweet when a man loses himself over you."

Later the Popsicle man came tinkling down the street, and Ty bought me a grape one. We sat on the porch stoop with the grasshoppers. "I told Daddy about Mama's hairy butt friend. Daddy believed me. I don't tell lies."

"You swear you're telling the truth? Cross your heart? Stick needles in your eyes?"

I crossed my heart. "I don't lie, Ty."

After I went to bed that night, Ty and Mama talked in the living room.

"Do people go to hell if they lie?" he asked her.

"There is no hell. Hell was made up to scare people."

"What about heaven?"

"Oh, everybody goes to heaven," she said. "We are born again and again and again until we become perfect people. Perfect people stay in heaven forevermore."

"Not what we learned in Sunday School, Mom. We'll be judged by God at the Second Coming."

"Oh, those religious people think they're perfect and know everything. But they aren't really evolved."

"Are you evolved, Mom?"

"Oh, yes. I am, but I'm not perfect yet. I'm looking forward to my next life. Next time I'll be different. Next time I will be a man."

Mama as a man? Hard to imagine. I can't imagine myself as a man either.

If I was a boy, I would be facing the draft like Ty and Chaz and Lester and all the guys around my age. I hear they are going to start using a lottery. A matter of luck versus an obligation.

Ty was not lucky. He is in Vietnam. Well, I don't know for sure where he is, but every time I think of him, my gut seizes into a knot. I wish I had his address.

Not fair. Why must someone be in a war he does not believe in? I wish Ty could be here. He loves the cabin, too. He didn't want to go to war. Why did Mama want him to go? She makes everyone I love leave.

JULY 7 TUESDAY

The aspens on the mountainside—skinny white and black trunks, leaves pale green and quivery. The last time I was here they looked like gold shooting out of the earth. That was October 3, 1961, the last time I saw Daddy.

We came down the mountains, and as I was getting out of the front seat of his blue Pontiac, he clicked my cheek and handed me a white box taped shut with "Happy 10th" in black ink.

I opened the box to my ring—curved white gold with diamonds on each side of the oval star sapphire. I gave Daddy a zillion hugs and kisses.

I think of the star as firmament from Daddy's soul.

I turn my hand, and the diamonds flash into the sky. How cool to see light traveling to light. Eight years!

Yes, ferociously hungry. Emptiness is such a heavy, dark feeling. I am always missing Daddy. Is he alive? He has to be. Has to be. I pray. I wish. I pray.

"Maybe he's climbing Mount Everest," Mama said. "Maybe he's fishing in the deep blue sea."

"Is Dad traveling?" Ty asked.

Mama shrugged. "Adventures may lead to being locked up in a dungeon."

"When is he coming home?" Ty asked.

"When he gets tired of the North Pole." She laughed.

"Have you done Santa Claus's chart?" I asked her being a total snot, and she said if I got his birthtime, she'd be happy to do it.

"Why is Dad gone?" Ty asked again.

She put on her bulldog face. "Can't we please not talk about him any more?!"

I picture Mama in her glider chair with the oakwood tray she uses as a desk over her lap, piles of *American Astrology* magazines on the floor next to her because Mama never throws them away. She lives on astrology and cigarettes and coffee. Women sit in the kitchen with her, drinking coffee, eating snickerdoodles, and going over life according to the planets.

Dishes pile up on the counter—coffee cups dominating. The black linoleum floor—white specks and sticky spots. The coffee pot always plugged in because nobody can drink more coffee than Mama, at least three percolators every day.

Mama works at the auto parts store. The neighbor ladies don't have jobs. They always make dinner, and they are married so they don't have dates. Mama quit cooking much when she started seeing Mister Floyd

Gross—the creepy guy Ty and I call Barf because he's a pervert and doesn't deserve a name.

Barf started taking Mama out to dinner three or four times a week, but the only sit-down restaurant I ever went to before I ran away to Wyoming was the Golconda Opera House Café with Daddy and lunch at Woolworth's with Mama.

Ty and I learned to cook for ourselves—boiled or fried or scrambled eggs, Franco American spaghetti, Campbell's soup, hot dogs. Mama said she hates cooking but likes baking.

She'd lean into the oven with the checkered mitt on her hand to pull out the cookie tray, her cigarette sticking out of the corner of her mouth, squinting to keep the smoke from getting into her eyes. She'd lay out the snickerdoodles on a plate and pour coffee and explain to her astrology clients who they are and where they can go with their lives according to their position on the earth in the universe.

Every day: Sitting in her glider chair, she adds and subtracts numbers, draws astrology symbols like the M shape for Scorpio and triangles, squares and lines on charts using her deskboard over her lap, living room draperies always pulled shut, her pole-lamp on, no matter if July's noon sun blazes down.

She flips her slipper back and forth—pink slippers with foam poking out of the little tears on the bottom. Her matching pink bathrobe with lots of little burn holes, overflowing ashtray where a filter sizzles and smells as bad as burning hair, her coffee mug with lipstick stains. Her coffee mugs—decorated with flowers that I named my dolls after. Lily, Rose, Violet and Poppy. The insides turn brown from her coffee, so she fills them with Clorox and lets them soak white.

Every morning at exactly nine-twenty Mama takes off for Turner's Auto Supply so as to make it by nine-thirty. Home again at three forty-five. Up early and up late. She says she will not waste her life sleeping. She says she will not waste her time cleaning up our house like the neighbor moms do either. Those moms don't have jobs, so they're home all day. Cleaning and cooking is all they have to do besides shopping, going to PTA, and considering buying a new vacuum cleaner, hairbrush, or bomb shelter.

One day I came home from school to a salesman in our living room on his knees spreading a giant brochure across the floor.

FALLOUT.

My favorite bomb shelter curved like a huge tube with bunk beds and stacks of wooden boxes plastered with signs saying Canned Food and Canned Water. My second favorite was not much different from the basement house nearby but more built into a hill instead of dug down into the ground.

On KIMN, I heard a commercial for new houses in Cherry Hills that would come complete with bomb shelters, and I wanted us to move there, but Mama said we didn't have the money. She said we were poor. I thought it wasn't fair people who had money would be safe from the bomb, but poor people would die. What did poor people have to do with the bomb?

When I complained about the injustice, Mama took my hands and showed me how to press my fingers against my wrist so I could feel my pulse. "Everyone has a certain number of heartbeats," she said. "When you've used up all your heartbeats, you die. But there's no way to tell in advance how many you have." My pulse vibrated against my fingers. "Rich or poor, old or young, strong or weak. It doesn't matter," she said. "We'll die when we've used up our heartbeats. Whether in a shelter or out of one. Now you see how we all are equal."

I felt better about not getting a bomb shelter, but I still imagined a playhouse with food and bunks and a lantern where Tina and I could camp. Ty said a tree house would be better, but in a tree house, you would hear the planes coming with their bombs; a bomb shelter would be quiet, like the basement house. Every time I saw a plane, my pulse would start pounding, no doubt taking days off my life. If only I could have been at the cabin in Golconda with Daddy where there's never a plane in the sky, I would have felt safe like I do right now.

The first time I ran away from home was the day after Mama slapped me and accused me of lying. I stuck crackers together with grape jelly and picked out a sweater from my top drawer. I wrapped the sweater and the crackers into one of Mama's silky scarves that she thought made her look glamorous. Then I went around the block from our house to the field that stretched to the horizon, where nothing was built but the basement house. I got down into the ditch and read my Casper comic book Ty got for me.

The basement house had a rim of concrete that poked up above the ground. The yard around it merged into the field—all weeds and crabgrass, no lawn. The people who lived in the basement house had to have been poor people. That's why they didn't build the rest of the house, and why they didn't have a lawn.

A lot of kids were playing around the basement house, and I stayed in the ditch and watched them. One kid would stand on a pile of bricks, and the other kids would pull that kid down. Whoever got the kid down would go to the top of the pile, and it would start all over. Their mother came up the stairs and hung overalls on the line. The kids all wore overalls, cut off at the knees into shorts, and none wore shirts.

When she finished hanging out the overalls, she came striding up to me where I was hiding in the ditch eating my crackers with grape jelly. She sat down on the ground near me and showed me how to make a whistle out of the long yellow grass. I can still envision her lips and teeth, soft pink lips without red lipstick and white teeth, not teeth stained with smoke and coffee. The kids all took long strands of grass and made whistles, too, and we blew a little symphony in the field. Then the basement mother asked me if I wanted to come into her basement house for a glass of milk and a sandwich. I'd eaten my crackers, but I was still hungry and thirsty.

We went down the cement stairs to the doorway. Dark down there. The curly-headed kids without shirts came in, too, and the littlest one hid behind her skirt while she was making sandwiches. The two biggest ones sat on each side of me on the bench at the table, staring at me like I was an alien and not saying one word to me. Weird, sitting in the middle having all those eyes watching every move I made. Even though we'd made that whistle music together, we still did not talk to each other. They hardly talked to each other either while I sat there.

But while she made the sandwiches, the basement woman kept smiling at me and asking me questions about where I lived and where I went to school. I learned they went to the public school—not like me and Ty who went to the True Christian school. Across the field, a brand new public school was under construction, and the basement mother told me all about it. It sounded modern, and I thought it would be fun to go to school there, but not if all my classmates would stare at me like these kids did. The basement mother filled my milk glass twice, and then she and the kids walked me part way home. My first runaway was a short experience. I don't think Mama even knew I was gone.

****

A bluebird lands next to another bluebird on the tall ponderosa, and the nuthatches go *hey hey hey*. I think the voices of birds are the voice of the spirit of the wilderness.

A lady brought a sick canary into Wally's clinic, but when he couldn't save it, she said its spirit was released to heaven.

I wonder if animals have souls. Two times when I was manning Wally's front desk, people brought in their dog to be put to sleep, one a collie; the other a mixed breed shepherd with blue eyes. The owners believed their collie had a soul when they said goodbye, stroking it and promising to it in a sad voice to meet again in heaven.

I understand when a dog is dying, ending its life ends its misery, but I don't understand killing stray dogs who are otherwise healthy because what if it turns out dogs do have souls?

That is like killing homeless people off.

Wally says I shouldn't get involved with the animals, or before long, we'd be living in a zoo.

Could be. Animals also have definite number of God-given heartbeats.

I vote animals have souls, too.

****

Worry started filling my mind when Daddy disappeared. Worry filled my mind fuller when Ty went into the Army. Then Chaz—zoomed off in the ambulance with the siren screaming, and if he listened, he could hear me screaming, too.

One worry after another. It's like my head is swollen with worry. Worrying about people you know is different from worrying about the flood and if it will take your house. Every worry adds to the worry room in my brain. Just like the bomb and not having a bomb shelter. Fire drills and bomb drills. The earthquake in Panama right after Mama told us that's where Daddy disappeared to. Then she said he was really in China.

I don't have to worry ever again all day about what Wally will want me to do when he gets home from the clinic. He insists wives must do whatever their husbands want. He says I have to get breast implants. He says a wife is subject to her husband, and if she scoffs at him, she is scoffing at God and will go to hell.

"I'm not scoffing when I say no." I said.

"You are." He put his forefinger on my forehead and pressed, looking me in the eyes. "You are expressing your scorn." His eyes are a pale brown, set close to his nose, with almost invisible eyelashes.

"Neither of us wants you to go to hell," he said.

I think I've already been, I thought but did not say aloud.

I don't feel scorn for him, but I can't convince him. He says a stubborn man is steadfast.

Another thing adding to my brainful of worry is getting pregnant again. I could be pregnant right now! What would I do? I don't want to have Wally's baby because we would be linked forever.

What if I had gone back home to Mama instead of going to Texas to get married to Wally?

What if I came through the door and she jumped up and set down her astrology board and cried, "Welcome home, Micky! I told Floyd to hit the road." What if she started calling him Barf instead of Floyd?

What if pregnant-me coming through the door made her happy?

What if she came to the hospital when I wanted her to be with me? When I was feeling the way I did when I stayed at Daddy's apartment and I'd miss Mama and miss my bed with two pillows and my soft pink blanket and my Puss & Boots lamp and my life-size baby doll named Poppy with curly brown hair. At Daddy's, sleeping on the floor in a sleeping bag on the living room in Denver was fun but not cozy like my own room.

The baby came October 15. Ten days after our wedding. I wanted Mama, and I wanted Chaz.

What if he'd never taken the yagé? Then he would have been with me, and he'd still be alive.

Almost a year since the parents came and got him taken away in the ambulance. Since that day I:

-got fired,

-evicted,

-married,

-had a stillborn baby,

-got smacked many times,

-worked in a vet office and cleaned countless cages,

-grew a garden,

-learned to drive.

-intentionally became a solotramp

What if Chaz stopped taking speed like he promised he would do since I was pregnant? Why did he take speed with the yagé ?
I am still angry.
So anger pushes into my swollen mind.

Forgive me. I am wrong to be angry with someone who passed on. I hope Chaz is watching me from heaven and does not feel my anger, just my prayers and my love.
The constant ache of missing him.
I find myself listening for his voice when I talk to him in my head.
Once upon a time we were happy. Chaz would play his Gibson, and I would write down lyrics, and we would sing together. I love his voice—deep, moody. You can feel his heart when he sings.
He told me my voice is rare since I can sing in three octaves. I'd never heard of octaves. I sing low, and I sing high. I sing soprano, and I sing alto, and between is mezzosoprano, I learned. Our voices are different, yet when Chaz and I harmonize, we start in the same octave. I love to learn about music!
We must have created at least twenty-five songs. He borrowed Nathan's extra guitar and started teaching me to play.
We had golden tickets to the Pop Festival, fifteen dollars for three days. We missed all that music.

Floss may have found them in your mom's purse and attended after all while you were dying, Chaz. I wish I knew exactly when you died.

****

I had a weird experience trying to cross Gangue Creek—I froze. I couldn't make myself walk across the log. It's about six feet up, not that high, so why can't I do it? My shoes are still wet from wading across.

I could see up the yellow, grassy hill past piles of boulders to the strangest house I've ever seen—a round house. I wonder how the rooms are set up. Two-story, windows all around. A balcony surrounds half of the second floor.

Nearby is a wood building like a barn. No animals around, no pasture. A picnic table covered in pine cones sits under a gigantic blue spruce.

New neighbors. They weren't there on my tenth birthday.

Daddy told me in the early days of Golconda just like in the early days of Denver, a fire burned up everything, so all the buildings on Night Street are brick. Fire prevention must be why the round house is the same type of concrete bricks Chaz used when he made me a bookcase.

Three shelves high. I kept a green bottle on the top, filled with some dried yellow yarrow and two sunflowers I found growing in a spot where something had been torn down but nothing was being built. The bookcase saved us tripping over my library books.

I bought a beginner's guitar book, and Chaz let me start on his Gibson and then borrowed Nathan's extra Yamaha for me. A bunch of people would come over to jam, and Floss and I would play instruments we made—a kalimba created of a paper plate and popsicle sticks, bongos made out of empty soup cans with balloons stretched over the openings, and a shaker made from a salt carton filled with jelly beans. We clapped together paint stir sticks and banged spoons on pots. Floss and I became known as the Percussive Girls.

I loved writing songs with Chaz. My favorite is 'Solotramp.' I think all of us are solotramps. We come into life and leave life alone no matter if other people are around. We seek others to make us think we're not solo, but we still are.

Everyone's experience is different. Two people go to the same place but aren't precisely in the same spot at the very same time. Not like your own spirit and your soul if they occupy the same space.

Colors we call by the same name. Yet can we be sure our eyes see color exactly the same? We'd still call what we're seeing blue or purple or whatever.

"I get what you mean by solo," Chaz said the first time I wrote the lyrics, "but how do you see yourself as a tramp?"

"I'm a runaway."

"So Floss is a tramp, too."

"Yup. A solotramp."

"I'm not solo when I'm with you," he said. He put his fingers on my wrist, over my pulse. I will never forget. He said, "Feel. Our pulses in unison."

The exact moment I fell in love.

"We'll be tramps together," he told me.

Oh! My heart hurts to think of that day!

My mind—filled with worry; my heart feeling like barb wire facing in.

Chaz was going to marry me. I married Wally instead, but Chaz had my heart.

Wally knows Chaz was my baby's father, yet he acts like Chaz was never a real person because he went insane and died.

Life changed overnight!—Creating music & going to concerts & window-peeking & planning our future. Then: catastrophe and sorrow. Yagé ruined everything. Yagé destroyed Chaz. My mind is like waves pounding.

I know it's weird but I still imagine he's alive, that I'll go into a store, and I'll see him getting cigarettes, or I'll go to a movie and hear his laugh behind me. God can do all things, right? If John the Baptist was raised from the dead, then why can't Chaz be?

Babies get born and die before you've held them in your arms. Or yes, maybe they already died inside you where you are all twisted and sad. You put them in the ground in a tiny box and spread flowers on the grave, and the flowers wilt and blow away on the wind.

Something's left. A hole in your heart.

A hole is something. Hole. Holey heart.

I need a hole in my head worry will run out of. I need worry to leave my mind forever.

I wish Chaz could have seen how our baby's face had no expression but still looked like him. He did not see the white fuzz covering her. Her eyes never opened. Maybe he takes care of her in heaven. Maybe that is God's reason. They are supposed to be together in heaven. But I'm not good enough to go there.

Wally says original sin is why he is tolerant of the things I've done because I would be unable to do otherwise since we are all sinners because of original sin. He says I must be tolerant of him also because if he commits a sin, he could not help it either. He says because he's been baptized, he has grace. He says good deeds cannot make up for sins; God demands only we are faithful to Him.

Huh! All the brand new babies through the hospital window! Saying they have sin is like saying a spring purple crocus is weed spawn. Once upon a time, Chaz and I were babies, too. So was Ty and Floss and so were Mama and Daddy—and Wally—and even Barf.

Everyone. Once upon a time, every person began as a sweet little baby without history.

I vote against Original Sin.

I vote for Innocence.

✳✳✳✳

Wally makes me clean the cages and checking room and fill in for Linda the receptionist at his vet office, all day Saturday. Now he wants me to learn bookkeeping so I can take over Linda's job and be with him all day, six days a week. He asked a bookkeeping woman from church to teach me. He doesn't want Linda to know.

Wally pays me seven dollars for every Saturday I work. At Rocky's I got a dollar fifteen an hour and a little money in tips every day. If Wally paid me seven dollars a day, six days a week, then I would have forty-two dollars a week, but no living expenses to pay.

I felt sort of rich after Chaz and Floss moved in with me—my share of the rent went down to twenty-five dollars a month. They paid fifty dollars, which gave me the money to buy records and magazines and clothes and posters. Of course, Floss was going to find her own apartment, so our share would go up later.

Wally said the landlord took everything to the dump. So I didn't have any clothes. Before we got married, Wally bought me normal clothes, but after the vows, he started replacing my clothes with clothes I would never choose.

I'm okay with the hot pants made from silky material with pink and purple flowers—cute and comfortable—but he often insists I wear the super tight green paisley ones that zip up the back. Super, super tight. His other favorite outfit on me is the tight black jumpsuit with rhinestones. He ordered both from his Frederick's catalog. A package just arrived from there last Thursday—two body-stockings and brown suede hot pants with orange and yellow stripes.

I did not bring those clothes with me. I grabbed some shorts and a couple tops and the paisley granny dress I was wearing the last day with Chaz. I did not bring the platform clogs Wally makes me wear with the hot pants. I brought only my muddy red sneakers I left on the back stoop. I would have come here barefoot if I had to.

****

I sit under the giant blue spruce. I see circles on the trunk where the lower branches were removed to make room for Ty's target for throwing his knife. In the meadow, the wind waves the orange sea of paintbrush. Beyond the shooting range, I see the start of the trail Ty and I scraped and dug up Fire Peak to the bristlecone, breaking our backs moving rocks. We painted our names with a rainbow of watercolor on a boulder at the top, but our names washed off in the first rain.

I wish my marriage to Wally would wash away like watercolor.

Ty carved our initials into the bristlecone, and they will be there for a long time because bristlecones live so long.

I wish Daddy and Ty were here.

I love how the night opens from the first star into a massive glittering blanket—just out of reach above the faint, dark outline of the surrounding mountains, glittering like a giant bowl of diamonds.

Now it is too dark to write.

JULY 8 WEDNESDAY

Dear Ty,

I'm at Daddy's cabin, and I've been thinking of all the happy times we had up here. We've hardly talked since the night we started planning your move to Canada. Do you remember that night? Mama'd gone to bed (supposedly), and we were in the kitchen, and you spread your map across the table and drew your route with a black marker. First you intended to stay at the cabin, then continue on through Wyoming and Montana to Calgary, Canada.

We thought Mama was asleep, but now I'm convinced she was listening to us from the hall. The second she came through the swinging doors, you closed your notebook and slipped it off the table. You tried to refold the roadmap, but roadmaps are so hard to fold back up. You told her you were looking up how far Golconda is to Canada (which was not a lie).

I hope being in the Army is okay for you. I remember Mama told us Daddy won a medal from World War II, and she said earning a medal was the best thing Daddy ever did and no one could take it away from him. How many times did she say he was a terrible husband and a cruel father? But he did one good thing (in her eyes) which proves no matter how bad you are, you can still do something great.

It sounds like Purple Hearts are awarded for injuries, so I don't want you to get one, Ty. I know you don't believe in this war.

I am in a rage toward Mama, Ty. Why don't I know how she talked you into going in the Army? How come you and I have never talked since then? Why did you start staying away from me? I'm mad at you, too.

But I know if you were here at Daddy's cabin, I would be glad to be with you.

What if she had never walked in on us and your plan worked perfectly? What if you had gotten to Canada?

What good, big thing has Mama ever done? She hasn't won any medals.

She promised to take us out for our own family dinner the night before you left for bootcamp. Then she said Barf had caught the flu, so we never in our entire lives went to a restaurant with Mama. Instead he exposed us to the flu while he took over Mama's bed and the bathroom half the time and kept coughing and blowing his nose and leaving Kleenex all over the floor.

You came home from bootcamp, your hair shaved off and your ears sticking out. Mama got out your baby pictures so we could compare you as a baldy man with you as a baldy kid.

You and I didn't talk. Hi. Bye. You spent most of your time hanging out with a girl I do not know who Mama kept calling your drinking buddy. Before you got on the bus to go back to the Army, you said, "Write me, Micky," and I said I would, and I did. Honestly—tons more than the two letters I mailed you.

After you got on the bus, Mama and I walked to the ice rink and watched the skaters. Cold, but the sun was out, so we stayed out of the shade. Mama told me when she was a little girl, she wanted to learn to ice skate, but not much ice in Clovis. She said she had roller skates, but way hard to look graceful, and she wanted to be lifted up and jump and do turns. No one at the rink was skating that way either though. Everyone was bundled into coats and scarves, and some kids fell back down every time they got up. I tried to imagine Mama a little girl zooming around Clovis on her skates. I asked her why we'd never seen a picture of her as a kid, and she said there used to be a photo album, but when her father and brother died of the flu, her mother burned all the pictures. She burned his clothes, too, in the incinerator.

Mama said, "She hated being without them, and so when she began the new life, she wanted to be rid of everything reminding her. At least she didn't burn *me* up."

Mama was ten when they died.

I asked her what she would do if you got killed, Ty, and she said, "I'm not in charge of how many heartbeats he has."

I do understand—if you used up your heartbeats, it wouldn't matter if you were in Vietnam or crossing a street in Las Vegas or if it was an atom bomb or a car accident. Death's the same, and that's what it means when they say "Your number's up." They mean the number of heartbeats, but I don't know who *they* are— the ones who make up the rules like God. They.

They say liberty and justice for all, so how can They force boys who can't even vote to be drafted and sent to war they don't believe in? How come They say Jesus loves the little children but then say babies have sin and kids need to be whipped? How come They say God loves you but say you're going to hell?

How come They say "it's all for the best" when your little baby dies?

Now you can fathom why you never receive a letter from me. I write troublesome things you would not want to read. But I hope you can feel my love in your heart, and I hope your heart is beating steady with a trillion zillion heartbeats to go.

Love,

Mick

P.S. I don't have to throw this letter away so Wally (my soon-to-be ex-husband) won't read it. I hope we will find each other soon, Ty.

Every time Ty would watch a war movie at his friends' houses, he'd tell me the whole plot, which had no girls. At Tina's house, her mom kept the TV on all the time, and as far as we could tell, the afternoon war movies on TV never had girls starring in them. But Daddy taught me to shoot like a boy. The cans we blasted are still all over the ground near our shooting range. I wish I could practice shooting right now. I want to find out if I am still a good shot.

One time I told Chaz I sometimes thought about shooting Barf, but Chaz said, "Whoa—extreme, Mick. Pretend he's dead. He's not worth going to prison over." I said, "You're right. Not worth going to hell over either." I told Chaz that Barf messed up our family, but I never exactly revealed to him that Barf laid himself down on me.

****

Next door to Wally lives a foreign man I call Mr. A. His accent is hard to understand, but he helps me with my garden. One day, turning soil with a little shovel, I joked if I dug too deep, I might dig into hell, and he laughed and got down on his hands and knees in my garden and touched my first bean plant breaking through the soil. "How does it make you feel to see this baby plant?" I said happy, and he said, "Heaven."

He told me no two leaves are exactly the same, and ever since I view leaves in a new way. I had never thought that leaves were like snowflakes.

I believe Mr. A will water my garden. Wally is right—gardening helps me feel better about life.

I told Wally that Mr. A has been helping me, and Wally called Mr. A bonkers and told me to stay away from him. I didn't divulge that Mr. A assumes Wally is my father.

Do the math. It is quite possible for a 36-year-old man to be father to a daughter who is eighteen. In fact, if my baby had lived, when she turned eighteen, I would be 36. Mama was 36 when Ty turned eighteen. So it's not bonkers for Mr. A to assume Wally is my father.

It does concern me that Mr. A thinks I resemble Wally. That means I'm homely and try too hard. Wally makes his pompadour hair-do every day, but he wouldn't pass for Liberace or Governor Love. His ears stick out, and his mouth is wide for his face; his eyes are pale brown and squinty, his nose kind of like a hawk how it curves down, but it gets super red.

When I am sorry for Wally, I think I love him. Sometimes I perceive a sad little boy though he is an older man. Wally's life hasn't been easy although you'd think so because of growing up with endless money. He didn't wear used clothes from the church sale, and he didn't listen to his mother haranguing about the utility bill. But sometimes the boys at his school would beat him up. Wally talked to me about the bullies while he drank a bottle of Jim Bean Single Barrel bourbon. He got beat up lots of times. His brother told him to act like a man and never cry.

His brother is a bully himself in my eyes. In the pictures of Wally's family, in three of them, his brother blocks him out by getting in front of him. In another, he makes finger horns above Wally's head. In another, he is pinching Wally's arm and Wally is making a face like it hurts.

An idea sprang in my mind, and I told Wally the bullies acted that way because they were jealous of how smart he is.

Wally's Adam's apple reminds me of Dwight's—a boy with thick brown glasses and a scar up the back of his head at our school and church. More than once the boys ganged up on him and beat him up. Our grade had twelve boys and two girls—me and Tina. Five of those boys were mean through and through, and the other six boys never stood up for Dwight.

I am sad for Wally the way I felt sad for Dwight. I can't be mad at him all the time.

To be clear—being sad for him does not mean I want sex with him. His book in the drawer of his nightstand—those positions creep me out. I hate it when he stops and pulls out the book because it takes longer when I want him to be done. Why is spanking in a sex book? Is there any difference between spanking in sex, spanking for discipline, and hitting your wife any time?

How much do I owe him?

It's gotten so whenever I see my life creaking on ahead forever with him, I don't want to live one more day.

I lay my fingers against my pulse and count my heartbeats. I don't own a watch so can't tell how many beats are fitting into a minute, but my pulse pounds fast.

I wonder how many extra beats Chaz put in with all the speed he did.

Mama said that we keep having lives until we're perfect. In that case, are the heartbeats you didn't use in your life waiting for your next life? An extra long life?

A short life like my baby's? What life was she on? Does being born dead mean being ever truly alive? Where is her soul? What if she didn't have a soul and that's why she died? Chaz didn't believe in souls, but Mama said that soul comes into the body with the first breath. I don't know if my baby had a breath before she died. Did she die in me or right after she came out?

Did Chaz die in the ambulance or at the hospital? Was Floss with him?

Does Chaz try to be with our baby in the afterlife?

What about the dogs Wally puts to sleep? Do dogs have souls? Do heartbeats count for dogs, too? People's beloveds?

Wally said nobody loves him, not even me. But the dogs love him fine at the clinic because he's gentle with them.

He never had a pet dog though. Neither did I, but both Ty and I wanted one. Our astrology charts are different, but Ty and I were always on the same side. Especially when it came to Barf.

Barf is the USSR, and the higher he builds the wall between us, the better.

I imagine a wall of concrete blocks going up to the sky between me and Wally, too.

I do not like being a part of Wally's family. At the wedding in Texas, his mother said, "Well, at least Wally has someone now," as if I was one little step better than nothing. I guess she doesn't realize Wally has friends. I guess she has no knowledge of the people who bring their animals to him to save their lives. Wally didn't have to marry me so he'd "have someone," despite his brother saying, "What did you do? Force her to get pregnant so she'd marry you?"

I was shocked he said that. Wally might have said, "It's not my baby," but he didn't.

His brother is handsome but not nice. He put his hands on my breasts when I was waiting for Wally in the hall outside the bathroom and whispered, "I'd like to fuck you." I try to erase the memory of his hands on me. He had no right to touch me. I did not owe him anything. I wanted to punch him, but I just crossed my arms and stood there glaring at him like a bulldog until he went away. I didn't tell Wally.

No matter if I dislike his family, I owe him. He bought everything necessary for my garden. He bought my Falcon. Did surgery on my jacked-up knee. Paid for my baby's funeral. The list goes on. I've been a hundred percent dependent on him. I am grateful.

I've been trying the scales. You know, fifty-one good/forty-nine bad?

I don't remember "death do you part" in the wedding vows. I don't remember his proposal. I do remember getting into his brand new red GTO and driving all the way to Texas. I know his brother was jealous because his car was a boring station wagon. Wally told me he intends to trade in his car every year. He said this is a cool way to remember your life. He said he'll always remember GTO as his wedding car.

I will always remember the Falcon: it will remind me of the good side of Wally and the bad side; it will remind me of soaring up the mountain and setting myself free.

****

Chaz and Floss and I talked about how we would choose to die. Floss said, "Shoot me in the head so it's fast." and Chaz said, "Take drugs and drift off to sleep and never wake up." I said I would like to die saving someone's life (you know, the one big, good thing that makes the whole life worthwhile?), and Chaz said, "So you want to be a heroine."

I said that would be a reason I had lived, and Chaz said, "No need to seek a reason for life. The meaning of life is living."

What a shaman would say, I guess.

Lester said the meaning of life is "Party." I wish I could write party the way he said it: "Parrteee!" He was supposed to be heading to Vietnam, but he said there was a psychiatrist in Los Angeles who could set him free, like say he was crazy or something.

I was a stupid girl. I got into a car with a stranger. I never told Wally or Chaz or ANYONE about Lester.

The past is true and cannot be changed. No matter how many wishes nor how passionate my prayers to lose my memory, the past keeps flashing, and then I'm reliving it. I wake up in the night having just experienced it over again. I want those memories buried so deep. God, please. God, please, please.

Here I am wanting a divorce and at the same time being mad at Mama for being stupid about Daddy, one of the few exceptional men in the world in every way. She could have quit astrology instead of quitting Daddy. Simple.

I keep thinking she knows if he's alive or dead. She's like Wally that way: she gets all smart aleck when we want an answer. Like "He's in a Pyramid, of course."

She wanted Barf to be single so she could marry him. Whenever he wouldn't be with her because he said he was with his wife, Mama would cry and play her records. Not only Strauss but Frank Sinatra and Dinah Shore, and Ravel and all the other ones she got each month from her album subscription (except for the Brothers Grimm that I asked her for).

Mama is like Wally. She makes up her mind about something and she won't change.

She made up her mind Barf tells the truth, and I'm a liar.

Every time he broke up with her, Mama believed it was because his wife was being pitiable and demanding and wouldn't give him a divorce, but how does she know he's really married? He could be lying to her and have other girlfriends.

I asked her if she ever talked to his wife, and she said, "Certainly not!"

"I think you should," I said, and she got all lofty: "It's not my role."

Tina is the only other person besides Mama and Ty to know about Barf. Tina wouldn't tell her mother he put his hand between her legs when he was being all friendly and giving the little kids in our Sunday school piggyback rides.

I told Mama he came into my room and stood overlooking me and lifted off my blanket, but she didn't believe me.

"I want a lock for my door."

"Don't be silly."

"I hate how you choose him over us," I told her.

"I don't. He's my soul mate. And so are you."

"Maybe his wife is his soul mate. Maybe she's your soul mate since you both want the same man."

"What a tangled web the world is," she said.

Maybe he was with his wife all those times he was breaking Mama's heart, but it's weird that his wife would accept his affair with Mama at all. I asked Mama if she'd done that woman's chart.

"I'll have to get her birth data from Floyd."

A couple days later I was standing in the hall with the swinging door propped open talking to Mama in the kitchen about her new record, the soundtrack of *West Side Story*. Barf came up the hall from the bathroom and started talking, too, right behind me. I felt him rub up against me, and I yelled, "Don't touch me!"

"Calm down, Micky. Floyd wouldn't do anything like that on purpose."

"It was on purpose!"

He swung through the door into the kitchen and put his arms around Mama. They both stood there frowning at me. So hard to hold my tongue and not break my promises to Ty and Tina.

How could Mama let that creep stay in our home even for one minute?

The next time he spent the night, Barf came into my room and knelt down by my bed. He started touching me under the covers. I screamed, and he jammed out of there fast. In the morning I told Mama, and she said it wasn't my fault that my dreams were so vivid. Moon in Scorpio square Pluto square Mercury, the Sun and Saturn square Uranus, the crazy planet.

After supper when he'd left, I demanded a lock for my door. Mama lit a Pall Mall and said, "I don't want to talk about this any more."

It didn't do any good. He was in our lives forever. And Ty wasn't there any more to stand up to him.

She carried her coffee mug into the living room and pulled her astrology tray onto her lap. I opened the closet beside the front door and grabbed my new coat we bought at Woolco from the final sales rack. I walked out of the house, slammed the door behind me. Mama didn't come after me. Despite it being 3 days after the spring equinox, it was cold and windy and snowing.

I cried my way past the houses where the snow dusted the lawns. A few blocks further, a major rush of snow spun into my face. Instantly, the storm turned into a blizzard. I could hardly see a foot in front of me.

I had never considered going into Tubby's Pool Hall before since it was supposed to be a hangout for guys with an evil eye out for other guys who want to rumble. I stood out in the dark with snow trying to blow me over and peered through the window. Seeing two girls playing pool reassured me to take a break from the blizzard and go inside. I have had a few occasions when girls wanted to beat me up, but the pool girls didn't come across as the beating-up kind. For one thing, they're obviously older since they had cocktails.

The beat-you-up girls hang on each other, and they're dressed almost alike in jean jackets and jeans. One of them takes the role of the boss. She always has her hair ratted up into a disaster area, and she wears white lipstick. I heard they wear their hair backcombed big so they can hide razor blades. If another girl tries to pull their hair, her hand will get all cut up. They make up an excuse to start a fight: "You were messing with my boyfriend, so we're gonna get you," but I've realized boys don't love them. Ty made them leave me alone when he came upon a group of them (I call the Goofus Gang) ready to beat me up. And then you could tell they were attracted to him! The leader gave him her phone number!

Unlike the beat-you-up girls, the girls in Tubby's were the kind of girls boys love to be with. The girls in Tubby's were what Mama would call wild girls because their skirts were short and they wore those cute white boots. They both smoked cigarettes and wore their blonde hair long and flipped up.

I got a seat on a stool at the counter in the back, with a cup of coffee (which I don't like but who can complain about a hot drink on a cold night?). Tubby had goodness to let me sit at the bar and drink coffee without playing any pool. Tubby is a little fat man with greasy black hair, a cigar stuck in the corner of his mouth like how Mama holds a cigarette when she's baking. The coffee cost fifteen cents, and I had three dollars and fifteen cents in my purse. I put in lots of cream and sugar. I won't drink it black like Mama does.

When I felt warm, I took off my coat and laid it over the red vinyl seat of the empty stool next to me. In the mirror against the wall on the other side of the counter, I observed everyone behind me. I admire girls who aren't scared of anything, and in contrast to those girls, I looked like a scared rat with dripping wet hair.

So why did Lester come up to meet me? He did stand out as I watched in the mirror everyone playing pool because his purple glasses dominated his face. Maybe he could tell I was looking at him.

He came over, pushed my coat off on the floor, and sat down on the stool beside me. I picked my coat up and folded it over my lap. Not the cleanest floor.

"Hi, beautiful" His first words shocked me since nobody ever called me beautiful before. He put a dime into the little jukebox next to the napkin dispenser and punched in "Itchycoo Park."

"Do you like this song?"

I said I did, and he said, "Do you have the record?" and I said, "No," and he asked, "Do you want to go to California?" and when I said, "Yes," he twirled his stool around to face me. "Do you play pool?" he asked, and I said no, and he asked if I've ever been to Missouri, and I said no, and he asked me if I wanted a ride.

At first I said no, but thought about the wind and snow blowing all over the place outside and how home was about ten blocks away. I thought about how it might freak Mama out if I came home in a strange boy's car, so I changed my mind. As "Itchykoo Park" came to the last "It's too beautiful," he zipped up his jacket, and I put my coat back on.

His old red and white Ford was parked across the street under a streetlight, and he held onto my shoulder as we ducked through the snow. He opened the door for me, and I skidded across the seat; then he got in and started up the engine, jumped out and cleared the snow off the windows. As we headed down the street, I gave him directions to our house. "Whoa, girl. I ain't gonna twist up directions and find myself lost in this stupid, snowy town. You can get what you need on the road."

I thought he was taking me home.

"Heya, heya, you said you wanted to go to California, so don't back out on me, okay? I don't like when a chick says one thing and does another."

"I didn't know you meant California right now," I said.

"I'm not coming back for you when you decide you're ready. C'mon. Let's go. Live on the beach. Be hippies. You like the idea, don't you? Ocean. No fucking snow. Let's jam out of this frigging snowy place."

The snow kept coming down, and he kept driving further and further away from my neighborhood. We stopped at a red light, and he said, "What you wanna do? Hop out right now? Go ahead. I ain't stopping you, beautiful. But I want you to come with me. I want you to."

Like being handed magic—leave the snow and ice and become a flower child. Leave Barf behind and go to a place with sunshine and flowers and an ocean and love. I forgot my obligation to sing solo "Enslaved in Sin" in church on Sunday.

I traveled down the highway in Lester's big red car with the red seats, the Animals pleading "Please Don't Let Me Be Misunderstood," and the snow streaming down while the lights of Denver disappeared behind us. Snowflakes bounced on the windshield, and the blades slid back and forth fast, and all I could see was the road leading somewhere I'd never been.

Lester explained the route: we would go to Wyoming, then head over to Utah, to Nevada, and across the desert to California. "Less mountains this route," he said. "I planned it good."

I started to tell him about Golconda and how the mountains aren't scary when you are in them. He said, "Yeah, and how many times do you go up in winter? I don't got no chains."

So we kept driving the Valley Highway toward Wyoming through the profusion of snow with the radio sounding more scratchy by the mile. At some point, we changed to Highway 287.

Lester sang along in a loud, flat voice with the crackly radio "Last Train to Clarksville." The car hammered louder. He patted the steering wheel. "Friendly car. It always makes that sound. Likes to talk to ya. Hey, open the glovebox for me, will ya? Ditch weed. Can't expect much from it."

I found a bread wrapper under a Wyoming map. He made a joint, driving with one hand, rolling with the other. I took a puff and coughed my brains out! The car started banging harder and harder, and then a loud pow! Lester managed to steer the car to the side of the road before the red machine stopped altogether. We were a long way from Denver with snow flying everywhere.

I got out with Lester to open the hood, but it stuck shut. Lester kicked a tire and called his car names like "red devil," and the snow fell hard and fast. The wind whipped my hair all over the place. A dark trickle ran out from under the car. My first touch to ground in Wyoming.

Why didn't I cross the road and stick out my thumb to beg a ride back from another stranger who would take me home again to Mama and Barf?

Well, Ace Teeter appeared like an old angel in a pickup truck. He flashed his lights, and Lester grabbed my hand, and we burst into a run. The snow blew into my face blinding me, and Lester pulled me along by the hand, and at this moment, nothing was more important in the world than to catch up to the back lights of the pickup truck flashing through the snow.

The passenger door of the truck hung open for us, and Lester pushed me up on the seat and climbed in after me and slammed the door shut.

"Couldn't leave a couple of sorry kids standing by the road in a blizzard," Ace Teeter said. "Though ordinarily I'd as soon run over them hippie hitchhikers. You ain't hippies, are you?" He squinted at us in the dim light and I guess he'd shove us back out if we said yes.

Lester brushed his sleeve across his snowy purple lenses. "Nope, me and my wife hate them hippies. I am a PFC with the U. S. Army." He squished my hand and gave me a look, so I didn't say anything. Ow. Wife.

Ace said that back at his garage in town he had a tow truck and could bring Lester's car in.

In shock, I kept my mouth shut! Ace drove down the white highway with the wipers pushing the snow off the windshield, which covered in white slush again in a second.

Soon we were in town, parked at his gas station. We got out of the truck and slid through the snow to the door. He unlocked it and we went inside to a dim room with a metal desk and a couple black chairs next to a little table. He didn't switch on the ceiling lights. "You kids make yourselves at home," he said. "No sense in your being out again. I'll bring back your car with my tow truck."

Lester gave him the key, and Ace headed back out the door. Lester rolled his jacket up and stuffed it behind his head. Through the space between his skin and glasses, I saw him fall asleep. I sat beside the desk, the ancient cash register, the heavy black phone, the ashtray heaped with brown butts, a stack of Laramie newspapers, and the snowy wind pounding against the dark window.

Instead of heading back outside into the blizzard like a smart girl, I covered up with my coat and tried to go to sleep, too. The next thing I remember is Ace Teeter telling Lester an estimated amount for fixing his car.

Lester went over to the black phone on the wall and started dialing. I went to the bathroom that reeked of Pine-Sol. When I came out, Lester still held the phone to his ear, his neck bright red.

He shouted into the receiver: "So don't send the damned money. I'll hitch it."

Then he said, "Yeah, yeah. I got a guy here to fix it. I swear. No sweat." His voice changed, got low and deeper.

"So how's Maria and the kid, huh? Tell her I'll be in touch, okay?"

He hung up and said, "Go to it, man. The dough will be here in the morning. Lemme sign that sucker, and tell us where we can find a cheap honeymoon hotel."

Lester stood over me and reached for my hand. I got up, put on my new coat, and followed him into the quiet night, the street wide with plenty of room for the wind blowing the snow. All of a sudden, Lester started making a noise sounding like an inside-out cough. I thought he was choking.

He has the weirdest laugh.

"Boy, is that asshole going to split a gut when we don't come back for the ole hunk a junk."

I didn't get it. He told Ace Teeter to do the work. He signed a piece of paper. He squeezed my shoulder so hard it hurt, even though he squeezed through my coat. "See here, I got a plan. My old man sends the bucks, but we hitch it on out of here for free. You're the bait, beautiful, see? Oh man, I am a wizard."

"But what about Ace?"

"I hate them geezers," he said. "They won't do nothing for you unless there's something in it for them. The only reason he picked us up was he saw us break down and thought it meant he would make some bucks. The only reason he doesn't like hippies is they don't got much money."

We were the only living things on the snowy street. No traffic. The cars parked on the side were covered by mounds of snow, and the snow blew into drifts and around the pink neon light blinking OPEN for the motel surrounded by semi-trucks. "Must be the place," Lester said, and we went through the door into a dingey, pine-walled room with orange plastic chairs.

Lester pushed the bell at the counter where we stood waiting. He pushed it again, and a light came on. Through a door behind the counter appeared a lady with a scarf wrapped around her hair rollers, wearing a pink and green flowered robe. Lester told her we were stranded and needed a room, and she said, "You poor kids. Eight dollars a night." Lester told her Ace agreed to fix his car and had recommended the motel, and she said "Ace is a good man. We'll make it seven-fifty." Lester signed some paper-work, and she handed him the key. "Fifth door down." She pointed outside, and we headed back into the blizzard. I cannot explain why I went along with Lester other than to say I could not stand Barf. I had no lock, and Mama believes everything he says.

Memory pounds in my head like a hammer.

The walls in the room—shellacked pine. A light bulb hung from the middle of the ceiling on a chain. A green and brown rag-rug covered part of the green linoleum. Painting of a cowboy riding a white horse through the desert with some cattle in the distance. I sat down in the only chair—light wood arms with a vinyl, turquoise cushion, a bit wobbly.

Lester started peeling off his clothes and throwing them on the floor. In a minute he lay on the bed naked except for his purple glasses. I had gotten out my comb and was combing my wet hair. What was wrong with me? Why didn't I simply head back out into the blowing snow to the office where I could start ringing the bell for the lady in rollers to help me?

That's why I have never told anyone what happened. No answer to the obvious question:

"When he took off his clothes, why didn't you run out the door?"

In some odd way, taking off his clothes didn't seem weird. While Ty never whipped off his clothes in front of me, we lived in a little house with only one bathroom. So when Lester started taking off his clothes, I assumed he'd change into something else to wear. But he lay naked on the motel bed and said, "Commere, beautiful. I'm lonesome."

I sat in the turquoise chair combing my hair, my hands shaking. He started playing with himself. I looked away from him and stared at the cowboy on the wall.

"You don't gotta be shy with me," he said. "Trust me. I won't bite."

I just stared at the cowboy, but before I came up with a plan or jumped up ran out the door, Lester rolled off the bed and came at me. "Maybe we're thinking the same thing," he said, and he pulled me up out of the chair and grabbed me in a bear hug. I felt his mouth on my neck. "Let's fuck, girl," he said.

I rammed my elbow into his stomach. He chopped me on the arm, ow! I grabbed onto the arm of the turquoise chair, and he broke it off the chair and twisted my arms behind my back and forced me across the room, pushing me from behind. He shoved me down on the bed.

I hit him with my fist. I bit his hand.

"I don't mind," he said. "You like it rough. I don't mind." He whacked me across the face, and I saw stars. By the time the stars were diminishing, I knew what was going to happen.

He was going to do It to me, and I couldn't stop him, and if I kept fighting him, he'd hurt me more.

I turned my face into the pillow. I didn't want to breathe his breath or let him kiss me or let his pimples touch my skin. His tongue licked my neck. It didn't help to kick at him. It didn't help to fight him. I managed to pull the sheet mostly between us.

"You owe me something for all my trouble," he said. "You know you do." He yanked my jeans down, and I held my legs together, but he pushed them apart and rammed into me. It hurt so much. Oh, God, it hurt. He kept jamming at me, and I protected my face with my arm so I didn't have to breathe his panting breath.

I concentrated on the sound of the wind rattling across the parking lot outside and beating against the window. I held my breath and tried to pretend in my mind that nothing was happening. But each ram at me hurt like being split down the middle.

Finally he got done and slid off the bed and went to the bathroom.

I got up and put my jeans back on. I sat down in the turquoise chair and wrapped myself in my coat. I felt like crying, but I didn't. From the bathroom, I heard water splashing. Lester started singing "Yesterday.'" His voice was flat and terrible. I wanted him to stop singing. No right to hurt my ears, too.

He came out of the bathroom and stood over me with a towel wrapped around his waist, grinning and wearing the purple glasses. "This is like a real honeymoon, ain't it, beautiful?" he said.

My body rocked, rocked, and I couldn't stop. "You wrecked my life," I said.

He laughed his inside-out laugh that sounded like coughing.

"You'll get used to it." He turned on the television, nothing but static, so he turned it off again and got back into bed, now with the covers over him. "C'mon and cuddle up," he said.

I shook my head and huddled up wrapped in my coat in the turquoise chair, its left arm on the floor. I can't explain why I didn't go looking for the lady in rollers. She didn't deserve to see someone as gross as me. In the dim light, the way the splinters stuck out got me crazily thinking of *Fantasia*—how the broom splinters become brooms and danced poor Mickey crazy—dancing in with water buckets until he's drowning. Poor Mickey—all those splinters and brooms and buckets, dancing and dancing and dancing . . . . I dozed off in the chair.

The motel shower was warm, not hot, more of a trickle than a spray. I had to put my same clothes back on afterward, and when I came out of the bathroom, Lester asked if I wanted to borrow a shirt. I said no, and he grabbed me by the arm and said, "Come, beautiful. Let's go for some breakfast."

To my surprise, it was daytime. Lester opened the door to powder pouring from the wind and blowing into the room. My wet hair from the shower froze on the way to the café next to the motel.

Except for me and Lester, I think all the customers were truck drivers. "Anything you want," Lester said, and I ordered scrambled eggs with hash browns and toast. Our breakfast arrived, and Lester squirted ketchup all over his eggs.

Sickening, like a plateful of blood.

My frozen hair melted onto the table-drip, drip. He talked with his mouth full, and I kept trying not to look at him because I didn't want to see my ugly self reflected in his purple glasses.

He kept talking about California. He said, "I'm gonna eat so much fruit when I get there, they're gonna wonder what stripped their trees. I like fruit."

I asked if they had fruit where he came from, and he said, "Of course, they got fruit. How do you think I learned I like it? They don't grow no oranges in Missouri, but oranges grow everywhere in California."

As Lester paid at the cash register, he pointed out a rack of rings to me. "Pick one of those out. Any one you like, beautiful." Only right for him to give me a present after what he did to me. So I scanned the rack and selected a ring with a black stone—shiny and shaped like a star. I did not predict the band would turn my finger green. "This here's your wedding ring," and he laughed that inside-out cough of a laugh.

I wish I said, "No, it's my apology ring," and made him beg for my forgiveness.

I could have asked someone in the café right that second for help.

I could have gone to the phone booth and called Mama collect to find out if she'd help me figure out how to find my way home. To her and to Barf.

I went back to the motel room with Lester.

The next time he wasn't so rough with me, maybe because I didn't fight. Nothing to fight about because what could he do to me he hadn't done to me already? This time he put his finger inside me and moved it around slow, which didn't hurt. Afterward we fell asleep on the motel bed, and I didn't wake up until I felt his finger moving around inside me again.

Weird to wake up that way—I didn't know where I was at first. A dark room with a man. Then he was standing over me, telling me to dress while he was gone, that we'd go out for lunch after he came back. He asked me again if I wanted to borrow one of his shirts. This time I did, a black shirt with yellow trim on the pockets. He left, and I washed off in the warm trickle in the shower stall. My choice: Lester or Barf.

When Lester came back, he'd picked up the money his dad wired. We went back to the café for hamburgers. The French fries made me happy. He said, "Sorry about that. I didn't mean to plug no virgin. You was, wasn't you?"

I acted like I wasn't listening and smothered the French fries in ketchup.

"Yeah, that's what I thought when I seen the blood on the bed. You know, a chick comes along with you, you figure she's up for a good time. I didn't guess you was a virgin."

"Well, you don't know me," I said.

"Now you're my girlfriend. You'll get better."

He bought a deck of cards at the cash register, and we went back to the room and played rummy. Every time I beat him, he pretended to throw a fit. He threw himself on the bed and smacked himself on the forehead. "Beat by a chick! I can't believe it! Beat by a chick." He'd crouch on the floor, and we'd play again. Funny Lester.

We went out again for supper, and the snow had almost stopped, with just a few flakes fluttering by. Lester insisted I order a steak. "Order the best thing on the menu. I'm going to treat you right." When the waitress asked how I wanted it, I had no clue what to say because I'd never eaten a steak before. Lester said, "She wants it medium rare."

Bloody meat in a pool of blood. I pretended I liked it because he was so pleased he'd gotten steak for me. Some truck drivers seemed to be inspecting me, likely because of my out-of-control hair and Lester's black shirt with the yellow trim on the pockets. Lester bought us chocolate bars at the cash register even though we ate cherry pie for dessert. My first time to eat in a restaurant three times in one day.

Back in the motel room, he did it to me again. He scrutinized me lying beside him with all my clothes off. "You're beautiful. You know that?" I didn't scrutinize him; I could see my reflection in his glasses. Mama always told me I needed braces and sometimes called me Bucky, yet in some way, Lester made it easy for me to pretend I was a pretty and cool girl. Another explanation for not escaping. That night I slept in the bed with him.

In the morning I got dressed and unsnarled my hair, and then we went out to find a ride. Next thing, Lester was talking to a truck driver, and then I was climbing into a blue Mack semi-truck to meet the driver Frank. Frank wore a red sweatshirt and blue jeans, had a jiggly chin, and spoke in a deep, growly voice. "Hey, beautiful," he said to me. How weird everyone was calling me beautiful! Lester climbed up behind me. "This here's my wife," he said and poked me with his elbow. I got it. A joke on Frank.

Frank rolled out of the parking lot. He told us 287 was made to connect Denver with Yellowstone, that 30 that merges with 287 is East-West while 287 is North-South. He said we could follow 287 south to Port Arthur, Texas, or follow 30 to New Jersey or Oregon. "Destinations from Laramie."

He was hauling machine tools from Indiana to L.A. We turned north on 3rd Street and passed by little houses covered in snow, shops and a bar, a church with a tall steeple, some motels, and then the country, flat and white as far as I could see. "Better known as the Lincoln Highway," Frank said.

Sitting up on the hump in the Mack truck between Frank and Lester hauling tools across Wyoming transferred me to a parallel world where everything was new. The vast white landscape beneath the vast cloudy sky, the idea of roads connecting all the states and cities. Vast connections beyond the horizon.

Sometimes in my dreams, I'm aware of the body of sleeping Michaela lying on the bed. The real Michaela is me in the dream—not the sleeping Michaela who is having the dream. I felt my sleeping self was back in Denver, and my real self headed down the road, seeing places never seen before with two men I didn't know. We rolled past snow fences and snow fields with brushes of yellow grass sticking up.

As we passed through Bosler, Frank pointed out the store where you can buy a new bed, chair or a new car. Otherwise, most of the buildings are falling apart, and he said it was a ghost town that was going to be worse with the Interstate soon to open twenty miles south.

Frank told us about another town on this highway (that we would not go through since it is north) named Home on the Range. When Home on the Range developed into a uranium town, he said, its name changed. The postmaster got feisty, and she'd return mail not addressed to Home on the Range. So the name didn't change after all to Yellowcake. She wouldn't let mail go to Jeffrey City either, which is what it got named after all.

"Why Yellowcake? Is there a bakery?" Lester looked excited.

"Maybe," Frank said, "but that's not what I'm talking about. Yellowcake is what they do with uranium for making nukes."

"I like yellow cake, but I like chocolate cake best. I don't like no white wedding cake. My mom makes tomato soup cake. Tomato soup from a can and raisins. It ain't too sweet like white wedding cake."

Frank lit one of his little cigars. He said he liked to learn about all the places he drove through. As we drove into Rock River, Frank said a star got killed here in a car crash. I might have seen her on *Howdy Doody* at Tina's house, but I never saw *Jailhouse Rock,* which surprised Frank and Lester since all girls love Elvis movies. The Texaco gas station was across the street from a tavern with red hand-painted signs for Cocktails and Budweiser hanging on front but no neon beer signs like at Tubby's. Frank said a long time ago, a couple hundred pioneers came through here & a blizzard swept up and wiped them totally out, but we didn't tell him that could have happened to us if Ace Teeter hadn't saved us!

Frank explained the scenery in his rumbly voice. He told us Butch Cassidy and Calamity Jane and even President Teddy Roosevelt stayed at an old hotel a couple hours or so north of Rock River in Buffalo. Butch Cassidy's hideout was close by. Along with his little cigars, Frank smoked nonfilter Camels, and when he wasn't talking, he was singing along with his 8-track tapes: Merle Haggard, Johnny Cash. I liked the Patsy Cline best. I guess Frank was close to Daddy's age. Periodically he took off his cap and rubbed his bald head. He had a pointy nose and grey streaks in his beard. He smoked the way Mama does—the second he put one smoke out, he lit up another.

All of a sudden I probably jumped a mile from BOOM and BOOM. I thought the same thing was happening to the truck that happened to Lester's car.

"Well, shit," Frank said. "What a damn crappy stroke of luck."

Right up the road in the middle of nowhere, a garage rose from the flat white landscape, and Frank pulled in. "Damn! We're lucky!" The BOOMS were two tires blowing out, one right after the other. A guy came out of the station and said they didn't sell tires. The next thing, he and Frank got into a rusty Chevy truck, and headed back to Laramie, leaving me and Lester hanging out in Frank's truck. A bit of snow danced in the air, making tiny rainbows as the sun pushed through the clouds.

Lester immediately started snooping through Frank's stuff. "Check this shit." He held up a gun. "A Colt 45. I ought to put this baby in my pack for safekeeping."

"I think you should leave Frank's stuff alone," I said.

"What if he decides to shoot us?" Lester stroked the gun. "Bet you'd be glad I got the gun and not him."

"If you take his gun, I'm going to tell him," I said, and Lester said, "I'd shoot you for opening your trap." He pointed the gun at me, and I could see right into the black hole surrounded by silver. "Do you want me to blow your brains out or would you rather take a bullet in the gut?"

I sat entirely still. I glared at him the way Ty glares, no blinking. I could barely see his eyes through the purple lenses. I reflected back at myself in his glasses. I looked like Mama—like a fierce bulldog.

He put the gun back. "Just shitting you. I ain't gonna shoot no chick. I ain't into killing people." He started laughing his inside-out-cough laugh. "Chick, you should see your face."

I wonder what his face would look like if he knew I actually shot a .22 at the cabin from the time I was six years old.

A knock on the steamed-up window; a hand brushed the snow away.

Lester rolled down the window. A woman's voice called up, "Does the lady want a cup of coffee?"

Not too fond of coffee but happy to leave Lester and the Colt 45, I grabbed my coat and pushed open Frank's door and jumped down. The truck was running with the heat on, and the cold outside surprised me. The woman tapping on the window introduced herself— Annie. She said she loved the plaid yellow, red, and orange of my coat, and I followed her to her tiny little house sitting behind the garage. She didn't invite Lester.

Her house reminded me of the basement house in the field around the corner from Mama's although it was above ground. Annie's house was one large room completely filled up by beds, a Formica table and chrome chairs, and the stove, refrigerator and a wringer washer. Despite the snow outside, the kids were running around in their underwear. Of course, they weren't cold because the oven made the room hot. The little house smelled like a bakery. While bread baked in the oven, Annie whipped chocolate cake batter, and I sat at the table watching her.

Mama baked cookies, but never bread. She always bought dark brown rye or wheat bread at the store, not Wonder bread like the other kids at school got in their lunches, pure white. Once she made a chocolate cake for Ty's birthday. She opened the oven at the wrong time, and the cake sank in the middle, so she filled the collapse with melted marshmallows. I told Annie that I made some Jiffy cakes but never one from scratch. Not hard to do, Annie said.

She opened the oven and took out two loaves of bread with golden brown tops. She reached up for a mug on a shelf above the sink and poured in coffee from the steel pot on the stove and handed me the mug and a thick slice of bread topped by a melting glob of butter. Yummy.

"I hardly ever entertain company," she said, "especially woman company. What a treat for me you showed up today." Texas accent, like Wally's.

Annie is not as tall as me so that may be why she called me a woman. Me being tall and her being short isn't the only way we're opposites. My hair's light; hers, black. I'm skinny as a shaved dog, and she is round and curvy like Marilyn Monroe. She smiled every second, and I no doubt resembled a big grump because Lester aimed the gun at me.

Annie said this was her anniversary. Only twenty-four and she had six kids. The oldest—a little girl with curly brown hair who was missing her front teeth. The rest were boys. To celebrate their anniversary, they were going to Laramie for dancing, and a woman from the church in town would spend the night with her kids.

Annie poured the chocolate batter into a round cake pan and a square cake pan and put them into the oven and told me she would make them into a heart by cutting the round cake in half.

She opened the curtain over the closet to show me her red dress with a ruffly skirt. It was her dancing dress when she first met her husband. "You wouldn't think this dress still fits me after all these kids, but it does. I swear, when I wear this, he remembers how he fell in love with me that night. Never mind nine months later, we had ourselves a baby." She laughed. "You can be sure we won't be having another one this time because he got himself a vasectomy. Our sixth anniversary present to us!"

A little one in diapers clung to her leg while she whipped up some chocolate frosting out of powdered sugar and cocoa for the heart cake. She sat down at the table with me, and pulled him on her lap. "The baby's still sleeping," she said, and I noticed the crib in the corner. "He's almost six months." The older kids were building a tower as tall as they were, and the other little one, wearing nothing but a green shirt, pulled a corn popper toy around the room.

Annie told me things always work out somehow and the best thing that ever happened to her was getting pregnant and leaving Texas for Wyoming. "Wyoming is a fine place. A little lonesome sometimes. But being a little lonesome beats watching your back every day like I did in Fort Worth."

Her ex-boyfriend beat her up when he found out she was seeing the man she was going to marry. He kept following her around and calling her up ten or twenty times every day even after she got her number changed. "Lucky to move!" I said.

She laughed about how yesterday when she was feeding the baby, the little one pushing the corn popper told her the reason she had two boobs was because they were like faucets with one hot and one cold.

She kept telling me stories about the kids that made her laugh so hard her words couldn't come out. Her laughing got me laughing, too. Who wouldn't love a laughing lady?

When the cakes were cool enough, she showed me how to remove them from the pans and cut the round one and put a half on each side of the square one, and lo and behold, she created a heart.

She couldn't be more jealous since I was on my way to California. She said they never had snow in Fort Worth in the spring, just like southern California.

Lester banged on the door and let in a rush of cold air. He said the truck was ready, and I needed to get a move on. He stood waiting for me, letting the cold air pour in.

I didn't ask Annie for help. I am so weird. I didn't tell her the truth about Lester.

"You lucky!" she said. "Tomorrow will be summer for you."

I left my new coat for Annie to keep warm, and she hugged me. I raced out to the truck and climbed over Lester. Frank gave me a toothy smile. Just as the truck started moving, Annie came running up to the window carrying a half a loaf of bread. Lester rolled down the window, and she handed the bread wrapped in waxed paper up to him.

"Hey, homemade bread," Frank said, and blew Annie a kiss, shifted gears, and steered into the road. I strained around to wave bye to her.

Lester tore off a large piece of the bread to pass over to Frank. "Dumb bitch," he said. "Look how she lives."

"You don't know nuthin about nuthin," Frank said, and Lester tossed the rest of the bread out the window. What in the world made him discard divinely delicious bread?

The sky opened from grayish sheets to puffs surrounded by blue, and we drove on where I'd never been before. Frank said the mountains in the distance were the Medicine Bow Range, so named because the Indians held ceremonies after collecting the wood they used to make bows. He talked about a plane crash that happened nearby, the worst crash in history. Sixty people killed, members of the Mormon Tabernacle Choir. "No radar," he said. "And a blizzard something like this one we just had—except in the fall."

"Hairy it snowed so late," Lester said. "Snow should come in winter, not spring. It don't snow in Missouri in the spring."

"Spring and fall is when the blizzards happen around here."

We got on Interstate 80, which is also called the Lincoln Highway and kept on driving across the gigantic flat landscape. The clouds hovered close, and finally hills developed. As we passed Rawlins, you could see a couple motel signs and some houses across the hills. Frank said Rawlins was home to the penitentiary, and people lived right next to the prison's fences. It had a "punishment pole" and if a prisoner misbehaves, they tie him to the pole and beat him with rubber whips. And the Old Hole, pitch black where they put a naked prisoner for weeks.

We crossed the 7,000-foot altitude Continental Divide. Lester started complaining about being hungry. "Not too bright to throw the bread out the window," I said, and he squeezed my leg hard. "Ow!" I reacted with an elbow to his rib, and he let go.

Frank opened a medicine bottle and shook out some little white pills and passed them across me to Lester. "White crosses will hold your appetite down for a spell." He asked me if I wanted some, too, but I did not because it seemed odd to eat pills instead of food. I hate taking pills.

For a while, snowy white hills jutted alongside the road; then flat with hills in the distance. Rarely a tree to be seen. Lester and Frank told each other jokes. One of Frank's was about two people who died and went to the Pearly Gates. One was a truck driver, and the other, a preacher. St. Peter let the trucker in but not the preacher. So the preacher asked how come, and St. Peter said the truck drivers had scared the hell out of more people than the preacher did. Lester shared a similar one about a preacher and a taxi cab driver. In this one, St. Peter says when the preacher preached, it put everyone to sleep, but when the taxi driver drove, it made the people start praying.

Frank asked if Lester was planning to be a preacher. Lester said not likely. We came upon buttes, and a sign for Eden, and I started seeing billboards with penguins.

The sun kept bursting through the clouds until the enormous sky was bright blue. Frank pulled into the parking lot at Little America and pointed out the penguin standing on a block of ice behind glass. That explains penguins on the billboards. The penguin is from the South Pole, and he died on his way to this truck stop with 55 gas pumps named after Little America, South Pole. Admiral Byrd, first to fly down to the Pole, was in a movie about Antarctica that was hard to film because of the freezing cold.

Inside, we sat down in the corner at a table with orange cushions on the chairs, and when the waitress came over, Lester acted sweet. "Get anything you want, beautiful." I put in my order for a hamburger and headed to the bathroom. The mirror showed my superfine hair as a total mess of tangles. I struggled to comb through the knots, and by the time I got back to the table with my hair somewhat tamed and my face washed, the food had arrived. I was hungry, and I'm sure I ate fast, but I don't think I've ever seen anyone eat so fast as Lester, almost like he inhaled his burger and fries.

When he got done, it was his turn for the bathroom, and it felt crazy to be sitting alone with Frank.

He leaned across the table. "I don't for one second believe you're married to that little creep." I didn't say anything. I dipped another French fry into the ketchup and popped it into my mouth.

Frank kept talking. "If I thought you was married to him, I'd advise you to git yourself a quickie divorce. But being's I don't believe it, I advise you to dump that chump." I started swirling another French fry around in the ketchup, and he put his hand over mine. Little black hairs covered his knuckles, and his hand felt sweaty. "You know what he was saying to me while you was in the ladies room? He was telling me for fifty bucks he'd let me crawl up in my bunk with you. You got yourself a pimp there, beautiful, and if you want yourself a pimp, you could do a lot better than that little asshole."

I didn't even know what a pimp was. I had never heard the word before. But it wasn't hard to figure it out. Lester was saying he would sell sex with me, like he owned me, like because I did it with him, it meant anyone could do it to me and he could get money.

"I'd rather give you the fifty bucks direct," Frank said, "but you look like the kind of girl who does it for love, not money."

"I never did it at all until yesterday," popped out of my mouth, and I started crying. Frank started petting my hand. "Aw, you poor little baby," he said. "Didn't you like it? Didn't that boy know how to treat you right? Didn't that boy know how to make you feel good? I got ladies all across the country, and there ain't one of them who'd complain. Ole Frank knows how to make a woman feel righteous good." I kept crying. He was so wrong, and I didn't know what to say about Lester. I wanted to be saved, but not the way he was saying it. I sat in the booth and cried and Frank kept rubbing my hand.

When Lester came back from the bathroom, Frank said, "Little lady here told me you ain't got what it takes in the sack, boy."

"Aw, what the shit's she know." Lester grabbed my hand away from Frank and twisted my wrist so it hurt. "I married me a virgin. What the fuck does she know?"

I wiped my eyes and blew my nose with a paper napkin.

Frank got out the medicine bottle and took out a couple pills and swigged them down with the rest of his Coke. "I wouldn't mind getting a couple more of them white crosses off you, Frank," Lester said.

'Well, you ain't going to," Frank said, and we all got up and went back to the truck. Cold outside. What a dimwit to leave my coat at Annie's as if California was just a couple miles down the road.

Lester and Frank argued. Their main topic claimed which was better: older or younger. Lester would say stuff like "Sure glad I'm young enough to get it up," and Frank would laugh and say, "Yeah, like a little baby worm."

"The U.S. Army don't think so," a comment that got them into a conversation about which was better—the Navy or the Army.

Frank figured it out.

"You on your way to that there war in Asia? I believe that's Fort Lewis, Washington, you're intending for instead of Los Angeles, California. Aren't they testing brains on you boys these days?"

"I got a stop to make first in LA," Lester said. Easy to tell he was mad. Bright red neck and flaming cheeks. Frank didn't let up on him.

"I sure will sleep better at night knowing you're defending my interests, boy. Yes, indeed, I'll sleep a whole lot better."

"I ain't gonna defend your interests, old man. The only interest you got is in whether to take an enema like all old men do."

Frank cracked up.

They liked to argue. I rode between them watching as we crossed into Utah, saying nothing.

Little cars. Land. Rocks. Wires. Poles.

Hills of red rocks, mountains.

We changed Interstates near Salt Lake City and filled up. Four hundred miles to Las Vegas. I craned my neck wanting to see the Salt Lake, but we were on I-15 South. From what I could tell, Salt Lake City looks a bit like Denver. A tall crane by a tall building under construction.

Dry mountains, no forests.

Frank passed out snacks—potato chips and Oreos. He stuck in his Patsy tape, and asked me to crawl back there and get his *Valley of Wild Horses* book.

I climbed up into his bunk, an enclosed space with a mattress and a shelf with books by Zane Grey and Louis L'amour. Before I found the book, Lester climbed up, too.

"Time for our nap, beautiful." He pushed me down on the mattress and stripped off his pants.

"No, Lester," I said, but it didn't do any good. He got my jeans slid down and pulled off one pant leg. I held my legs together, but he pushed them apart.

"Hey, Frank, I'm fucking her. I'm slipping it in. Sure feels good. You sure you don't want some, Frank?"

Frank didn't answer. I lay on my back with tears rolling out of my eyes. Frank kept on driving, not saying a word, and Patsy kept singing in her pretty woman voice "Crazy." Lester pushed inside me, up and down. It didn't take long, a relief. He got off me and fell sound asleep.

I tried to fix my pants again and forced myself not to hear Lester's snores and just lay there crying. The next thing I remember, the truck was stopped and Frank's face was right there. He had his hand inside my shirt and was running his hand over my chest lightly and saying, "Oh, you pore baby. You pore baby. You're so beautiful. You deserve better than that." He kept crooning to me and touching me soft. He kissed me light little kisses all over my face and neck and unbuttoned my shirt. "You're so beautiful," he said over and over. He climbed up next to me, and I realized he had no pants on. "Ole Frank ain't gonna hurt you," he said. "Don't worry about a thing." The soft way he touched me, the pretty things he whispered to me, Lester sleeping beside me. I didn't try to stop Frank when he pulled my jeans down again. I held my breath and let him do it. Lester slept on.

I lay in the dark a long time between both of them snoring. Then I pulled up my jeans and crawled over Frank and maneuvered down to the seat, dirty and sick to my stomach. Two days before—a virgin girl who had never even had a date, and now two men had done it to me. I stared out the window at the dark sky fathomless, and Lester climbed down, too. "Don't say nothing," he whispered to me, and he started going through Frank's stuff again, hunched over and quiet.

I didn't want to be any part of that. I yanked the handle and opened the door and jumped down, which I guess is woke up Frank.

He shouted, "Get out of my stuff and get out of my truck!"

"Don't hurt me, man." Lester jumped out of the truck, too, with Frank right behind him. Fat Frank without his pants chasing Lester. I ran down the embankment and hid in the ditch, so I couldn't see them, but I could hear them. Grunts and thuds and scraping noises, groans. In the background the motor of the truck. I waited to hear the gun go off.

I knew it would, and I put my hands over my ears and huddled down in the ditch and waited to find out which one, Lester or Frank, was going to be dead. If

Lester survived, he would come after me and shoot me because when I jumped out, I made the noise that woke up Frank.

Even after I heard the truck roar away down the road, I kept waiting for the sound of the gun.

I kept my hands over my ears for a long time. I heard a car on the highway. Stickers poked me. A dazzle of stars and a half-moon in the blue-black sky. Quiet. I took my hands off my ears and listened harder. My heartbeat. Little rushes of a tiny animal running on the ground. I shivered. A chill in the air.

After a bit I heard a moan. I stayed in the ditch and listened. Lester started cussing. He said all the cuss words, and between saying them, he made moaning and grunting noises. He yelled, "What the fuck is this life about?" and I came out of the ditch.

In the dark, I could see his shape crawling around on the ground. "Help me find my glasses," he said, and I got down on my hands and knees near him and began feeling around for them. The dirt felt like wet sand. "That fucker. Fucker busted my glasses. Fucker drove off with my pack, too. My fucking papers are in there." He found his glasses, the frame bent and the purple glass broken out of one lens.

We both sat on the ground beside the road. Lester started crying. "Damn this life. Damn it all to hell. I got a sweetheart, I got a kid, and they're going to send me to Vietnam. They're going to make me kill people. I got nothing against those people. Damn it all to hell. And now I don't got my fucking papers. What the shit am I supposed to do?"

I sat on the dirt. Lester cried, and I felt bad for him, but didn't know what to say or do.

Suddenly he said, "What the hell are you just sitting around for? You got to get us a ride."

"I want to go home."

"So go the fuck home then. I ain't stopping you."

"Where are we?"

"How the fuck do I know? All I know is it's fucking cold, and the sooner you stick out your thumb, the sooner we can be sleeping in a warm place."

Not much traffic, but I got up and went to the road and stood shivering and waiting. A semitruck like Frank's passed, sending me back in a whirl of wind as I held out my thumb. A few cars passed without slowing. At last, a long black car slowed down and stopped. Lester popped up behind me.

The pretty blonde girl at the window shook her head at Lester and said to the driver, "Never mind. Let's go." Lester said, "Aw, come on. I'm a serviceman, and we just got robbed. Guy beat me up and stole our car. I don't usually look so bad. Come on. I got to get to my base."

Lester looked bad. Beat up. His broken glasses hung on one ear. I stood behind him, my arms wrapped around me, trying to keep warm. She unlocked the back door and let us into the car. Soft leather seat. The driver with black hair circling a bald spot on the back of his head flicked ashes off a silver cigarette holder. The girl kept turning back to us, her eyes outlined in black, her hair a long, blonde flip. We cruised down the highway in the comfortable black car, and Lester started asking questions about Las Vegas, telling how he'd always wanted to visit. She said she was a dancer. Lester said, "Can you hook up this chick here?" and the girl laughed. "Dance?" The guy driving laughed, too—likely because I was a mess.

"Just drop us at a motel," Lester said as we began to see the lights of Las Vegas. "We got to get cleaned up and get some sleep."

The guy turned into the first motel parking lot. We got out, and I said, "Thanks," and Lester gave a thumbs up. We started walking to the main door, and Lester said to me, "Well, at least I got something out of Frank." The inside-out laugh. "About $500 and a bottle of white crosses."

We checked into the motel, and for once, Lester didn't touch me. "Anybody ever tell you that you was a jinx?" he said and rolled over and went to sleep. I curled into a ball on the other side of the bed.

I woke up to him letting in light from outside as he came through the door. I'd been sleeping so hard I didn't realize he'd gone anywhere.

He sat down on the side of the bed next to me. "Now listen," he said. "Somebody's gonna be coming in a few minutes. You don't got to do nothing. All you got to do is keep your mouth shut. Now shoot into the bathroom and comb your hair."

Weird to think someone was coming to this motel room. I figured I would take a long bath while they talked or whatever.

Clean bathtub, warm water. The tiny bar of soap accompanied a miniature bottle of shampoo. I took a long bath. When the water cooled, I added more hot. I loved feeling clean again. It occurred to me that now I knew how to hitchhike, I could find my way home—or to California.

I hated putting on my same dirty clothes. Lester's wrinkled black shirt with the yellow trim, my jeans with stickers in them, my bra with a broken strap. I dropped my black-dirt socks into the trash. My own shirt was in Lester's pack that disappeared with Frank, and I'd thrown my dirty panties away. I put back on those yucky clothes and came out of the bathroom my hair wrapped by a fresh white towel. Lester and the strange man were sitting in the orange chairs by the window. "See, what'd I tell you?" Lester said.

"Okay."

I was confused.

"I like her. You can wait outside, man."

They both stood up. I was looking back and forth between Lester and the stranger.

"Remember what I told you," Lester said to me, and he flipped open the door and walked out. I didn't have a clue what was happening. The man slid the chain lock on. My eyes took in this guy. A bit taller than me. Puff of blonde hair. Reddish-white skin. Bolo tie. Thin eyebrows arched, giving him an expression of surprise. His yellow buck teeth made him ugly. "So let's do it," he said, and he unzipped his pants—corduroy pants, no belt. And then I got it: I knew Lester had sold me.

The man let his pants fall and he stepped out of them, and dropped down on the bed. I bolted past him to the door. "Hey, where are you going?"

I struggled with the chain, my hands shaking, my fingers slippery.

I flung the door open. I ran. The white towel blew off. On the walkway Lester was sitting on a bench smoking. I sped past him. He yelled, "Where are you going, bitch?" I faced back over my shoulder to see if he was chasing me. Brakes shrieked.

I got creamed.

I remember flipping into the sky, but I don't remember landing, and I don't remember how I got to the hospital. I don't remember telling someone how to reach Mama, but by the time I realized I was wearing a cast on my knee, Mama got her wish to fly.

She checked me out of the hospital and took me in a taxi to the airport. She flew back to Denver with me on the seat next to her.

Mama was not happy.

"Do not talk to me, Michaela. I don't want anything to ruin my trip in the sky."

I didn't say a word. In fact, I have never told anyone about my trip to Las Vegas. I'm ashamed of that trip. Shame crimps my heart.

Lester blew an unrepairable hole in my life. He might as well have pulled the trigger when he aimed Frank's gun at my face.

****

It rained for about 15 minutes; lightning struck all over the sky at once over and over—a lightshow with a constant rumble of thunder. Now the rain is stopped. Water drops are sparkly patterns on the aspen leaves.

Fire Peak stands like an enormous, solid God, changing colors but never changing shape.

I once told Chaz everyone needs God. "Just to have something to look up to."

"If I want to look up, all I got to do is lie on my back."

"But who do you look up to?" I asked, and he said, "Don Juan and Carlos Castaneda."

I intended to read *Don Juan* but I really preferred to read books about kids like *Harriet the Spy* & *The Outsiders* & *Little Women* & *A Wrinkle in Time*. My list could go on and on.

Too dark to write any more.

JULY 9 THURSDAY

Fire Peak is stunning. The snow on top sparkles so white, I need sunglasses. I love being up early in the mountains. Newborn day. No past to shape or change its color. Every minute a tad warmer. I measure degrees on the backs of my hands. The breeze whooshes through the trees and birds whistle and chatter. I am positive Chaz would love the Land of Golconda.

I dreamed last night I had two brains. I dreamed I could take one brain out of my head and put the other in, sort of like changing a light bulb. But instead of throwing the old brain away, I tucked it into a velvet box similar to the one my sapphire ring came in, but much larger, with an attached key.

When I wound the key, the box began playing the opening Strauss music for the movie *2001*.

Wally says dreams are meaningless, a collection of images from what your eyes saw that day—half of which never register in your consciousness—so your mind tries to make sense of them.

Mama said dreams hold keys from your subconscious, so you should try to remember them and figure out your brain's messages to you.

Daddy never dreamed. "I sleep like the dead," he would say.

"That might mean a blank mind," Mama said, and he said, "Better blank than full of mumbo jumbo."

Floss said dreams are messages from your Guardian Angel, and nightmares are devil messages.

My nightmares are like life itself. Like life repeating and repeating. My nightmares weren't like that when I was with Chaz very often, only when he was gone.

Sometimes Chaz couldn't sleep and got up in the middle of the night and didn't come back for a whole day and night. In his sleep, he'd twitch and shake Mr. Squeak. He babbled, putting words together making no sense, like saying all the words from a movie but not in order. But that didn't prepare me for when he took the yagé .

He told me sometimes I cried in my sleep. Sometimes I'd wake up relieved I was not traveling in a Mack truck or that Barf wasn't standing by the bed watching me. One time I woke up laughing, but the joke wasn't funny in real life. I remember asking: Why in the world did I crack up about my teeth falling on the ground and turning into blue crystals? Chaz said teeth magically changing into blue crystals was a cool image. He said dreams are part of creativity.

I once dreamed my nose started growing after Mama told me that when you get a nose job, they break your nose and then set it right. You'd be under ether, she said, so you would be unconscious. I don't know if she meant me or was just telling me about the procedure, but ever since, I hold up mirrors so I can see my nose from both sides. Chaz said nothing is wrong with my nose, but it is big. Ty has a big nose, too, just like Daddy's. Mama's nose is tiny—her eyes dominate her face. Wally's nose bends forward at the tip and turns bright red whenever he gets mad at me.

One time he came home to me playing records I'd checked out from the library—dancing, like I used to do when I'd play Mama's 78s—Tchaikovsky and Chopin and Ravel. I love to lift my legs and arms and float them into the air with the music and pretend I'm a ballerina. Mama never cared if I played her records, but Wally walked in and exploded. His nose turned red as the bloodwood, and he yelled at me to never touch his stereo again or I'd be extremely sorry.

I didn't play *his* records. I gathered the albums (including the soundtrack for *Brothers Grimm*) together and walked back to the library since now I had no way to play them and it was not my permitted library hour. I vowed to save my money to buy a record player of my own, and that's what I was about to do when God sent me the GO message.

I took out a new book from the rack of books by the checkout, which I began reading that night. It opened with a girl stealing her mother's wedding dress, but after I got up the next day and made breakfast for Wally, the book dematerialized. After looking everywhere, I finally went to the library to find out how much the lost book cost, but the librarian said it was turned in two days after I checked it out.

Wally took it back to the library himself, and I didn't get to read it. It turned out when I check out a stack of books, some he decides I can't read and returns them. Once I hid some books in the Falcon, but next thing, the library welcomed Wally and my hopeful reading material back.

I can understand not wanting someone else to use your stereo, but what right does someone else have to control what you read?

Or control what you wear ?

Or what you own or what you like?

Or who you are?

Wally reminds me of Mama. She was critical of me all the time, and Wally does, too. But I have no clue how he chooses the books to return and the ones he allows me to read. He took back an Italian cookbook, for goodness sake! And he likes Italian food. We've gone to eat with Billy and Mary Ann at Gaetano's several times. Mama never made one Italian dish, which is why I checked out the cookbook he wouldn't let me read. Mama would have let me read it and try a recipe.

In the seventh grade, my feet jumped three sizes in one month from 5 to 8, and Mama said, "Your feet are almost as big as your father's. His feet are ugly, don't you think?" Then not much later, I dreamed my feet grew so huge no shoes would fit. I woke up freaking out and threw off the covers and checked out my feet (which have remained all this time size 8).

On my thirteenth birthday, she said, "I can't believe you don't need a bra yet. I wonder if you'll be mistaken for a boy. Hmm. You have muscular arms. Were you meant to be a boy, but something happened in the womb?"

Another time, scrutinizing me, she said, "I keep wondering if they mixed the babies up at the hospital. You aren't like me at all. Where in the world did you get that voice?"

I wanted to see pictures of her when she was my age. What if I do have a different real mother? But everyone says Ty and I look alike. Ty has a super voice, and some people think I have an okay voice, too. The choir director Madge asked me to sing the solo at least a dozen times. But there were only twenty singers in the choir.

Inside my head, it sounds like I can perfectly imitate Barbra Streisand.

Mama never heard me sing solo at church because she won't go. Does she think my voice is bad? I would like to hear it recorded so I can hear how it sounds on the outside of me.

How can I keep Mama or someone else from influencing my dreams? My interpretation of the two-brain dream is a message that right now I need a survival brain instead of regular brain.

****

Ty helped me make a cave in the cluster of thick sumac along the back corner of the fence, my best reading spot in the summer. Bizarre to be reading *Charlotte's Web* in your hidden cave and overhear someone talking about you. "Those poor kids," I heard Mrs. Grant say. She was talking to the neighbor Mrs.

Donahue, across her back fence. "Just watch. Down the road, they're going to have serious problems. Isabel doesn't care if she ruins them. His car's parked in the driveway more nights than not. She carries on an affair right under their noses. Those kids are headed for trouble."

His car—Barf's car. Those kids—me and Ty.

But when I went into the house, Mama pulled out a deck of cards and ask me if I wanted to play a game of Rummy, and she said, "I made some brownies. Would you like ice cream with one? Oh, at the library today, I picked up a couple Nancy Drew books."

I thought: Those neighbors are mean. We're not headed for trouble. Mama does care about us. No wonder she doesn't have anything to do with them. No wonder she never does their astrological charts.

****

I took a Mason jar from the cupboard to fill at the creek, and I saw the neighbor man in waders standing in the water with a fishing rod. His little girl played with a doll beside the creek. He waved at me. I couldn't see his face because he wore his hat pulled down so all you could see was his ponytail. I waved back. I couldn't tell if the little girl noticed me. I am sure they are the round-house people. I didn't see the mom.

Ty would be surprised to see the new motel at the edge of town near the mine pits. Across the road from it, the ground is plowed up with a bulldozer. Golconda is changing.

I parked around the corner from the Opera House Café. Since I have waitress experience, I decided to ask about a job. I intended to order the cheapest sandwich, too—most likely grilled cheese.

The café was full of people, but I got a little table by the door.

The red velvet rope still blocks off the front staircase. One time as a little kid, I asked the waitress Rosie what was upstairs, and she took me by the hand, undid the rope, and led me up the red carpeted staircase. A black rug with a border of pink roses stretched from one end to the other of the hall. She opened one of the transom windows with stained glass designs. We went into a room with a white twill bedspread on a white iron bed, and across the room on the marble top of a white dresser was a book about the Gold Rush.

When I first walked into my apartment in Denver, I instantly thought of this room because of the daisy wallpaper and the woodwork with carvings of flowers.

But that was about the only similarity.

- Our bed—Mr. Squeak—brown metal

- black and white striped mattress similar to the one here in the cabin.

- a long, brown cloth over our bedroom window that faced a brick wall about six inches away.

-    the bookcase Chaz built for me, Chaz's stereo,
     lots of records, his guitars

-    a green & white checkerboard linoleum floor

Wally told us we were lucky the old gas stove in the kitchen didn't blow up. You had to light it with matches. The little freezer held two ice cube trays. The day after defrosting, the freezer was covered with layers of frost. No room for frozen food. The refrigerator leaked Freon and had a weird odor.

Seventy-five dollars a month—reasonable for an apartment with a bathroom with a clawfoot bathtub and a rusty pedestal sink that was missing its hot water handle, and a living room with a brown Naugahyde foldout sofa where Floss ended up sleeping—across from another sofa that was uncomfortable. In the bedroom, we plastered posters on all the walls.

In the café I recognized Rosie the second she came over for my order of grilled cheese and iced tea. She didn't recognize me. No surprise since I'm not a little kid anymore and haven't been here for eight years. I know I look different. Mama always kept my hair really short, and now it's long, and I'm wearing my granny dress. When she brought my tea and grilled cheese, I asked her if she needed a waitress. She said, "Do you sing or tell jokes? Are you 21?"

Confused, I shook my head. I managed to say, "I like to sing."

"Sorry, you caught me at a bad time. The tea is free." And she darted off to another table.

I thought of how Boss at the Rocky always complained he was almost ready to go out of business. "One more month, one more month," he'd groan, even though all the seats were taken.

"Sorry," she said as she passed me. "Crazy." She hurried off to another table and then sped back into the kitchen.

So she won't give me a job. I have to think of something else. I'm glad I didn't introduce myself. I left the money on the table with a 15 percent tip.

Outside, walking to my car, I saw the man who was fishing lift the little girl out of an orange truck. I waved my fingers at them, but I don't think they saw me. The little girl has strange eyes. I wonder how she sees. I guess one of her eyes doesn't move. It's turned inward. Her hair needs combing—wild! Like mine!

Rosie's ponytail—black, smooth like it never tangles, down her back past her waist. Tangles are a puzzle. How do you untangle them without damaging your hair? Floss would sit for hours sliding apart a hair up its length. She liked to see how far she could split a split end before the two sides parted company.

****

I've been sitting in the shade under the blue spruce that shades the cabin snipping my split ends with manicure scissors I found in the buffet. I snipped off my nails first—dirty from gathering wood although I've washed my hands in the creek. The water is so cold, I could never take a bath in it. If I can keep staying in the cabin, what will I do for a bath? And what will I do for a job?

If I follow the track where my Falcon is parked, I'll come to the road. If I follow the road, I'll come to Golconda—a grocery store with a post office, a hardware store, a realtor's office, a red brick school, a firehouse., and a bank. On the other side of town are hundreds of abandoned mines.

If I walk across the meadow, I'll see kinnikinic and paintbrush. I know the long needles and scent of ponderosa pine and the shape of the bristlecone on the mountainside. I know the feel of dirt and pine needles under me and the sun on my face. I know the rumbling of the creek and the icy bite of water that yesterday was snow. Fresh.

If I go to the highway, I can drive out of the mountains and back down to Denver. I know a house where Wally attached cuffs to a board to hold my feet. In the backyard of his house I planted marigolds and tomatoes, and this same sun warming my legs here is burning up my plants unless Mr. A is caring for them. I know all these things, yet I don't know where I am in this life. I don't know how to figure out my future. I don't know how to stop my memories from taking me over.

GODISNOWHERE

****

Chaz and I used to always spy on people. We'd walk around the neighborhood at night looking into windows. We saw a guy reading in a throne-like chair beside an old-fashioned lamp with light bulbs looking like candles. A fighting girl and guy shaking their fingers in each other's faces gave us the exact lyrics for our song "Better."

You can't stay here tonight

You have to go now, go now, go now

A night by myself—better, better, better.

I've been wanting to leave you so who cares what you think

I've been wanting to leave you, Oh! you stink.

Go now. Go now. Go now.

Better, better, better

We cracked up creating that song. I wish we had a recording of it. I would love to *hear* how we sounded together. I'm betting on great harmony. Otherwise, Chaz wouldn't want to sing with me!

****

I waded across the creek to spy on my new neighbors but still no sight of the round-house mom. I hid behind scrub oak, and the fisherman sitting on the picnic table playing guitar didn't look my way. I liked it! His thumb plays the lower three strings for rhythm while his fingers pick melody. I've not gotten to see people play guitars since Chaz. I loved to scrutinize and try the techniques myself.

The little girl played under the picnic table, her voice creating dialogue for her dolls. She uses grass and wildflowers as their food, and her dolls fretted a bear would get their dried meat. Tweety voice and wild, white fluff for hair.

I want a camera. Not only would I take pictures of the man playing his guitar and the little girl scurrying dolls around (so the bear won't get them), but pictures of Fire Peak at sunrise, and the bristlecone that shows life and death at once with the pointy branches and the green fronds, and the cabin with the moon-house and shooting range, and I'd send the pictures to Ty.

What a blast it used to be to come here—leaving our little dome-roofed school and Mama and Barf. We'd drive into the mountains on the curvy road and end up here.

At night diamonds sparkle the sky. The puff of wind surges through the trees. Always in the distance, you can listen to the endless ripple of Gangue Creek. Ty and I would take our sleeping bags outside and lie on the ground watching for shooting stars. We could reach out and grab one if only our arms would stretch another foot.

****

I picture Mama dressed up in her long-sleeved, green taffeta dress she made for herself in the olden days before astrology took over all her sewing time. Backless, a white satin belt. Sparkly rhinestone earrings, her hair in a French twist with little spitcurls in front of her ears.

At the beauty shop earlier while her hair was being fixed, I played with black kittens in the back of the shop by the hairdryers. Mama wouldn't let us have pets. At home Barf (this was before we named him Barf, shortly after I'd seen his hairy butt in Mama's bed) came in with his hat on and shiny shoes and smelled like Old Spice.

Mama made drinks from Jack Daniel's whiskey and Duffy's Lime Rickey. She gave me a glass of Duffy's Cream Soda, and I felt grown up getting a drink, too. Ty was camping with some of his friends in their underground cave they dug out. I sat in a chair that matched the ones around the dining table except with arms like a king chair, drinking my cream soda. So adult listening to Nat King Cole and Bing Crosby on the record player! When Mama said it was bedtime, I got into my pajamas and kissed her goodnight. She was wearing red lipstick, and her breath smelled like Jack Daniel's, her soft cheek like powder.

I fell asleep to Frank Sinatra singing "I've Got You Under My Skin" thinking he was singing to a bug. What else gets under skin? I fell asleep listening to Sinatra and Mama and That Man (as we called Barf then) talking and laughing.

I woke up, and it seemed spooky. So quiet. First I went to Ty's room but since he was spending the night in the hole he dug with his friends, his bed was empty. Mama's bed was empty, too. I turned on the light in the bathroom. In the kitchen, I turned on the overhead light, and in the living room, I opened the draperies and switched on Mama's lamp and sat down in her chair. Through the window across from Mama's chair, lights shone at the Grants' house next door.

I went outside, and That Man's car was not in our driveway. I crossed the driveway to the Grants' house and rang their doorbell. Mr. Grant opened the door, and I asked if he knew where my mama was.

Mrs. Grant joined Mr. Grant at the door. They brought me inside, and they asked questions about where Mama could be and where my babysitter had gone. I told them I had no babysitter and how Mama was dressed in the green taffeta and how That Man Mr. Gross was with her and they were drinking and listening to music and telling jokes. Mr. Grant went over to our house to investigate. When he came back, they started talking about how late it was for a little kid to be up. Their clock pointed to 10:20. The weather forecast was on TV. Mrs. Grant took me into the little bedroom she used as a sewing room and put me to bed on a couch with a flat pillow and wool blanket. "You need to go to sleep now. Children should not be up so late."

I wanted to be home in my own bed, but I was happy that the Grants had taken me in. I didn't have to be all alone. I wrapped up in the wool blanket and listened. "I wonder what time the babysitter left," Mr. Grant said.

"Or if the little girl was telling the truth and there was no babysitter," Mrs. Grant said. "I wouldn't put it past Isabel."

"Well, you know her better than I do. Should we call the police?"

I clutched the hard pillow in the dark feeling scared. When I stood up on the couch, I could see through the window the lamp shining next to Mama's chair and the stack of astrology magazines on the floor next to it and her little table with her ashtray and paper and pens. Weird view of our house.

Cold air pushed in through the gap between the glass and the wooden frame. My breath turned to steam on the window, and I wiped it with the sleeve of my pajamas. I shivered. I could hear the Grants talking, the people laughing on the TV, the train whistle from far away. The TV went off, and the Grants took turns in the bathroom. They went to bed. I lay back down but couldn't sleep. I stood back up on the couch and stared into our house at Mama's chair trying to get up the nerve to run back across the yard. A car came down the street and turned into our driveway.

It was a Yellow cab, and the driver got out and opened the back door and carried Mama into the house. She was limp, and I thought she must be sick. I wondered if I should tell the Grants she was home, but I didn't want to wake them. The driver came out of the house, got into the cab, and backed out of the driveway and took off down the street.

I got down from the couch and slipped out of the room and out the Grants' front door and ran across the driveway. Our front door wasn't locked, and inside, Mama lay on the sofa, with a splash stain on her green taffeta dress like a glass of water had spilled all over it and lipstick all over her face like it was randomly smeared on. She wouldn't wake up when I asked if she was okay but mumbled and turned over so her face was in the sofa pillow, her French twist undone.

I went into her room and peeled her bedspread off her bed and dragged it into the living room and covered her up. I pulled off her shoes and sat on the floor by her, but she didn't wake up. After I closed all the curtains, I curled up on the floor but kept shivering, so I crawled under the part of her bedspread that drooped on the floor and fell asleep near her.

Next thing I knew I woke up in my own bed. I got up, and in the kitchen Mama sat at the table with the *Rocky Mountain News* and a full coffee mug. Her French twist and spitcurls were gone, and her hair flipped like she'd just taken her rollers out.

"Where were you, Mama?" I asked.

"When?"

"Last night. Where were you?"

"Here all night playing cards with Floyd."

"I got up, Mama, and you weren't here."

"You are a silly little girl, Micky. What a funny dream."

I ran at her and punched her with both fists. She pinched my hands together. "Stop being such a brat, Michaela, or I won't buy you the tights and leotard you asked for."

I do have spooky dreams, but I swear I did not dream Mama was gone. *I wouldn't put anything past Isabel*, Mrs. Grant said.

The next day, Mrs. Grant came over. She never comes over.

Mama sent me to the store for a pound of burger, so I don't know what they talked about.

Mama ordered me the tights and leotard we'd seen in her Montgomery Ward catalogue—both white and black. I got to dress like a dancer and play her records and pretend I was a ballerina.

After I'd had the tights for awhile, That Man (i.e., Barf) put in a request: "How about if you put on those black tights and dance for us again, Micky."

I went to my room to change my clothes, but Ty followed me, and when I told him That Man wanted me to dance, Ty said not to change but dance in my slacks. I went back to the living room, and he said, "Put on your costume, Micky, your black tights." And Mama added, "Don't you want to wear your costume?" I went back to my room to change, but Ty was waiting for me.

"Don't do it, Micky," and hustled me outside telling Mama that we were going to ride our bikes.

We hardly ever rode bikes together. He had a three-speed with a hand brake, and my bike was little with training wheels. He went slow enough for me to follow him around the block to the field close by the basement house, to the hole he and his friends had dug for a clubhouse.

Boards lay over the top. This was my first time I went down there.

After he set up the boards over us, except for slants of light that made us look like zebras, it was dark. We sat on the dirt floor, and he told me he was going to tell me a secret if I promised I would never tell anyone.

"I do keep secrets, Ty. Remember my stellium in the 12th House? Mama says it means I can keep secrets," and Ty put his hands on my knees and stared into my eyes and told me Barf was showing him how to put a box kite together and pulled out a five-dollar bill. "He offered me five bucks to touch his dick."

I screamed, and Ty hushed me. I asked him if he was going to tell Daddy. Ty said, "Nope, it's a secret between you and me."

"But Ty," I said. "That time Mama called me a liar when I saw him in her bed with her, when I told Daddy, he made me feel better."

"What'd he do?"

I thought hard. "He knocked Mama down. He'd do the same to her dumb friend. I know it."

"I mean it, Micky," he said. "I'll blow your brains out if you tell Dad or anyone."

And he told me why: "I can't tell Dad," he said, "because I took the five bucks."

I felt sick. "Did you touch it?"

"I touched it," he said. "Next he offered me five more bucks if I'd kiss it."

I felt sicker than ever and didn't want to know, but he said, "Don't look at me like that, Micky. I didn't. Next thing he would ask me to suck it. Stay away from him, Micky. Stay away. Stay away. Stay away. Don't ever be alone with him, and when you change your clothes or take a bath, lock the door. Do not go back to your room wrapped up in a towel ever, and don't wear your tights and leotard around him. I'm dead serious."

From that day on, we called him Barf because he didn't deserve a name, and I stayed away from him. Every time he asked me if I wanted to ride along when he went to pick up a pizza, I said no. If Mama went into the kitchen leaving me alone with him in the living room, I'd jump up and follow her or go to my room or go outside or call up Tina and ask her if I could come over.

One night Mama was in the shower when he arrived, and I let him into the house and ran past him out the door into the front yard. Ice cold and dark, and no one else outside in the neighborhood. Even though I was freezing without a coat, I didn't go back in until surely Mama was out of the bathroom.

Once Mama prepared supper while he sat at the table playing solitaire with a deck of cards (missing the nine of spades—thanks to me), and she needed tomato paste and decided she'd hop into our car and rush over to the store. I told her I wanted to go with her, and she said I should stay and keep an eye on the pan on the stove. I started whining.

"Why can't I do one simple little thing without it getting complicated? Why can't I run to the store for a can of tomato paste without it turning into a dramatic production?" She went to her bedroom for her purse, and by the time she got into the car, I was sitting on the seat next to her, but she didn't make me get out. "I mean it, Micky. I am not buying one other thing besides a can of tomato paste."

"Okay," I said, and we rode peacefully along the half-dozen blocks to the grocery store. I still wonder why she didn't ask me to ride my bike over or ask Barf to do the errand since he was losing at Solitaire while she was preparing supper.

I had to be mindful not to give away Ty's secret, and I won't lie—the ride to the store was one of the times when the secret wanted to jump off the tip of my tongue. I clenched my lips together to keep from making Ty's confession.

So hard to live like that—keeping a secret and trying to keep as far away as possible from someone who often comes to your house—who IS the secret. Now I'm older, I think Ty should not have kept what Barf did secret.

Mama always stands up for Barf. She let him into our lives and chose him over us.

Would knowing Ty's secret change her mind?

I made up a crazy, dramatic scene in my mind of Mama sitting in her chair wringing her hands saying, "I'd do anything if my Micky would come home again. I would give up Floyd." I'd envision her on her knees praying, "Please, God. Return my child to me. My children are first in my life" instead of looking at his astrology chart trying to figure out when he'd leave his wife and marry her instead.

I have a brain that sees good and a brain that sees bad.

The good side of my brain likes to remember how she sat on the kitchen floor painting Easter eggs, how she whistled as she hung clothes on the line, sang "Heart and Soul" in the shower. I'd come home from Daddy's and she would show me a blouse she was making me from a new pattern or a plateful of chocolate chip cookies.

The realistic side of my brain sees her sitting in her chair studying the astrological charts, frowning as she draws astrological symbols on paper and smokes one Pall Mall after another.

My negative brain sees Mama throwing up in the bathroom after she drinks too much. She is passed out on the couch, her face turning swollen and ugly.

Her body without clothes next to Barf.

Sinful to hate Barf, but I can't think of anywhere in the Bible hating someone like him is wrong. In Leviticus, it says you can't hate your brother, but Barf is not our brother.

My bad brain sees how God partly hates me because in Proverbs, it says that God hates wicked imaginations and feet that turn to mischief.

Before Barf came into our lives, we didn't imagine what mischief was. We tried using mischief to make him want to leave and never come back. We cut the seams in the pockets of his coat he left hanging on the back of a chair in the dining area. I smeared jam inside his hat. Ty put a crawdad in his glove compartment; I put a dead fly in his mashed potatoes—Ty sprinkled cinnamon in the bowl of his pipe. Ty stole his car registration and burned it in the incinerator.

Ty wrote in the dust on the back window of his Buick Riviera: "I'm a pervert." I scratched a nail file on the tail gate of his other car, the Nash Woody: *pervet.*

Which made Ty take his knife and etch in an r. I will always be able to spell pervert.

It was fun to be bad and carry out mischief. Our couch sat in front of the picture window, with plenty of space behind it so the drapes could hang free and not be squished. I kept lots of toys behind the couch—dolls, my tea set, stuffed animals, bits of food like crackers or popcorn or sugar cubes. Mama never cleaned behind it. Like my hideout in the sumac in the summer, behind the sofa was my private little spot.

I would throw bits at the back of Barf's head when he was sitting on the couch thumbing through the *Rocky Mountain News*. On the rare times Mama cooked dinner and he came over to eat, Ty and I would start whining about the food because we heard him say that he hated kids whining. If Mama served pork chops, we'd whine we wanted Franco American spaghetti; if she served Franco American spaghetti, we'd whine hamburgers. Ty would pick his nose at the table and say odd facts: "Did you know that cats like to eat placentas?" "Did you know that everybody swallows a gallon of snot every week?" "Did you know a tapeworm inside you can be 35 feet long?" "Did you know that long ago people crushed up mouse brains and used the crushings for toothpaste?"

I whined I needed a kitten, and Ty would support me saying the kitten could grow up to kill mice so we could make toothpaste of their brains. We'd argue to give us an excuse to hurl food at each other and we could make sure Barf got a blast of it before Mama stood up all tight-lipped and sent us away from the table. We would throw fits about having to go to bed.

"I'm too old for you to tell me what to do!"

Evil fun. Ty and I would get the giggles and laugh so hard we couldn't stop.

"Hard for a woman alone to raise children," Mama kept saying. Did she ever suspect it was tough for her kids to have Barf hanging around?

The bad side of my brain remembers bad.

Mama would dress up to go out with him. Spiky heels and bright lipstick. "My earrings pinch. This necklace chokes. Bracelets are like chains." But she wore her jewelry, and she smelled of Chanel #5 and cigarette smoke and whiskey and coffee. Frown lines between her eyes.

Skirts and sweaters to her job. Complaining because she had to go out in the daytime. Back on with her pink bathrobe, coffee stained with burn-holes.

She called me a liar.

My good brain:

Daddy.

His red hair windblown and sticking out all over his head, smoothing it down with his hand. He stands with a group of men, all listening to him like he has the most important things to say in the entire world. Spooning corned beef hash from a can into a frying pan and cracking eggs on top. His arms around me teaching me to shoot, his freckled hands helping to steady the gun. His face getting solemn when he talked about the Lord. His orange hunter jacket, his fishing boots holding him up in the fast waters of Gangue Creek.

I loved how he would take us to the movies. *Ben-Hur, Davy Crockett, Old Yeller.* In *East of Eden* they talked about repentance and how someone can be bad through and through.

At school and church, they taught us that the wages of sin is death. Who is the sinner? Me and Ty for our mischief and hard feelings? Or Barf for wanting to do sexual things with children? I never found where in the Bible it says doing sexual things to kids is wrong. Maybe that didn't happen in those olden days when God was actually showing up on earth.

The closest I came to blowing Ty's secret was when I told Mama what Barf did to me after she brought me back from Las Vegas. I was lying on the floor doing homework, and they were in Mama's room, supposedly having "private conversation."

For homework, I was doing a crossword puzzle about the government. I was on "number of Supreme Court Justices", and suddenly he was lying on top of me. He put his hand over my mouth and whispered in my ear: "Someday you'll love me the right way, ugly girl. My way."

Then he got up and left out the front door and drove away.

She came out in her pink robe wearing her pink slippers and went right to her chair.

"He just laid on me, Mama"

She looked at me and pulled out a chart. "I'm so tired of this. I'm going to see why you are making this up, Michaela. Could it be the stellium in Libra with Neptune opposed to Jupiter and conjunct Mars?" She opened her fat blue astrology book.

Under my breath: "I'm not the only one. All you need to do is ask Ty."

"What? What did you say?"

I turned my back on her and walked to my room and got my suitcase out of the closet and never said another word to her.

I packed fast. I could hear her chair creaking in the living room and I heard on the radio that a whole lot of sheep in Utah had suddenly died. The news completed, and Bobby Goldsboro started singing "Honey."

I untwisted a metal clothes hanger and slipped into Mama's room and used the hanger on the lock on her jewelry box to get my star sapphire ring. I wish I'd done so long ago. It opened easily. In the tray on top next to the ballerina, my treasure. I slid the ring on my middle finger of my right hand. I carried my suitcase to the living room. Shaking, I took deep breaths to calm myself. I tried to concentrate on how it felt to finally possess my ring.

Mama wasn't calm. She was rocking hard back and forth hard in her chair. I set the suitcase on the floor and got my coat out of the closet.

"How can you say something dreadfully awful about Floyd when he is such a dear man? You always want to ruin it for me. So selfish. You ran away and lost the beautiful coat I bought you with money—a gift from him."

Knowing that made me glad I'd left my coat with Annie.

Holding the sapphire made me feel strong. I put on my coat.

I did not say one word. Silence equals strength.

"You don't know how hard it is to raise two kids all alone. You don't know what it's like to be a mother."

Blah, blah, blah. Complain, complain. Always about her.

"If you walk out of here now, don't expect I'll come and pick you up in Las Vegas or anywhere, Michaela."

I could predict everything she was going to say before she said it. Her hard, hard life. Her only son now in the Army (and whose fault is that, Mama?). The big red-headed hypocrite who tried to force religion down her throat. But she painfully cooperated and sent us to Christian school to keep the peace. She tried harder than every woman to be the best mother, cooking, washing clothes, sewing and working a job to keep food on the table and never got any appreciation for anything she did. Ho hum.

I put on my old brown coat.

"Don't I deserve a little happiness in my life? How could you try to destroy that with your lies? Floyd's an honorable man. Look at his chart! Capricorn rising with a strong Saturn! You are cruel."

I slid on my gloves and grabbed my suitcase by its handle and walked out the door, leaving it wide open.

She screamed: "All you ever do is run. But you can't run far enough to get away from your sinful self!" She jumped up from her chair and I looked right into her bulldog eyes before she slammed the door shut in my face.

And that is the last time I will ever see her—with squinty eyes and smoke-yellow teeth, snarling.

****

Andre the Angel

I decided to go into Golconda again to see if there were any maid jobs at the new motel. I bathed more or less at the creek and cleaned off the spot on my granny dress and hopped in my Falcon, but when I was making the turn from the cabin track to the road, it stopped. I kept turning the key, but just a whir noise, and the engine wouldn't turn over. I wondered if I could be out of gas although the tank was full when I left Denver.

I got out and tried to push the car back because my front end was out on the road, but it would not budge. Then a snake moving by my foot startled me, and I caught on a root and took a fall, and twisted my bum knee. Man, did it hurt. It seems that when you injure something, it never gets one hundred percent well.

I sat on the ground watching the snake, dark gray with yellow stripes and giant black eyes. It must have been almost three feet long! It slithered away and pushed itself up a boulder and found a place to sun. My knee kept throbbing, so I limp-dragged back to the Falcon. There I was—a half mile from the cabin on a road hardly anyone drove with my broken-down car and a hurting knee. I stood on one leg, leaning against my car, stroking my knee, and looking down the road wishing help would appear.

Yes, I did wish on my ring.

It worked!

Andre came bumping toward me in his orange truck, with little Jori on the seat beside him. His truck whirled up the dirt, and he came to a stop in a cloud of dust, swung open his door and jumped out.

Andre took care of everything. He tried my ignition, lifted up the hood, lifted me into his truck—and put me on the road to heaven.

I got the answers to my questions about how his house is set up inside.

The ground floor is a workshop and storage for recording equipment. Upstairs, the living room is crowded with two amplifiers and four speakers, electric guitar, acoustic guitar, and a gorgeous black piano with Schimmel in gold letters over the keys.

Heaven.

I stretched out in a swath of blue pillows on the sofa with a rubber bag filled with ice over my knee. Jori brought me her DeeDee doll with stand-out blue eyes and one of those hilarious Flatsy Patsy dolls with long white hair and red boots.

Andre called the Golconda garage and took off to meet someone to check out my car, and Jori and I played with the DeeDee doll and the Flatsy Patsy. Jori has voices for both of them—DeeDee's voice is squeaky, Flatsy Patsy's bossy.

She brought out books I haven't read before, and I read to her until Andre came back home.

An ignition coil's on order, and it should be in tomorrow. I asked how much it will cost, and he said not to worry about it, but I am worried because I might not have enough $$ even though he said it is not expensive.

He started fixing lunch, and I helped Jori put together the TV trays, sitting with my knee stretched out with ice. Jori said she liked the deer and campfires on the trays—dark woodsy green metal, deer peeping out from the trees, campfires burning, a repeated scene all over the tray. Back when we stayed at Daddy's apartment, we used TV trays all the time once he got some chairs. His TV trays were black with pink flowers. Daddy never got a table to eat on. The furniture that he carried in that truck from Clovis, he brought to the cabin.

Andre put plates on the TV trays with tuna sandwiches and pickles and slices of apples and Fritos with dip made from sour cream and Lipton onion soup. He sat in the brown easy chair instead of at the rectangular table that separates the living room and kitchen. In the center of the table is a sun made from orange and yellow tiles, and all around are blue tiles.

They ate faster than I did. I was still eating my tuna sandwich when the two of them started batting a yellow balloon around. Jori giggled like crazy, and I thought about when Ty and I would get the giggles and Daddy would click us on the head to make us stop.

In comparison to Andre's, Daddy's living room was bare except for his maroon-colored Bible on his coffee table next to a wooden cigar box with a picture of a redhead girl in a circle with the words Red Dot. Inside the lid was the redhead again and "Don't cut or bite—it's ready to light." Ty and I were curious about what "cut or bite" meant.

Andre has a cigar box, too, but he made it into a guitar with a hole on the top and a neck with three strings attached. A chordophone. His cigar box says Romeo y Julieta, with a picture of a blond girl on a balcony and a young man in white pants climbing a rope ladder. The neck of the chordophone is made of aspen, and Andre said it is not an enduring piece of wood, but it is from the aspen grove east of the meadow.

Nothing religious in the round house—no Bible anywhere, no cross hanging on the wall like in the cabin. One of the songs Andre and I figured out we both knew was "Turn Turn Turn", which is a religious song. After we sang that one, Jori danced around and shook a maraca while he kept the rhythm on his cigar box guitar and I beat out the rhythm on a bongo drum while we sang "Dancing in the Street." Fun. The chordophone sounds like a real guitar.

Jori's only five, but what a genius on the piano. She played the first part of "Pink Panther," and what Andre told me was "Rondo Alla Turco" (I asked him how to spell it), and he told me it was by Mozart and is also called the "Turkish March." I never listened to Mozart's music before, and now you can be sure that when I get a stereo, I'll get some Mozart records.

Andre said Jori started playing when she was two, and her mother plays piano with a band that tours the world. Clear now why I didn't see any mother around because she's on a tour. When Jori played what Andre told me was Nocturne in C sharp minor by Chopin, I watched how she dramatically raised her arms before delicately touching the keys. Who would believe a little kid could do this? Stunning!

I told Andre I sing all the time at the cabin since no one has to hear me, and he said people would like to hear me because my voice is unique. I told him I would like to listen sometime so that I could judge it, and he told me that when he has his recording studio finished, he'll record me! Heaven!

He invited me to spend the night since it would be better to stay off my knee as much as possible.

The night in the wedge-shaped room was like nothing I've ever experienced—bookshelves filled with books all the way to the ceiling—Thackeray, *Dune,* all the books of the *World Book Encyclopedia*, Bertrand Russell, Catch 22, *House of Mirth*—I could read all year and not be half done. Lavender sheets, a fat pillow, a fuzzy cream-colored blanket, a thick fluffy rug on the cement floor, and a cactus on the windowsill. The echo of the Nocturne in my head. The environment was so sweet, it scared me.

Will God punish me for being happy and peaceful because I haven't atoned for my sins?

Solomon says in Ecclesiastes God gives to people who fulfill their vows to God's word, but to sinners he gives travail.

Travail means torment.

My eighth-grade teacher talked about Solomon and the sin of vanity. She said mirth and pleasure are connected to vanity. She was always stern. No mirth and pleasure, it seemed. Why is mirth connected to vanity? The dictionary on Andre's shelf defines mirth as gladness and gaiety. I would think if a girl is vain, she would not truly experience gladness, not real happiness. Of course, she would be glad when she gets praise.

Sorrow beats laughter and the wise won't be remembered any more than the fool, it says in Ecclesiastes. Mirth and vanity and grasping in the wind.

If everything does go in the wind, why shouldn't we experience mirth while we're alive? Know life as much as we can? Someday I need to study the Bible more. Chaz would like a conversation about this.

Atonement is hard because how can I know God decided I atoned? The key could be if travail goes away.

My good side of my brain says God is rewarding me for my efforts at atonement, which is why this joy of staying in heaven with my angels Andre and Jori. My bad side of my brain asks if I add to my sins by experiencing mirth and pleasure. Which will result in travail. Or hell.

Chaz didn't believe in hell. He said long ago people made hell up to freak people out so they would behave better. Mama would agree with him. If they didn't believe in hell, people back then would do whatever they wanted, and society would be at war all the time. I said, "Aren't we at war anyway?" "Yup. And war is hell, right?" Chaz said.

Andre told me Robert McNamara was the person behind the Falcon. He said McNamara used to be the Secretary of Defense. McNamara convinced Ford to invent the Falcon because everyone was buying Volkswagens, so Ford needed an economical car. Such different jobs: designing cars, designing war. I wonder what Mama would discover in his astrological chart.

Andre said it was ironic that McNamara would buy anything for war, but for peace, he wanted luxury stripped away like with my simple car. Andre said he's the head of the World Bank now and he's trying to end world poverty.

I never heard of a world bank. It must have an endless source of money if a bank for the whole world. It should be easy to do away with poverty.

I hope the war will conclude. I don't think changing to the lottery instead of drafting will end the protests at colleges unless the war ends. When the National Guard shot the students in May, Wally said they were un-American and didn't deserve a college education. He was showing me a picture of the girl kneeling and screaming by the dead boy, and he said, "This ought to make you glad you're not going to college."

His saying this reinforces why I can't talk to him.

Chaz gave me hope about going to college someday. He told me if I didn't go back to high school, I could take a test to make up for dropping out, and some colleges would accept it. He said my high school education was limited anyway by the church that runs the school, but I read so much I would be likely to pass the test. He said I could go to Emily Griffith. He said he would help me. Chaz went to college the year before we met. Then his conscientious objector status went through, so that's why he worked at a hospital.

Nathan who moved into Floss and Chaz's old apartment gave Chaz *Don Juan* by Carlos Castaneda. Nathan wants to be a shaman, and he said he saw shaman qualities in Chaz, though Chaz was not religious. A shaman is a holy man. When Chaz got taken over by the yagé, he experienced travail. I wonder if his mind changed about hell after that. I wonder if his mind is still lost. I keep seeing the whites of his eyes look like they were tattooed with little red lines.

Chaz wore his hair like Andre in a long, brown ponytail, but Andre doesn't talk while he's playing his guitar. Chaz was the most talkative person ever. Even while he tuned his guitar, he talked. Sometimes he'd spend more time tuning than playing.

He talked about everything—what he did all day, who he ran into, what he wanted to buy, what was happening with his friends, what new music he'd heard, what he heard on the radio or read in the newspaper, what he'd like to do with his life, what's wrong with the world, what's right with the world. It was like he expressed all his thoughts as they raced through his mind. He did talk ten times more than I did. Floss said that was because of the speed, and when he was off it, he was more of a listener.

If I had told him the truth, would he still want me? I am ashamed for not telling him because he had a right to know if he really loved me with all my warts. I kept my trip with Lester and Frank secret from everyone. Chaz thought I was a virgin.

We had so much fun together. We loved to roam our neighborhood. Shabby houses divided into apartments like the one we lived in next to piles of rubble where some of the rundown houses were being torn down and replaced by empty lots or construction sites. You couldn't guess what you'd see from one day to the next. The sidewalks were broken red flagstone, so in the dark we had to be careful where we stepped. Chaz tripped once and grabbed me, and I went down, too, and we both had to wear Band-Aids on both knees to work.

Around the block is a stone mansion—rundown with some stones fallen onto the ground and peeling paint around the windows. I don't want it to be torn down. One time when Chaz and I peeked into a window, we watched two women dancing to slow music with their arms wrapped around each other. The room they danced in was almost empty with a long, wooden floor and a chandelier with crystals making rainbows over the wall.

Like ours, most places had a dome or bare light bulb hanging from the middle of the ceiling. We liked to check out how people decorated their apartments: Tapestries bought at the head shop spread over car seats; tapestries attached to the ceiling; tapestries over windows; tapestries over mattresses on the floor. Beads hung in the doorway of one apartment; in another someone had painted a blue peace sign over a whole wall. In the house with purple shutters, a gigantic spoon and fork hung on the wall above a wire spool table. Next door to us: a seven-foot pyramid made from Coors bottles. More than one candle in a wine bottle covered in dripped wax, and any sounds we made were drowned out by huge speakers everywhere, bass rumbling into the street. Lots of young people cluster in this area because it is cheap. Some old people, too, but never little kids or middle-aged.

I loved the music spilling from the apartments— anything from Johnny Cash to the Zombies and Hendrix. I could go on and on—so many musicians! I love music! I love people getting together spontaneously in the park to play music. Lots of people jamming on guitars, harmonicas, flutes, recorders, bongos. The park is supposed to be closed late at night, but the cops never kicked us out. Chaz and I would soar so high on the swings, and it was like flying when we'd leap off.

Chaz carried his Gibson with him everywhere (even to his job sometimes!), always ready to jam. Floss carried guiro scrapers and our other percussive devices in her purse, so she'd get them out for us. Fun to make the devices with Floss. She was really creative. Hanging out making music. The best times.

Floss didn't understand why anyone would make a big deal about sex any more since we could get a prescription for the pill. She went with me down to the phone booth to set up an appointment at the free clinic. So dumb. I thought my boobs were growing because I was getting older, and my irregular period meant I did not notice when it stopped. I was already pregnant. If not for Floss, I don't know how long it would have taken me to learn about the baby. I was dumb: I thought since I didn't get pregnant from Lester or Frank, I wouldn't from Chaz either. Plus, taking speed, he couldn't finish lots of times.

After Mama brought me home from Las Vegas, anxiety reigned like a giant in my mind. I prayed and prayed not to be pregnant from Lester and Frank. I thanked God so much when my period started. With Chaz, I kind of didn't think about it. We felt natural together, especially with our pulses beating in unison and our voices wanting to sing together. Getting pregnant surprised me, but wow, something he and I created? I was a little scared but mostly surprised and delighted, and Floss started jumping up and down for joy.

Unlike me and Ty, Chaz and Floss did not look alike: he was tall; Floss short. He had thick eyelashes; her eyes are closer together, and her long eyelashes a pale gold, almost invisible. Chaz and Floss moved alike though, their hands waving through the air to emphasize whatever they're saying—and they would both talk all day and night, on top of each other, getting louder and louder. Sometimes I had to say, "**Come** on, you guys. It doesn't matter who's right."

Who's the best guitar player? Who's the best drummer? What's the best 3.2 club? Who cares?

That was the trickiest thing for me and Floss pretending to everyone we were 18. We had to always find an excuse for not going to the 3.2 clubs. At first I believed she was eighteen, and she believed I was. What sprang the truth was when we were talking about getting our high school diplomas and how old we were when we dropped out. Then we each knew the other was a runaway, too. When you're kinda living a lie, it's better when you're living the same lie with someone else. One night we met someone in the park from Pueblo who said he could get us fake IDs if we went down there. If not for our decision to hitchhike to Pueblo the next day, I probably would never have met Wally.

A man and woman on their way to Santa Fe picked us up in their station wagon two minutes after we got on the Valley Highway, and a couple hours later, they dropped us off at the exit close to the Pueblo address Floss had written down. Guess she wrote the numbers wrong, however. The house was vacant with a board nailed over the front window. An ancient refrigerator sat on the porch and an old toilet was half buried in the tall weeds growing on the driveway.

Wasted trip. We hiked back to the Interstate and with a break in traffic, we ran across the highway to go north. In seconds a creep in a beat-up Lark stopped for us. He jammed off the next exit instead of continuing north. "Gotta get gas," he said. He drove under the Interstate. "Gas station—over here."

The Interstate runs down Pueblo's east side; it would not be outlandish to buy gas on the west side, so I didn't have an immediate panic. I sat in the middle between Floss and him, and he put his hand on my leg and moved it up. I shoved his hand off and nudged Floss with my elbow.

As we slowed for the stop sign, she flung open the door.

The guy grabbed my messed-up knee and twisted. Man, did it hurt!

I shot out after her screaming in pain. Turned out he dislocated my kneecap on my bad knee I injured when I collided with the car in Las Vegas.

He screeched off. We cheered to see him go. Floss flipped him off, and we collapsed on the curb, me in pain, Floss frustrated about the wrong address and thus not seeing the cute Pueblo guy she met in the park, both of us dying of thirst.

Tall yellow grass swayed in the hot breeze; in the distance rose the enormous smokestacks of the steel factory. Hot. Dry. Few trees. At the corner a bunch of men stood smoking in the shade of an elm. Just beyond them—a red brick one-story building, originally someone's house, with a sign hung above the door: FAITH MISSION.

Floss jumped up. "Let's go there for help. Come on!" I limped after her as fast as possible, but my knee equaled agony. We passed by those men who said gross things to us like "Suck me off." Floss stuck her tongue out at them and said, "Oooh, skanky" and held my arm.

She helped me up the porch steps to the door. Inside, the man behind the desk pushed a ledger forward and said: "More and more runaways lately. Sign in here. We won't release your name. First take your shower and be deloused. Supper's at 5:30, and once you sign in, you can't leave until seven a.m. tomorrow. No drugs, no alcohol, and we check." He said all this in a bored, reciting voice—hypnotic—Floss picked up the pen to sign in.

I yanked the pen out of her hand. "We don't want to check in."

He looked surprised. "What do you want?" Water. I-25 on-ramp.

He gave us drinks and directions.

Every excruciating step shot pain all through my leg. My knee swelled like a balloon and felt stuck and couldn't bend. Since Floss is little and chubby, leaning on her was like leaning on a pillow I could squash or tip over. By the time we finally reached the entrance ramp to the freeway, the desk man surely was setting out supper at the mission.

Hitching meant we risked meeting another creep, but Floss stood and I sat with my leg outstretched on the asphalt at the top of the on-ramp with our thumbs stuck out. Late afternoon sun burned down on our heads. No shade. Then a blue Polara with the top down, the back seat filled with Texas fruit, stopped for us.

Skinny older guy with a pompadour hairdo; long, scrawny hands on the steering wheel. Coolest car we'd ever been in heading to Denver. The wind blew through our hair; Floss and I felt like movie stars. He told us to call him Wally. In his Texas accent, Wally invited us to enjoy his peaches.

Every time he went home, he said, he brought back Texas produce. Floss climbed over the seat into the back and got us each one. The juice dribbled down my chin and down my arm. Sweetest, tastiest, peachiest ever. Floss and I had not eaten since a couple pieces of toast for breakfast. We obliged when he said we could eat as many as we wanted.

He asked if we were lucky hitchhiking. "We met creeps! Look at my knee!" He glanced down at it and said, "You need to have that knee looked at." I wore cut-offs; my knee matched the denim blue and looked the size of a softball.

I didn't know in those days when Wally says something, it means I'm going to do it. When he dropped us off at our place, he said it again. "I'm going to make sure you get that knee looked at." The next day, when he knocked, I got up and limped to the door and let him in, then back to lying on the davenport across from Floss's Naugahyde bed with our only ice cube tray wrapped in a towel on my knee, dreading going to work in the morning. He said, "You're going to get that knee fixed."

Floss and I introduced Wally to Chaz. After he did surgery on my knee (and I had to take a whole week off from the Rocky), Wally started coming over to play canasta with us.

How I met Floss: I had the bad habit of reading while I walked. I was reading *June Morgan and the Skyscraper Mystery* coming back from the library, and I bumped into Floss right in front of the apartment. We started talking—I mean *she* started talking. The night before she had seen *Bonnie & Clyde* at the drive-in, so she burst into telling me the whole plot. Funny Floss. Waving her hands around to emphasize her points, she flung her keys right into the bushes, and the next thing, we were crawling around on the ground under the shrubs looking for them among cigarette butts.

The shrubs in front of our apartments are the same kind of the shrubs between the church and Tina's house where I tried to sleep on my first runaway night. After that experience, I will always feel sorry for animals who have to sleep outside in every weather.

I've never told anyone about that night, not even Floss. I don't know Floss's runaway story either.

That night after leaving the scowly-faced Barf-soul mate, I took clothes out of my suitcase and layered up and tried to sleep like a racoon in those shrubs. First I went to Ty and his friends' dugout, which would have been a perfect place to crash, but it was crushed in. I expected the church to be unlocked, but my expectations were crushed when I tried the door. I believe churches should be open to people all the time since everybody sometimes needs to pray, but Tina and her parents were off on a retreat so I couldn't ask them for help. They came back at the worst time ever.

The first person I saw after the sun came up and I crawled out from under the bushes was Freddy who lives next door to Tina on the other side of the church. He was walking his dog and ended up sneaking me into his bedroom.

I stayed in his closet practically all day.

After he took off for school, his mom watched all the soaps while his little sisters who weren't in school yet kept barging into his room. Fortunately, they didn't try to come into the closet, and I got sleep, curled up on top of his dirty laundry and under his four white shirts and two jackets on hangers. The day passed, and when he got home, he snuck me into the bathroom and then brought me some food. Later we lay on his bed with the radio playing, whispering to each other. I kinda explained to him why I ran.

Since Freddy became Tina's boyfriend, I hardly ever saw her. He went to the public school, but I've known him practically my whole life because he'd do stuff with Ty and the other guys. I kept trying not to make blurbling noises, and Freddy rubbed my back like a friend telling me not to worry, how everything would be okay. He kept rubbing my back, and then he started kissing me on the back of my neck. That freaked me out. He reminded me of Lester and he was Tina's boyfriend! So I got back into his closet and wouldn't come out until he promised not to kiss me again. We ended up sleeping side by side on his twin bed, close together, but he didn't touch me again.

In the morning, he went out to the kitchen for breakfast, and fortunately, his dad and mom and little sisters all got into the car and drove off. Freddy came in and told me the coast was clear. Never so glad to see a bathroom! I fixed myself up a little, but my suitcase was still hidden in the bushes. Freddy gave me a bowl of cornflakes, and I wolfed it down.

He put the Beach Boys on the record player in the TV console. Jesus slumped on a cross on the wall and looked peacefully asleep. More likely he passed out from all the pain. I sat down on the sofa ready to figure out where to go next. Then all of a sudden, Tina stood at the front door screaming at the top of her lungs, "I hate you! I hate you! I hate you!" She didn't knock—or maybe she did, and the Beach Boys drowned it out since the sound was turned up loud. I was shocked. Where did she come from? Tina screamed at me, not at Freddy.

Sitting there with my mouth no doubt hanging wide open, I watched her come raging into the room. Her eyes turned black.

I kept saying, "I didn't do anything. I didn't do anything," until the weirdest emotion came over me.

Suddenly I hated her back. Perfect Tina. Perfect Tina with her perfect life. Perfect Tina, home from a perfect retreat. Perfect virgin Tina, so pure she could be chosen to be the mother of Jesus. I would never be a virgin again. Perfect family who locked up the church so no one in need could get in.

I jumped up, ready to run out of Freddy's house, but Tina grabbed my hair. We started fighting. I mean real fighting. Her fingernails went down my bare arm. I shoved her hard. She surged forward and grabbed my hair again and pulled. I kneed her in the stomach. She slapped me. All the while we screamed in each other's face—"You think you're so perfect!" "You betrayed me! You betrayed me!"

I don't know what Freddy was doing.

But in his living room, Tina and Michaela, best friends since the first grade, lost their friendship in one screaming half-hour of one cold morning.

Tina spun around and ran for the door, stopping for just one last second to scream,

"Michaela, God calls you Miasma—you stink. You have no right to live."

Freddy chased out after her leaving the door wide open. My hatred turned inward against my boiling soul—my heart felt on fire, like sizzling oil. What did I have to love about my life?

That was the last time I saw Tina.

I left Freddy's and got my suitcase from under the shrubs and stole the first *Rocky Mountain News* I found at someone's door. I trudged past where the underground house used to be and went down in the ditch where no one could see me to read the Help Wanted ads. When I saw the one for the Rocky, I was off to the bus stop, carrying my suitcase. No experience required.

****

Like Mama, Chaz preferred nighttime, and he liked the city. "You don't know what is coming at you in the country. Lions. Bears. The mountains and those curvy roads. If you're not watching all the time, you could go down a cliff."

"But you have to watch out in the city, too, for muggers and cars."

He started writing lyrics: "I want streets with corners you can cross every block / Pavement, smooth asphalt, sidewalks."

I interrupted, "Except the broken-up sidewalks?" This could be a duet! "I want Fire Peak and the Milky Way / the aspens dancing, the sound of the creek." I convinced him he needed to see Golconda. We planned to go the weekend after the Pop Festival one year ago.

Last year started perfectly. Minimal, I guess. I went to work, turned 17 in October, sang a lot, started learning how to play the guitar, wrote songs, played cards, jammed with people, bought clothes, always had Floss to talk to, loved my Chaz. Perfect.

No, nothing's perfect. Chaz and speed. My life collapsed.

My lesson: be grateful for the good; never take good for granted.

I still talk to him in my mind. I sing the songs we wrote together. While he played or tuned his Gibson, I wrote down the lyrics in my notebook; he experimented with chords and rhythms. We never finished "Rivers."

A flood changes the world

makes it never the same

Gullies and streams rage

rain is to blame

for carrying houses away

bashing them into bridges

the bridge comes down

a sheet of mud down the ridges.

We were trying to make the flood a metaphor for a broken heart.

Chaz didn't experience the floods of '65 because he wasn't in Denver yet. At least that's what he told me.

Rain that summer came down in giant buckets. The street looked like a fast river. Nightmare. The Platte River is like a sewer, so the flood was not just broken roads, washed-out houses, submerged cars, and floating gas tanks. Repulsive! At one point, we heard two explosions. Mama's house came through okay though, and so did her car.

I had never thought before about how we actually lived on a little hill. Tina and I took a bike ride after— so much stuff encased in drying mud: stoves, a jukebox with records strewn around it, a pillar surrounded by a crane near what used to be a building site, TV sets, steel lockers, the list goes on.

Chaz and I got in this major conversation about Noah and the Flood when someone opened a gift shop called Noah's Ark. In addition to their different styles of Bibles and a variety of crosses with and without Jesus, they offered a lot of toys including a piggy bank in the shape of an ark with cartoon animals painted on and a wooden ark with cutout animals and a Noah doll. Chaz said Noah and the flood was a fairy tale because so many species on earth eat other species.

"And it'd be impossible to fit them all on even if they didn't eat each other."

"But God can do the impossible. Because God created life."

"A myth. A legend. What happened to Zeus? Doesn't the impossible happen in fairy tales?"

I checked out a large fairytale book from the library. He loved the art, but he didn't see most of the stories as meant for kids. "Hansel and Gretel. They go back home of all places to the people who got them into the situation in the first damn place. Happy ending?"

Chaz gave me a new way of understanding of all those stories Ty used to read to me.

He didn't like how the woodcutter comes and rescues Red Riding Hood. "Red's got to fight her own battles like the rest of us. The writer should include a knife in that basket so she can use it to protect herself. If the woodcutter hadn't been nearby, what?" He cracked me up when he started railing on Cinderella's father. "Where was that dude while those bitches treated her bad? Too close to home, man. The dad was off making bucks and forgot all about his kid. Hell, he didn't go to her wedding. Bet he showed up quick enough though when he found out she married the prince." And Rumpelstiltskin: "Here the little dude saves the girl's life. She makes a deal with him, but due to his help, she becomes Queen and then uses her power against him, rips him off. Stiltskin should become King. We need to change these stories, Mick. Yeah, we can keep the impossible. Three wishes and a prayer."

Chaz began rewriting the tales. He'd write for hours in spiral notebooks. I wish I knew what happened to them. I hate the idea his parents would throw them out, but the way his mom tore through the apartment packing stuff, I wouldn't be surprised.

The day I met Chaz

When I got home from work, he was sitting on the front step waiting for Floss since he'd left his key inside. (Is there something symbolic about missing keys and meeting those two?) Gold wire glasses. Wavy dark hair past his shoulders. He made me immediately feel sparky. By the end of the night, we were still on the porch talking about everything. Chaz had magician fingers, long and pointy. When he held my hand, he'd draw me into his gestures, which helped me understand his inside self.

From the first, Chaz didn't want me to be with anyone else, and I didn't want to be. But before he moved in with me, girls were always coming over. I'd sit in my apartment reading and waiting for him to arrive home from work hoping to see him. I could always tell when he was parking outside by his van's rattle. Sometimes I'd hear a girl's voice talking as he unlocked his door. He worked as an orderly at the hospital and got off at eleven, so often he'd go to a bar or nightclub after. (His fake ID said he was 24.)

Chaz and Floss's apartment was smaller than mine although it had two bedrooms—the size of closets holding twin beds only. It had a newer refrigerator that did not leak Freon. Two closets and a back porch, which is why it cost more.

Nathan moved into their apartment when Chaz moved in with me. Floss was going to take over Nathan's tiny studio upstairs, but his old friend beat her to it. So Floss took over the foldout Naugahyde couch and got our one closet. The other couch had claw feet but kind of beat-up with saggy pillows and a spring that would stick you if you sat in the wrong place.

Our bedroom: Mr. Squeak under a peace sign. Chaz's speakers corner to corner. I guess we could have been more tidy like how I kept my books and stuff on the bookcase Chaz made, but we didn't really have any place to put our clothes. Our bedroom used to be the dining room of the house so it didn't have a closet. We used the two hooks on the wall, but mostly we strewed our clothes around on the floor, so it always looked messy.

Where Chaz, Floss, and I lived is entirely different from Wally's neighborhood: baby trees with trunks you can almost put a thumb and finger around. My Falcon is the only car parked on the street or in a driveway. Everyone else seems to have a two-car garage. Wally's house is the small rancher, third house on the circle. In the field nearby, the mountains look like a blue and white wall when they're not smothered in the brownish-yellow cloud (smog).

Mama's neighborhood: small brick houses with tall trees like the maple in the front yard that turns red in the fall.

Daddy's neighborhood: near downtown on Acoma, in walking distance from my apartment but in a blond brick building instead of a decrepit old house.

Chaz never called me a jinx the way Lester did, never called me a social dud the way Wally does. In fact, he said I was a good listener, and he told me that if I get the nerve up to sing in front of lots of people, I am destined to be a star. I thought about that yesterday when I sang with Andre. Chaz believed in me. He said he was in love with my voice, and I felt like that about his voice, too.

Ever since the ambulance, when I think of Chaz, my heart throbs like a giant bruise being beat on by a mean person.

Where are you now, Chaz? If you had lived and gone back to the apartment, you would find it empty because Wally told me the landlord evicted us so if we went on the premises, we could be arrested for trespassing.

Most of all: Will you remember me? Do souls keep memories of the people their person loves?

When I prayed for Ty, you'd say, "You're wasting your time, Mick, but if it makes you feel better, put a word in for me, too." I know it doesn't work that way with God, but I can't stop putting in positive words for you.

Does God listen to only the good girls? Maybe he laughs when somebody like me puts in a request. Laughs and turns his head away to keep an eye on the good girls trying hard to be good, not the girls who do anything to survive.

No, I am wrong.

Survival. God is helping me survive. God told me to GO—flashing over the pointing blue arrow.

God didn't tell me to leave Mama's, but it was easy to get my job and survive.

When I first started working at Rocky's, I would eat what people left on their plates. How starved I was then! Every cent I made, I saved for rent. No sheets, no dishes, a suitcase full of clothes, the same clothes I piled on me that night I tried to sleep under the shrubs.

I spent tips on a loaf of bread and sat on the chair by the tippy table in my kitchen and ate the whole loaf. The customers at Rocky's weren't big tippers. A quarter was major.

Twenty-four cents for a loaf of bread left me 20 cents of the fortune I saved for next month's rent. Rocky paid me $1.15 an hour, and I got tips.

Survival calls for the boss pinching you on the butt and scraping grease off a grill and listening to old people talk crazy. It starts becoming the normal life after a while.

After the early breakfast when everyone was gone to work, the old people would have "brunch" they called it. Miss Elizabeth must be ninety years old. She'd pull up her dress and say, "I used to be a dancer. Look at my dancer's legs." Her white legs were sort of muscular for an old lady. Mr. Blick required three ice cubes in a glass of milk every day and started crying if I forgot to bring him his milk the second he sat down. Louie kept forgetting if he had any money left from his pension check and kept accusing his son-in-law of stealing it, never mind his daughter and son-in-law live in California. Mr. Howard always left me a nickel for a tip and always grabbed my leg.

I filled the customers' coffee cups while they talked at each other.

Mr. Howard (who I call "Mr. However") would say, "Once I had a suit made by the tailor, Ephraim Felt." Miss Elizabeth would answer, "I did have a muffin for breakfast, dear. What did you have?" He'd answer, "However, black socks are best."

The only time the people made sense was when one would say, "This hamburger's well done. I asked for rare." They'd all chime in: "Mine's well-done, too. I want rare." Or I'd give them their ice cream and they'd eat it, and I'd clear off the dishes and fill their coffee mugs, and one of them would say, "When are you going to bring ice cream, waitress?" They'd all join in. "Yes, why are you slow? We want our ice cream." It didn't help to tell them I'd already served it. Boss would say, "Don't worry. Give them some more," and raised his ice cream prices.

Maybe they were just teasing me, but I walked out every day swearing I would never grow old. If I eat ice cream, I want to remember I ate ice cream. I don't want to remember wanting it; I want to remember having it.

Getting late. The orange streaks above Fire Peak are fading.

Sleeping here in the cabin far exceeds sleeping with Wally. No need to wake up to someone taking off my clothes or getting on top of me or pushing his thing into my mouth.

I want to stay here forever.

I hold my sapphire ring to my lips, to my forehead, and then against my heart. I wish so strong that Daddy will come.

Wishing on my ring is different from praying because I can feel my wish in my fingertips while lately my prayers seem to go out in space.

Too dark to write any more.

JULY 10 FRIDAY

Once I write down my memories in this notebook and bury them, they'll be laid to rest. My burying spot will be the moon-house—what we called the latrine.

The past is gone. I'm surviving. But haunting hasn't stopped. Last night I awoke to the ambulance siren even though there are no sirens out here ever. Worst is when I have to live my freakout times all over again. Maybe if I write more about the party, it will help although I realize it could become worse instead with a nightmare every single night.

Nathan's birthday party was part in our apartment, too. People everywhere. The music on the porch between our two places conflicted: for example when I came home from work, the Doors' "The End" came out Nathan's door and Floss's favorite—the Temptations' "Runaway Child Running Wild" came out of ours.

Turned out the songs were prophetic.

I got home in the afternoon, and a lot of people were already there. In the bedroom, I pushed a couple of the large bricks we used for a nightstand in front of the door so nobody would come in and see me changing out of my Rocky clothes. I put on a new loose, white top to cover the baby bulge. The shorts were tight around my waist. I stacked the bricks back into a nightstand and set the alarm clock and ashtray back on top and went looking for Chaz.

I found him in the kitchen. He and Nathan had matching green bottles that looked like 7Up. "Yagé tea," Chaz said to me.

"The healer," Nathan said in his dramatic voice.

"Wonder how it will go with the speed." Chaz emptied the bottle with his head back and scowled like he'd taken a bitter drink.

"What is it?" I asked.

"Yagé. The Tea. Shamans use it, for spiritual growth and healing. Ayahuasca it is also called."

I asked why they were taking it since it didn't sound party-enhancing.

"To become better people. To awaken our shaman side."

"For your birthday party?"

Nathan said. "A man should live for his acts. Yes, I'm a Gemini." He and Chaz danced around the kitchen singing, "Ayahuasca, ayahuasca, ayahuasca—tastes like marasca, tastes like marasca!" They started popping maraschino cherries from the jar on the counter into their mouths and danced around singing until they both ran outside and started throwing up on the yard. Floss cracked up and called them "Masters of vomit."

Nathan went back inside to clean up, and Chaz washed off with the hose we'd found in a trash can, even washing out his mouth. Leaky hose—I was soaking wet, too. We squirted each other and laughed so hard. We were dripping wet as we walked over to the store to get him cigarettes, talking about if we should move to Mexico where he could learn more about being a shaman, or go live on the beach with our new baby.

Strolling back talking about everybody who'd be playing at the Pop Festival at Mile-High, all of a sudden, at the sight of a Mary statue in a neighbor's front yard, Chaz experienced instant terror. "Look. Gnome."

He stood frozen pointing at Mary. He panicked and burst into a run down the middle of the street. I ran after him. He stopped short in the middle of the street and started lighting a cigarette. He lit the lighter again and again and again, until it ran out of fluid. He kept clicking and showing me the spark.

I talked him into going back to the apartment. He wouldn't go inside, so we sat on the porch between the two apartments with people partying all around us. Chaz grew silent, which was extra weird. Drool ran out the corner of his mouth. He kept flicking his lighter to make the spark. I didn't know what to do, so I sat with him. Everyone said he'd come down. "It will be like twenty-four hours. If he doesn't come down in twenty-four hours, you can worry." Nobody else had tried yagé

.

I went inside to find Nathan, and there he was in his apartment stretched out on his bed in his own world, too, his girlfriend stretched out on her back beside him. She gave me a thumbs up, so I looked for Floss and brought her outside. Sitting down next to Chaz on the porch, she talked to him, but he kept staring into space ignoring her like she was invisible, his eyes rolling back in his head.

She flipped out and tore off down the street to the phone booth on the corner.

Magic? Within two hours from the time Floss ran down to the phone booth, their parents came driving up in a Plymouth Valiant station wagon with a Colorado license plate.

But they're supposed to live in Chicago?

The second they came onto the porch, it seemed that everyone at the party fled like they do when the cops come—running out the door and down the street. Nathan drove off with his girlfriend. By then, I'd convinced Chaz to come inside, and he was sitting on the living room floor spinning records on his finger, breaking them on purpose! His rolled-back eyes made it look like he had white marbles for eyes with red lines. Spooky!

I don't think he recognized his parents. His dad slapped him a couple times, and when his head hit the floor, he stayed sprawled between the shards of the records he'd broken, not saying a word, just a moan like maaaaaaaaaah.

Floss and her mother took off to the pay phone to call for help, and his father kept poking at him. Chaz turned over on his back on the floor and stretched his arms above his head, his eyes still rolled back. I kept repeating to myself, "24 hours," and looked at the alarm clock in the bedroom and grabbed a pillow to stuff behind his head. His dad went out to the front porch, came back in, and went back out, pacing until Floss and her mother returned.

The siren screamed. Their mom dashed around the apartment grabbing anything she thought was theirs and stuffing it in a bag. The medics lifted him onto a stretcher. My last sight of him—being pushed into the ambulance, strapped to a stretcher, his eyes rolled back, red and white.

I sat on the living room rug wiping my nose on his wrinkled work shirt, beyond miserable. My tears soaked Chaz's shirt. The yellow circle on *Electric Ladyland*'s label kept going round and round, the needle continuously clicking. I finally got up and turned the stereo off and tried to kneel on my good knee to ask God for an angel.

The door was unlocked, and moments later Wally walked into the mess. "Wow. What's happening? I came by to see how you kids were doing." He sat down on the floor beside me. I started crying again. "Disaster area!" He unwrapped my knee and asked, "What do you need?"

Chaz and Floss—gone. Pregnant. Trashed apartment. A roomful of records my psychotic boyfriend had methodically broken into pieces and scattered all over the floor. Empty beer bottles and pop cans and sticky spots from all the people who partied in our apartment.

This man sitting next to me in the disaster area held my hands like an angel and asked me what I needed. Then Wally pulled me to my feet and took me home with him.

I did not go to work again, and I did not get to attend the Pop Festival.

Wally told me Chaz died.

"They tried to save him," he said, "but it was too late. Thankfully he didn't suffer too much. His brain went dead, and every organ quickly followed."

My heart broke in a thousand pieces.

After my baby was stillborn, Wally took me to a grief counselor who attended his church.

The counselor talked about how God always hears us and how God doesn't give us what we want because we asked for the wrong thing.

So what is the point in asking?

Never mind "Ask and it shall be given to you." If we ask for the right thing, God had it planned to come to us whether we asked or not, and if we ask for the wrong thing, we'll be ignored. It drives my brain crazy sometimes to try to understand God.

According to the grief counselor, God planned for my baby to die.

Miss Hull, my Home-Ec teacher, believed that the way God takes care of the birds shows we can trust God to take care of us, just like we can trust our parents. I wonder what else besides parents Miss Hull could compare God to. What about kids whose parents do not take care of them? Does God already doom the kids to punish them for some reason we can't understand?

Original sin, Wally would say.

I wonder if God doesn't pay much attention—like neglectful pet owners who don't keep up with the shots.

I should feel sinkingly ashamed for this thought.

Chaz liked how Don Juan said: "What is the sense of knowing things that are useless?"

If God's a lie, no reason to bother about anything except what makes you happy.

Miss Hull said God punishes to teach lessons.

Did God punish Chaz for not believing? For wanting to find a shaman? Wanting to be one? For avoiding a war he does not believe in? The Sixth Commandment says not to kill. So God had to be happy about Chaz's anti-war choice. Except Satan hardly ever killed anyone in the Bible while God killed everyone but Noah.

Would God want American people to kill Vietnamese people because they aren't Christians? Chaz and I never met a Vietnamese.

Did God punish me for my pranks on Barf? Are those pranks why my baby died? Or because I broke the Fifth Commandment and hated Mama?

Why no commandment commanding parents not to lie to their kids? How come no commandment about lying in general? Yes, false witness, but more!

I look at reasons to understand what's bad or good. If the reasons are fair, then good. If the reasons hurt people, then bad. For Mama, the reasons people act the way they do are shown in astrology. For me, it is easier to forgive someone if I know the reasons they were hurtful than if they have a stubborn Mercury in Taurus.

I did not stay angry with Tina. I know she was hurt because Freddy was unfaithful. I wrote her an apology mail right after. I did not include my new return address because she might share my address with Mama.

Wally may not realize he's hurtful when he calls me names or slaps me. He says he's training me to be a good wife. Wally says he tries to be godly. On the positive side, he has done many good things. Not just for me but for all the people's pets at his clinic.

Is he godly?

Why no commandment that we be kind to animals?

Why no commandment forbidding slapping your wife for nothing?

A commandment against raping girls? Why no commandment forbidding torture?

Has life gotten worse since the Bible was written down?

G O D I S N O W H E R E

One night a baby was born dead in Denver, Colorado, to a teenage girl who wished she was not going to have this baby because her daddy was dead. If I were a little baby, I would want my mother to want me instead of wishing I would go away and never happened. I killed my baby: My wanting her to go away after Chaz died, wanting her to dissolve.

I don't believe Mama wanted me. I wonder why I wasn't born dead. She said they gave her a drug that made her go out of her mind so she didn't remember I was born.

I didn't have any drugs. I moaned and pushed and pain increased for hours. The nurse closed the door and said she didn't want my screams to go down the hall. I thought I was dying; anything that hurt that much had to kill me. All alone I turned inside out in that green room on a hard bed with chrome rails.

Mama said they kept her in the hospital when I was born for ten days. It was the best rest she ever had, no one to take care of, nothing to do—meals brought to her on a tray while she read magazines all day in bed. She told me her ideal life would be staying in bed as long as she wanted, reading and doing astrology charts and finding answers about the world. It would be lovely if she never needed to cook meals or take care of kids or go to her job every day.

Every time Barf went back to his wife, Mama said life is nothing but disappointment. I hated it when she talked like that. Once I yelled at her: "Then why don't you just do yourself in if it's so bad?"

"Because I have to take care of you."

I felt ashamed for breaking the Fifth Commandment. So the next morning, while she was still sleeping, I ran out and picked a yellow tulip for her and put it in a cup of water. Yellow tulips are the cheerfullest things and mean the end of winter. I made toast. Some coffee had cooled off in the percolator, and I heated it up in a small pan on the stove and poured it into my favorite cup, decorated with a red rose. I snagged her working tray from nearby her chair and loaded everything on it. The tulip looked happy next to the plate of buttered toast smothered in strawberry jam and the red rose coffee cup steaming. I carried her tray to her room. She woke up and blinked at me, then curled into her pillow and fell instantly back asleep. I left the tray at the end of her bed so it would be there when she woke up.

Problem though: she ended up kicking it and spilling the coffee, making a brown stain on her white chenille bedspread. She was furious. Later on she was mad all over again at me because strawberry jam on her tray stained an astrological chart she was working on.

I believe she was happy when I ran away for good.

Once upon a time a baby was born in Denver, Colorado. Red and yellow leaves fell to the streets, and the grass turned brown. Other animals have babies in the spring when the days are growing like their babies. Even arctic seals do this. But people have babies in the autumn like rattlesnakes do. Is it a good idea to bring a baby into the world in the fall when everything is about to die?

The October baby grows up catching her mother in bed with a creepy man. She attends a tiny school and a small church where the minister pounds on the pulpit. The choir is made up of old people, but she loves to sing with them. She ends up on the porch of a mountain cabin with her notebook and pen to keep her company. She practices scales. No one to listen. She can sing as loud as she wants. She listens to the creek and the brush of wind that makes the wildflowers sway. She will write her memories that torture her and then bury the notebook in the latrine. This

October, on her nineteenth birthday, she'll be a free and happy solotramp.

****

No one but Mr. A to keep me company ever since Chaz took the yagé . Weird to live with people and not really *be* with them. Wally does not keep me company. He owns me.

When Wally first brought me to his house, he gave me my own room with a foldout couch and a red capsule with a glass of water to relax me. The first night I slept for hours and hours. I woke up without a clock and realized I needed to be at work. Wally told me I wasn't working at the Rocky any more. He said I was fired because I slept late. He said he called Rocky's to let Boss know and tried to talk him into giving my job back, but Boss refused. No final check. Maybe I should write him a letter asking him to send it to me. Not fair to have me work for nothing. I could use every penny. I will need to make money to buy food.

I wonder if it is possible to grow vegetables up here. I love learning to garden.

The back yard at Wally's house: a large patch of dirt where nothing grew, so I bought a pack of marigold seeds. I planted them in a trench I made by pushing the dirt apart with my forefinger. I dropped in the seeds and spread the dirt back over them. I filled the tallest glass with water and poured it over the seeds. I didn't know the next door neighbor Mr. A had been watching me until the next time I filled the glass and he called over the fence: "No no no, girl. What are you doing?"

It turned out the dirt I planted in was the dirt from down deep when they dug out the basement and dumped it in the yard.

"Why do you think nothing grows in it?"

I said because it was a brand new yard, and he laughed at me and went and got a wheelbarrow filled with black dirt and brought it through the gate and dumped it near my trench. "You tell your dad to order topsoil for next year for the garden."

He showed me how to replant my seeds, and repeated, "You tell your dad about the topsoil."

Mr. A is an older man with a foreign accent. He wears overalls like a farmer and has flyaway white hair and a gray beard. He told me in the old country he'd had an acre for his garden. His old country was Poland. I can't spell or pronounce his name—why I call him Mr. A.

Last month I borrowed from his compost pit to fertilize the sweet potatoes Wally keeps trying to make me eat.

I told Wally what Mr. A had said about the basement dirt and topsoil, and next thing, Wally ordered some sod for a lawn, and in just hours our dirt yard became grass. He hired a truck to deliver topsoil so I could have a garden, and he ordered a maple tree and an oak tree and juniper bushes. One day we went to a nursery, and Wally let me choose another maple. I love the red and orange colors they turn in the fall.

Wally bought me more seeds, too—cosmos and bachelor buttons and zinnias and zucchini and peas and beans. When the seedlings started coming up, he said it was right the garden was taking my mind off things.

For him, taking my mind off things means taking my mind off Chaz and the baby. But gardening never took my mind off either one of them. Kneeling in the garden pulling out tiny weeds before they have a chance to get started gave my mind a lot of time to think. I talked to Chaz in my mind. I wanted a sign that he could hear me.

At first, I didn't want to weed my garden because I was curious what the little weed plants would grow into. Mr. A said it was better for me to pull them. I said God lets the weeds and wheat grow up together because if you pulled up the weeds, you might pull up the wheat, too. He laughed and said a weed is just a plant growing in the wrong place, neither bad nor good in itself.

He said Jesus did not give lessons on gardening. No, the sower sows the word.

He went into his house and came back with his Bible and read the Matthew parable to me in his Polish accent. At the end of the world, the angels harvest and pluck out everyone who is evil and throw them into a furnace where they gnash their teeth.

Mr. A is Catholic.

To my knowledge, I never met a Catholic before. My church doesn't like Catholics because they idolize Mary and saints and the Pope, but I guess I like Catholics fine because I like Mr. A.

Mr. A said we should think of each person as a whole wheat field instead of trying to judge whether people are wheat or weeds. "In your garden, you want to take out the weeds while they are tiny," he said, "Because yes, indeed. If you wait until they are big, they will be too hard to take out without messing up the whole thing."

Picking little weeds is like dealing with little faults before they overcome everything.

I asked Wally what he thought about the Sower parable. He said, "Micky, philosophical questions have no answers. I'm not letting you have a garden so that you can be philosophical about sowing seeds."

I looked up philosophy in the dictionary to better understand what Wally meant. I guess he meant I shouldn't think about my garden and life at the same time. He wants gardening to take my mind *off* life. But when I am outside digging and planting seeds and pulling up weeds, all I think about is life.

I don't know how to think about anything else.

I told Mr. A what Wally said, and he laughed. "Your father is a practical man. He is a scientist, no?"

"No, he's not a scientist. He's a veterinarian." I never told Mr. A Wally isn't my father. It seemed beside the point.

"A veterinarian is a scientist." He said not all scientists are philosophers, and not all philosophers are scientists, but philosophers and scientists can grow up together like weeds and wheat.

"Which one would be thrown into the furnace?" I asked, and Mr. A cracked up laughing.

Although Mr. A was too hard for me to understand sometimes, and his accent made it harder, I liked to think over his remarks.

My church gave rules about how to behave well and get to heaven. If you break the rules, you go to hell. Simple. Except one thing—if you break the rules, you may *possibly* be forgiven and wind up in heaven after all. The tricky part. You can't know if God forgives you or not. His voice does not thunder down the mountain saying, "You are forgiven, my child."

In Wally's church, it's not so much about forgiveness but more about salvation, God's grace only. They give you blood and body of Jesus from the Last Supper if you've been baptized. Wally said he assumes that I am not baptized since Mama is not a Christian. I like listening to their choir that Wally won't let me join.

****

When I heard the sound of a car, for a silly second, I expected Daddy.

I was gathering bullet shells together for a game I made up. I set up cans at different distances and tossed shells into them. The closest can is worth one point, the second two points, and so on. I got a shell into the number ten can, but I couldn't hit the eight and nine.

Of course it was not Daddy who drove in. It was my angels—Andre and Jori bringing back my Falcon. Andre jumped out and tossed me my keys. Jori jumped out and zoomed over to me carrying a paper bag filled with all sorts of yummies.

Andre asked about my knee and squatted down and unwrapped the Ace bandage with pine needles stuck to it. I was surprised how swollen it still is because the pain isn't that bad. "You need to stay off it," he said. "Damn foolish to walk back over here when you had a choice."

"Don't say bad wuds, Daddy," Jori said.

"How much is it?" I was going to give him the rest of my money if necessary.

"I don't want your money. Favor, okay?"

"I don't want to owe you anything," I said.

"Well, now you do. We filled up your tank, too, so you can get going wherever you're headed. You never know. Maybe I'll need you someday!"

I was stunned as he swooped Jori onto his shoulders and broke into a run, bounding past my Falcon and across the meadow toward the creek with her on his shoulders. I yelled thank you after them, and I was alone with a salami and cheese sandwich, a couple nectarines, a jar of orange juice, and a lot of chocolate chip cookies. I need to show my gratitude.

Wally's right. I am a dud with people. I am not polite enough.

Right now no one is going to hire me because I'm limping and using a stick for a crutch, but I want to sit in the Opera House café and drink a glass of iced tea and listen to the customers talk. I want to watch Rosie's experience carrying the food on a big tray she balances on one hand. At Rocky's I used small trays.

I've tossed enough of the zillion bullet shells at cans. I can only write so many words on a piece of paper. I can only stay at the cabin all by myself for just so many hours. Even a solotramp can experience the voice inside my head getting too loud and memories swarming.

Even the rumble of the creek doesn't drown them out.

I need to go where there are people. Not to talk to them, just to be near them so I don't feel as if I'm the only person alive on the earth. I wish that Andre and Jori stayed longer to visit.

I will use a long stick as a crutch and make my way down to the creek and wash up, then start up my repaired car and cruise into town for the assurance that other people do exist.

****

Bad news. This is what happened: I went to the café and when Rosie came to wait on me, she said, "Hey, are you the girl who asked about a job the other day? I could use you if you're still interested."

I can't tell you how excited I was to hear that even if I had to tell her that it would be a couple of days till I could start because of my knee. Next thing in walked Andre and Jori who came right over, and Jori asked, "Did you eat all the cookies yet, Micky?" I had to admit I ate them all.

Andre and Jori sat down with me. I remembered Jori likes dolls, so I started asking her what their names were, and she was off telling me about the dolls' lives— that is, Juanita is from Mexico; Rapunzel lives in the woods where Hansel and Gretel live; Dolly is going to be president. How these imaginary lives come to life in her imagination stuns me.

Then Andre interrupted: "Does the guy who owns that cabin know that you're camping there?"

Before one word came out of my mouth, he said, "I don't think I'd let that sonofabitch find me over there if I was you. Greedy bastard. Buying and selling this town."

"Oh dear, are you staying there?" Rose asked. "He's going to turn that cabin into a sales office for cabin sites."

"One-acre to five-acre cabin sites," Andre said. "Did you happen to notice the survey lines? Fire Peak Estates. Year-round cabins. Easy to reach his new ski area."

I sat there dying. I need to get out of Daddy's cabin. The guy in charge of changing Golconda owns it.

Customers threw in their opinions. A guy with a cigar said, "They do opera over there in Central City. No dinner. Just opera. You could think about doing that, Rose."

A guy with a white beard said, "I went to the melodrama over in Cripple Creek a couple weeks ago. We were all booing and hissing and having a helluva good time."

A woman in a pink muumuu with red flowers said, "Golconda would die without some effort. Now it gets to be reborn."

"Reborn as what?"

Men started cussing, and it was clear some were mad. I remember how it used be when Daddy would get into these conversations. I asked Jori if she wanted to go outside. Even though I was interested in knowing what was happening, I remembered how bored we used to be as kids and didn't want her to suffer, and Andre had plenty to say against developing Golconda.

Outside on the boulders, I turned Jori on to the Rock Game.

We each have ten rocks, and then one hides a few in her hand while the other guesses. If you have three rocks in your hand and she says four, then you give her one more to make it four, but if she says two, then she has to give you half her rocks. A long time since I've played Rocks. I hope I had the rules right.

Jori's hand is tiny, so it was easy to see how many she was holding on her turn. I was wrong on purpose so she'd win. I remembered how often Ty beat me at it.

Jori told me her mom lives in Denver when she "isn't on tour." She asked me how come I don't live with my mommy, and I said that it didn't work out, and she said that it didn't work out for her either. I asked her if she likes Rosie, and she said, "Yes. I wuv her. She's nice. She gives me dolls and wets me kween tables." Jori's voice is cute. R's and L's, I don't know what else.

Andre and Rose suddenly appeared, and Rose asked Andre if he wanted her to come by that evening, and he said yes. Then they kissed. So I figured he wasn't married to Jori's mom. Jori told him she "wearned a new game," and he said babysitting her while he was in there growling like a maniac paid for my car. Then he scooped her up and deposited her in his orange truck, and off they drove.

"Sorry about the scene in there," Rose said. "I hope you don't change your mind about the job. We're quiet people—until we're all in the same room."

"I'm glad for the job!"

"The cabin owner won't be back for a couple days," she said. "Don't think you have to be out of there tonight. It will be okay."

I hopped back in the Falcon and drove off without getting my iced tea.

I'm devastated this place is going to be a sales office. I think Daddy would be sick if he knew. Now I know what those posts in the woods are for. Surveying. Boo hoo!

I don't have enough money to rent a place, but Rose hired me, and I'll be able to camp out and save up for rent before winter comes. I'll start looking for a camping spot immediately. Yea! I can always sleep in the Falcon.

Evening
WOWOWOWOWWOOWWOOWWOWOW!!!!!

Omigod. The best possible thing in the world has happened!

I'll just tell the story.

Rose and Andre and Jori drove over checking on me, and Jori wanted them to learn how to play Rocks, so I taught them that, and then Andre had a pistol in his truck, so we got to use our old target setup. We shot for at least an hour! And after a few shots my hand was steady and I blew some cans under the ponderosa pine.

I taught them my new shell game. Rose tossed a shell that landed in the #10 can, and she laughed and said, "I for one am glad to be trespassing on Mike Abel's property." MIKE ABEL!!

I couldn't believe what I heard.

Daddy is in charge of all the development! Some stranger didn't buy this cabin. Daddy still owns it!

ECSTATIC!

Of course, I had to explain to them that Daddy disappeared and how Ty and I have been desperately longing to know where he was, but nobody could have calmed me down. I'm WILD with excitement! Rose suggested I go to his real estate office in the morning and ask Madeline when he's arriving. Madeline is his secretary. I don't think I can sleep tonight! I'm sure I can't!

I'm beyond excited! I'm trembling and my whole insides are feeling it!

Andre will end up liking Daddy. Who wouldn't be happy for new jobs in town and new people? What if they change Night Street to Abel Avenue!

Just as I was about to be convinced that Chaz was right and there was nothing to believe in, I found Daddy! My prayers are answered, my wishes fulfilled! Thank you, God. Thank you, thank you, thank you. I don't know how I could be doubtful.

It will be impossible to sleep tonight. My heart keeps pounding a million beats a second. I just can't stop jumping and yelling and laughing and screaming.

Never in my whole life have I ever been so excited. THRILLED! The absolute best day of my entire life! I can't write any more.

Oh Daddy! I LOVE YOU!!!!!!!!!

Amen, God!

AMENAMENAMENAMEN

PART TWO

JULY 12 SUNDAY

A gunshot reverberated across Gangue Creek. Andre rolled onto his back. "Sounds like my Ruger we were practicing with Friday afternoon. Damn. I don't recall putting it back in my truck. Do you?"

"No." Rose lay still beside him and listened for another shot. Gangue Creek rushed down the mountainside; finches congregated and tweeted in their loud voices on the balcony railing. The gun fired again just as Jori skipped into the bedroom chattering: "Cows say moo, sheeps say bah. What do deers say?" She climbed up onto the bed.

"Deer kind of grunt," Andre said as he raised Jori on his feet and floated her across the bed, his green plaid pajama bottoms sliding down his legs. In a deep and dramatic voice, he sang the children's bluebird song. Laughing, Rose dodged the flying child and slid out of bed and into Andre's robe hanging on a hook on the bedroom door. Jori giggled and flapped her arms. "Now I'm a bwuebid fwying in and out the window!"

In the kitchen, Rose started the coffee percolator and lit the oven to bake the cinnamon twists she left rising in the refrigerator overnight. Through the skylights, sunlight drenched the round house. In the bathroom, the amber bottle-wall filtered the light like caramel-colored stained glass.

In blue-footed pajamas, Jori slid past the bathroom and across the pine living room floor to the piano. Listening to Jori playing scales, Rose stopped keeping an ear cocked for another gunshot.

She tied back her dark hair, buttoned up her flannel shirt, pulled on her Levis, and fastened her turquoise horseshoe buckle. While the cinnamon twists baked, she whipped eggs and sizzled a cut of ham in a Teflon frying pan, reminding herself to bring Andre a cast iron skillet. He sang "Summertime Blues" at the top of his voice in the shower; she poured coffee into two Cathay cups with a green atomic design, drizzled vanilla icing on the golden-brown twists, and dished scrambled eggs topped with melting cheddar onto plates with green atomic borders. The morning sun poured through the curved span of living room windows over the piano where Jori ran the scales, faster and faster.

His wet hair combed back, Andre carried the plates to the round dining table, and laid them out around the mosaic sun. Jori closed the piano, grabbed her napkin, and tucked it into her pj top for a bib. "We need to take some bwekfast to Micky."

"I need to run over there and pick up my Ruger. It has to be there. It's not in my truck."

"I love her voice," Rose said.

"Yes, major talent." Andre spread butter over his second cinnamon bun."So tasty, Rosie. You just gotta open a restaurant."

"Wosie alweady has a westwant, Daddy."

Rose laughed. "Thank goodness I have a little helper to tear up lettuce for salads."

"How ever did Rose make salads before we moved up here?" Andre stirred sugar into his coffee.

"Wosie always knowed how, Daddy!"

"Super shock that Micky's father is Mike." He frowned. "The last thing we need is to turn Golconda into a tourist mecca."

"But Mike has investors," Rose said. "And his Plan"

"When did he first start coming up here, Rose?"

"Ten, twelve years ago for sure." She diced up Jori's ham and set the plate in front of the child.

"Really? I thought he moved up here around the same time I did."

"Yes, that's when he actually moved here. He took over the abandoned western store and opened a real estate office and put a bed in the back room. Sometimes he sleeps out at his cabin."

"Yeah, I thought it was Mike the first time I heard Micky's car."

"Late fifties Mike lived in Denver and came up here in the summer. He built the cabin and would come up to camp and bring his kids. Never saw their mother."

"So you met Micky way back then."

"I did! About Jori's age. Brother two or three years older. I didn't associate her with Mike. I was thinking she was a summer high school kid camping with her family."

"Me and Micky has yewow haih Do you think we wook awike, Wosie?"

"Hmmmm. Kind of you do." Rose laughed. "Man, isn't Micky lucky she doesn't look much like Mike? Flames of red hair shooting in all directions and masses of orange freckles?"

Andre cracked up.

"She's my best fwend. I want to pway dolls with her and pway the Wocks game and weed stowies."

"Last night when she sang, I remembered how he'd bring the kids to the café and pretty much forget all about them while he met with investors. Just like now, he was hot on selling his vision of the ski resort. I'd escape from the arguments out the back door whenever possible. I remember those kids sitting on the boulder singing 'Rock of Ages' and 'Tumbling Tumbleweeds.' Her brother had a great voice for a kid. Mike said it was sissy for boys to sing. That statement got attention. People started shouting out stars' names to him."

After breakfast, Rose packed cinnamon twists into a paper bag and filled a thermos with orange juice. Andre bounded off with Micky's breakfast, across his property toward Gangue Creek. The water was fast and clear and cold. Last April he'd dropped a log over the creek, and now he sprinted across and vaulted up the hill on the other side. Running outside in the mountains on a Colorado summer morning fueled his spirit. Mike's cabin sat on the other side of the meadow, and he strode through the long grass and blooming wildflowers and past Micky's Falcon parked on the track. The cabin door was wide open. Andre knocked on it and called her name.

No answer.

On the porch floor at his feet lay a black spiral notebook. Nearby under a quartz rock was a folded piece of lined paper with very large dark blue letters: *If you are one of the remodelers, do not read this. Just give to Michael Abel.*

Micky must be off with Mike since her Falcon is parked here, he thought, but the note seemed strange. Why not just give it to Mike herself? He stuck his head in the door taking a look for his gun. Not seeing it, Andre decided to run on up the trail criss-crossing Fire Peak, assuming she'd be back by the time he came back down the trail. He set the thermos and sack with cinnamon buns on top of Micky's notebook.

What a fabulous morning—the brief rainstorm yesterday gave the plants a drink that spurred them into madly blooming. The meadow and mountainside exploded in colors, pastel blue and purple and brilliant orange and yellow. He'd explored the trail several times. At the top was a bristlecone pine that must have been as ancient as the Utes' arrival to the Golconda area at least five centuries ago. Some idiots had cut their initials into it.

It was a fairly steep run uphill, and the snowfield above was eye-stingingly bright. His pace was steady. He rounded the trail just before the top and slammed to a stop.

Micky. Sprawled on her back on the ground beside the trail. Her chest heaving up and down under the blood-soaked cotton of her long dress.

"Micky!" He leaped to her. Not conscious. She must have slipped and fallen on something sharp. Blood all over her dress. Her breath caught in her throat making a gurgly sound. Andre did not stop to investigate. He slipped one arm behind her neck and the other under her legs, and picked her up. Holding her close to his chest, he bolted down the trail, intent on getting her down the mountain fast. Her breath was raggedy, and he kept talking to her along the way. "It will be okay. Hang in there, Mick." She didn't answer but kept making little moans.

By the time he reached the bottom of the trail, his arms burned from her weight. He managed to get the back door of the Falcon open, then laid her as carefully as possible on the back seat. She made the same gurgling and moaning sounds and did not regain consciousness. He darted into the cabin to find her car key and a took quick glance around for his Ruger.

Ah, there was the key on the small table by the iron bed. He swept it up, then grabbed the thermos, sack, letter, and notebook and jumped into the driver's seat. Her Falcon started right up. He bounced and bumped down the track leading out to the road. He could hear her ragged breaths, and drove as fast as he could the two and a half miles toward the doctor's office on Night Street in Golconda.

****

Rose hadn't explored Andre's studio construction lately, so Jori gave her a tour. "Awmost done! For the bands," she said of the largest room. Next the control room where the mixing console was covered by a heavy plastic sheet, then the machine room, the isolation room, and the small vocal chamber. "This is for wecording Micky," she said. "She sings pwetty."

Outside Jori found a broken rhodochrosite with pink and white spirals. Hard to make jewelry from the rhodochrosite (the Incans believed to be blood of their ancestral rulers turned to stone). Her current project was a necklace made of the petrified wood she and Andre found on a day trip to Teller County. Just as Rose decided they had waited for Andre long enough and she should take Jori home with her to take care of her horse Partner, Micky's Falcon rumbled down the lane, Andre driving.

"Micky!" Jori tossed down her dolls and raced over.

Andre got out of the Falcon, looking bushed. It felt like ages ago when he first left to take breakfast across the creek. "Where have you been, Daddy?" Jori scolded. "Where's Micky?"

He dropped to his knees in front of her. "Micky's gone to the hospital. In Denver."

"Wow." Rose frowned. "What happened?"

"I took her into town to the doctor." He lifted up Jori. "She just had a little accident."

"Was it that knee again?" Rose asked. "I was afraid she might hurt it after all the jumping and dancing around last night."

"I'll talk to you about it later. After Jori's mom picks her up, I'll head over."

He retrieved the thermos and Micky's notebook from the Falcon. The letter to Mike had slid under the front seat. The back seat was bright red with blood. He handed the notebook to Rose. "Would you mind looking through this, Rosie? See if there's an indication of anything Micky might need?"

"Sure," she said. "I'll peek at it as soon as I take care of Partner. Hey, I need to scram." She had already put her overnight bag into her truck. Andre popped Jori onto his shoulders. Rose stood on tiptoe to give him a kiss, and Jori kissed her on top of her head.

"Tell Pawtner hi."

"I'll see you guys later."

Jori's unstyle-able blonde fluff floated around her face. Andre, wearing cut-off jeans and a brown suede floppy hat with a braided leather headband, kept Jori on his shoulders as Rose got into her truck. Rose jounced by Micky's Falcon, waving at them. She happened to glance down to a huge stain of blood on the back seat.

I hope that was already there, she thought. It looks like blood. Nah, I bet one of her friends spilled something. I'll have to tell Micky my perfect formula for getting rid of red stains.

Rose bounced down the track to the road lined by mine tailings.

Her blue Victorian cottage sat by itself at the top end of Snow Street overlooking downtown Golconda. Partner was grazing the pasture next to her house, and the moment she drove up, he tossed back his head and trotted to the gate. Rose considered Partner a soul mate and talked to him all the time.

After giving him an apple for a treat and filling his water trough, she put on coveralls and went into his stall to clean and replace his straw bedding. Partner nuzzled her shoulder. She walked him to the grooming area and took down her bag. Making circles with the curry brush all over his body and combing out his mane, she talked to him as she worked: "Did you miss me? I spent the night with the guy I'm always thinking about."

When she finished and fed Partner, she stripped off the coveralls and kicked off her shoes on the enclosed back porch of the house so she wouldn't track anything in. In the kitchen she filled a turquoise plastic tumbler with iced tea.

Gorgeous July Sunday—cloudless sky deep blue, wildflowers everywhere—fireweed, paintbrush, yarrow—the lightest breeze sent aspen leaves dancing. She carried her iced tea and the notebook out to the front porch and settled into the cushions on the pine chair. Partner kept his eyes on her from under the honey locust tree. She opened the notebook.

"Rose?"

Sheriff Runyon came up the walk. He stood at the bottom step of the porch and wiped his sweaty forehead with his handkerchief. So hot today. Although the Sheriff came into the café every morning for breakfast, he had never come by Rose's home in her memory.

"Hi, Sheriff!"

"I need to ask you a question." He wiped his forehead again and folded up and returned his handkerchief to his pocket.

"Sure." Confused, she came down the porch step.

"I'm not trying to be snoopy, and I hate asking you this. I'm asking you as sheriff, not as a neighbor."

"What in the world?"

"Did you spend last night with Andre?"

Stunned, she wondered what this was about.

"Yes, I did."

"Were you over at Mike's cabin Friday night?" He pulled his handkerchief out from his pocket and wiped his forehead again.

"Yes. Mike's daughter's staying there. She'd hurt her knee, so we were checking on her."

"What did you do there?"

She thought back. "Played a rock game Jori likes. Um. Sang some songs. She's really a good singer! Practiced shooting. Andre left his gun there."

"Okay. Thanks." He turned with a quick wave and strode off toward downtown.

"Bye," she called after him, puzzled. She glanced at her Timex. Where's Andre?

Until he came into her life, Rose was alone. Her boyfriend from Grand County was drafted, his convoy ambushed, and he died at the age of 20. After his death, she developed a strong opinion against the war in Vietnam. But she kept her mouth shut.

"To each his own," her mother used to always say. Meaning if you run a café, you never want to alienate customers.

Rose was not fond of Mike. She remembered complaining to her mother when Mike said to the crowd in the café: "Hey, do you want to hear a hilarious joke?" Everyone became silent and waited.

"Women's rights!" he brayed.

His laughter boomed. A trickle of laughter moved through the café. Rose spun back to the kitchen, but he called, "Hey, Cute Thing, how's about some more coffee?" She had an urge to empty the pot over his head, but she held her infuriation inside and refilled the cups at his table with careful determination so not a single drop sloshed.

That night Momma said, "I am so proud of you, Rosie. You have the power of restraint."

The sun, the cloudless sky—so hot. Rose went inside to her bedroom to change into a light cotton dress. What a relief to get out of her jeans and flannel shirt. In the kitchen, she added ice to her tea and snagged a couple molasses cookies she'd made from bran, molasses, and carrots for Partner.

Lots of cars downtown. Busy Sunday. If her café were open, she would be serving lunch to all the church members right now. She hoped whatever took Micky down to Denver for medical help would be cured quickly. She really needed a waitress.

She figured Mike must have rejoiced to see Micky after all this time. But why did the Sheriff ask what she did at Mike's cabin and whether she spent the night at Andre's? The gunshots reverberated in her head. She plopped into the pine chair on the porch and picked up the notebook. Micky's handwriting was small, a combination of cursive and print. She'd drawn on many pages—flowers, houses, faces, doodles. Some pages had rows of numbers like she was keeping score.

Curious, Rose began reading. But a sick feeling washed over her. This girl's been going through hell—being tied up and photographed! Rose snapped the notebook shut and carried the cookies to Partner who was standing in the shade nibbling on grass, his black coat gleaming.

The afternoon sun blazed down.

"Where is Andre? Why do you think he asked me to check out Micky's journal? Did he start reading it himself? Crazy! Huh. Mike's little girl. The last time Mike spoke to me, he suggested I change the café to a night spot with a burlesque show and name it Little Las Vegas." She saw Partner smile as if he were laughing.

"Not against the law in this county. You should take advantage of it," Mike had told her.

That's the reason Rose responded to Micky's job inquiry with "Are you 21?" She was joking. Truly, she need a server since her current one quit last week and moved to Denver, but not a summer temp from one of the families renting a vacation cabin. She wanted someone who could take over the café totally once in a while so she could explore more of the world with Andre instead of only day-tripping.

After reading the first few pages of Micky's journal, Rose saw a different picture altogether: sickening. It will be better for her now that she's come to Golconda, Rose thought. It has to be why she asked for a job.

Micky said she hadn't seen Mike for eight years. Where the hell was he all that time? Why had he left Micky in a mystery? If he had started the ski area eight years ago when he was constantly talking about it, he wouldn't be quite so late to the game today. Well, one place he's been Rose did know about—Nevada.

Mike's wife and little son lived in Las Vegas, he claimed. He had not yet brought them to Golconda but constantly showed pictures of his little redhead son—a cute tot about two years old. Oh, Mike! Pushy. He talked Old Jake and Esther who owned a couple hundred acres abutting the property his cabin sat on into selling their land to him—before they talked to anyone about what the property was worth. He could be convincing, that's for sure.

Rose scanned the horizon. Almost three-thirty. Jori's mom must be late. Or Sheriff Runyon might be speaking to Andre, too. While downtown looked busy, the road coming into town from Andre's was quiet. Sure, the sheriff was doing his job, but what difference would it make to anyone where she slept last night? What did it have to do with visiting Micky at Mike's cabin? Did it have something to do with hearing the gunshots?

With Partner looking comfortable in the pasture, Rose settled back into the chair on her porch. She picked up the notebook and read the first page again. So personal; she felt like an intruder: "Here I am, about to write freely in a notebook no one else will read." Oh well. She read on.

****

Andre sat on the floor in Jori's room, helping her pack. Jori ran to the window looking for her mother's car, then zipped back to the chest and grabbed socks and shorts and t-shirts from the drawers and put them into the suitcase on the floor. She looked around for more to pack.

"Takes a lot of room," Andre said when she topped the pile with her pillow. "Don't you have a pillow at your mom's?"

"Yup, and it's gween." Jori took the pillow back to its place on the bed and opened the closet door. "You don't need your jacket," he said stopping her from putting her winter coat into the suitcase, too. "It's the middle of summer so it's hot, and not only that, but you're going down in altitude. Do you know what altitude is?"

"Wike when you say, 'I don't wike your attitude, so cheeh up'?"

Andre laughed. "Attitude and altitude are two different words. Altitude is going up or down the mountains. Attitude is your state of mind."

"What is state of mind?" she asked and climbed on the bed to get her two-headed lamb.

"How you think," he said. "How you feel."

"Okay," she said. "My awttitude was cheeahed up." She carried over the lamb she'd given two names to— one for each head—Yips and Bips.

Andre glanced through the suitcase in case she needed anything else and clicked the snaps shut. "Come on," he said. "Let's go outside."

"Is Mommy here?"

"I don't know." He grabbed a guitar as they passed through the living room. Outside, in the cloudless sky the sun was the hottest it had been all summer. He sat on the table under the tree with one foot on the seat and the other crossed over his knee and began tuning his guitar. Jori darted past Andre's truck and Micky's car to see if her mother was coming.

She skipped back. "I don't see her, but my altitude is excited."

Andre laughed but didn't correct her, and she climbed up on the table beside him. "Pway 'My Gil,'" she said. This was not the Temptations' song but one he had been writing to Jori all summer and continuing to add verses. The latest verse was "my girl made mudpies to take to the bees," based on a real experience, and he started singing it. Jori giggled, and a long, blue Eldorado with a sun roof came into sight on the track.

****

Rose could not put Micky's journal down again until Andre's truck kicked up dust on the road and he pulled to a stop in front of the house. The sun flashed off the orange fenders in a wave of late afternoon heat. He was wearing shorts and a tee-shirt with a pack of Marlboros folded into the sleeve though he didn't smoke often. Wordless, he came up the porch steps, pulled her into his arms, his muscular strength against the thin cloth of her summer dress.

"I'm sorry it took so long."

"I assumed Tess arrived late." She touched his cheek. "Mmm, you smell good." Andre's hair was tied back and still damp from his shower. "Sheriff Runyon came here a little while ago. He asked if I spent last night at your place. Andre, what happened? Why would he ask me that?"

"Oh, God, Rosie." He got his cigarettes from his sleeve and flopped down into one of the chairs on the porch. "I didn't want to talk in front of Jori."

"Is Micky going to be okay? What happened?"

Andre fumbled to open his cigarettes. "I'm not even sure what happened."

Rose sank down into the other chair. "Did you read her journal before you gave it to me?"

He shook his head.

"Why did you ask me to read it?"

"She got shot."

"Shot!" Rose gasped. "What? No. How in the world would she get shot? Crazy. No!"

"You remember the shots we heard this morning."

"Yes."

Andre leaned forward. "Consider—if someone shot her, we may have a killer up here."

"Oh, jeez. Who would want to shoot a teenage girl?" Rose stood up and paced. "She was over the top with excitement about seeing Mike after all those years."

Andre tamped his cigarette on the table. "Huh. Mike. That asshole. I dashed over to the real estate office to tell him right after I dropped her off at the doc's. I suppose he's gone down to Denver by now, but he didn't seem in any hurry—except to meet his client."

"Probably wouldn't stand a client up. But omigosh, he must have been over the top thrilled to know she's here!"

"I don't think so. He struck me as blasé. I'm a father, too. If anything happened to Jori . . ."

"I know. I know. Oh! I can't believe Micky was shot!" The gunshots resounded through Rose's mind.

"With my gun."

"Oh, no!"

"She wasn't at the cabin. So I left the breakfast on the porch and decided to run up the trail on Fire Peak. Near the top, I found her. Drenched in blood. I assumed she fell."

"I swear, we need medical helicopters in this state!"

"We do."

"What happened?"

"God, I wish when we heard the shots, we investigated." His shoulders and neck were unbearably stiff. "I didn't notice my Ruger lying right next to her."

Shot. Unbelievable. Rose flipped his lighter and lit his cigarette, and he took a long drag.

"Andre, she ran away from her husband."

"What? Husband? That kid has a husband? Would he try to kill her?"

"I can't imagine." Rose frowned. "Of course not. How would he know you left your gun? He didn't know she was here. She was shot by your gun? You're sure?"

"Pretty sure, yes. Runyon and I went back up, and it was lying on the ground beside the boulder where I found her. Absolutely drenched in blood. I may have hurt her more by picking her up."

"What choice did you have? You had to get professional help."

"Guess you're right." He took another long drag and stamped out the cigarette in the Folger's coffee can filled with sand Rose provided as an ashtray.

"As soon as Doc said she was shot, I ran to Mike's. That asshole had his feet propped on Madeline's desk reading the *Rocky Mountain News*. The first thing he said was "How do you know she's my daughter?" I said she told me and that she was fucking excited she was going to see him again, and he said, "I'll be right over, but I'm waiting for a client."

"Did he look shocked she'd been shot?"

"Surprised, I guess. By the time I ran over to Sheriff Runyon's office and we got to the Doc's office, they were putting her into the emergency van. I thought Mike would be riding down with them, but he hadn't come, and by the time Runyon and I got into the squad car to go back to the cabin to investigate, Mike hadn't shown and his car was still parked in front of his real estate office."

"Oh, dear."

"After Runyon and I came back into town, Mike's car was gone, so I assume he did head down to the hospital after all."

"Of course."

"Maybe he took off with his client to show property instead."

"Well. Maybe Mike had to call her mom first to let her know so he didn't rush to to the doctor. Did you tell Sheriff Runyon he was her dad?"

"I did."

"No doubt he remembers Mike bringing Micky and her brother up here."

"The second we got to the spot where I found her, Runyon sees my gun lying on the ground and said, 'Obviously the weapon.' I was shocked I didn't see it.

My Ruger. He gets out his Polaroid and takes several pictures of the site, and puts my gun into a bag and starts questioning me."

"What did he ask?"

"Why I went up the trail, why she had my gun. After I told him everything, I didn't want to tell him you spent the night, but it came out when I told him about hearing the shots this morning."

She sat down again and leaned forward, put her hands over his knees. "He was apologetic about snooping into my private life."

"Hard to keep a secret in a small town. Hey. You like my new shirt? Runyon sent me over to the Penny's store to buy a new shirt and pair of shorts."

"Good of him. So Jori wouldn't see the blood."

"Well, yes, but more to keep my clothes as evidence. Maybe he really thinks I shot her."

"Oh! No way! Can Micky talk?"

"She might be able to by now. She was unconscious the whole time. Ragged sounding, but every breath she took gave me hope. So much blood."

"She'll tell the sheriff you just left the gun, Andre. She will be all right. You saved her."

"I hope so." He felt exhausted. "Anyway, after I dropped off my clothes with Runyon, I drove her Falcon home. I'd forgotten all about the notebook I picked up, but I figured you could read through it and see if she indicates who shot her. Now we know—it must be her husband. Who is he? I gotta tell Runyon."

"No! It's a diary!"

"I should have given it to him in the first place."

"No! Unless she dies, her diary is private."

"Evidence, Rose."

"No! She wrote that Wally knows nothing about Golconda. Plus, no way he'd know you left your gun there, right?"

"True."

"She wrote that she felt safe here because she'd never told him anything. Let's wait, okay? If we give her diary to anyone, that should be Mike or her mother."

"Not Mike." Andre lit a joint and took a long drag, and Rose told him about Micky's prayers and her life with Wally.

"Damn. You wouldn't think a cute kid's life would be like that. We really should give her diary to the Sheriff, Rosie."

"No. Because Wally might be able to find her if we do. Imagine it: they question him, so he asks where she is now. And takes her back." Rose held the notebook against her chest, feeling tears starting. "We're holding this for her," she said. "For the solotramp."

"Okay, okay. Where is her mother?"

"Denver, I guess."

"Her brother?"

"She thought he went to Vietnam."

"When will he be back?"

"They go for a year," Rose said. "I think she lost touch with him."

"Was her brother her enemy?"

"No. No. Absolutely not."

A shadow spread over the pasture as a cloud passed over the sun.

"Imagine if you did not run up that trail—she could be dead this very moment right up on Fire Peak. No one would know."

"True."

Partner stood by the fence looking as though he were listening to every word. July's late afternoon sun burned down and the cloud disappeared, and in the shade of the porch, an alpine breeze picked up.

"How about early supper?" Andre asked. "I'm starving. I'll grill some burgers."

"Good to have someone else in charge of the cooking for a change!" She led the way to her kitchen. "You want to hear something super bizarre? Mike made the kids go to a Christian school,"

"Whoa. Mike chose their school?"

"Yup."

"A Christian school? Unreal. No, I wouldn't think of Mike as religious."

"Yes, but get this: her mother is an astrologer. Sounds like the kids went to the religious school because of her astrology. The paranormal evidently offends Mike, so he made sure the divorce required the kids go to the church-school."

"I can't imagine Mike as being churchly."

Rose laughed. "Anything but, I'd say!"

"It would be maybe less bizarre if he shot her."

Rose's breath caught in her throat. "No. Beyond bizarre."

"This crap with Mike is irritating."

"Mike's been irritating all the time I've known him," Rose said.

"It totally seems to me that he's hiding something."

"Hmm. I dunno. He's always outspoken."

"Has he ever told you where he was all those years?"

"Okay." She laughed. "You've got me there. No one knows."

"What if," Andre said, "he tried to kill her because she could expose something about him?"

"I do not like to imagine that."

"Where was he all that time?"

"He says his wife and little son are in Las Vegas. So I've assumed that's where he's been."

"If so, what would keep him from being in contact with Micky and her brother?"

"Well, sometimes a new wife wants her husband to have nothing to do with the past."

"In Sheriff Runyon's career, Rosie, how many people have been shot around here?"

"There was a suicide a couple years ago."

"No murders?"

"No! Golconda isn't like that!"

"Still—maybe Runyon suspects me. My gun."

"Had to be an accident."

"Or a suicide. Or attempted murder."

"This makes everything different. Like we won't instantly be just like we were when we woke up this morning. I hope she's telling them what happened right now."

"Hope so," Andre said and took another long drag on his joint.

PART THREE

AUGUST 1970

Coma: Micky lay in a hospital bed.

Her impounded Falcon sat on the vacant lot next to the sheriff's office.

Mike claimed Andre tried to murder her; Andre continued looking at Mike suspiciously,

Sheriff Runyon decided she tried to kill herself.

The sound of gunshot echoed in Rose's brain again and again. What could cause Micky to try to kill herself when everything was looking up? Wally. Rose could not stop thinking that when it came to Wally, Micky said suicide was her worst desire. But Wally couldn't know where she was. She left that night, and she was gone. Disappeared from his life.

Plus, she wrote that she wanted to die saving someone else. Thus Rose was convinced that it was a freak accident. Horrible.

A beautifully talented girl who should be singing for the whole world to hear.

She read the journal again and again and started locking her door when she slept alone at home. Rose became more convinced not to reveal Micky's journal. Not only did Micky (and Ty, too) deserve privacy from everyone else, but most definitely she would not want Wally being notified of where she was.

It played in Rose's mind to give the journal to Isabel so that she could give it back to Micky as soon as she awakened. But Isabel told Micky that her mother destroyed anything that would remind her of Isabel's father after he died, and Rose feared Isabel may have the same characteristic. Micky had a right to write in her notebook and throw it in the latrine herself when she woke up.

Bad enough that Rose had read it.

Not used to feeling guilty nor having her conscience tapped, Rose decided to visit Isabel. She took the unusual step of closing the Opera House Café for two days in August, and she drove down to Denver, adding a day to her drive-for-supplies day. Andre drove, and Rose got to be the passenger and look down cliffside.

First stop—St. Anthony's Hospital.

Moved out of intensive care, the window in her room overlooked Sloan Lake, and Micky lay in her hospital bed surrounded by a pulled brown curtain. Eyes closed, hair spread out on the pillow, breathing regular, she wore a blue nightgown with lace around the cuffs and looked to be in a deep sleep. Rose touched her forehead and whispered, "Come on, girl. Time to wake up."

Rose started humming, and Andre joined her singing, "What a Wonderful World."

"Are her eyes flickering?" Rose asked, stroking Micky's hand.

Andre shrugged. "I can't tell."

"I'm here, sweetie," Rose said. "We're here for you."

They then drove over to the Kings' house where Andre's parents lived. He was taking the unusual step of introducing a woman to his parents, and they'd be taking them out for dinner tonight.

"You're sure you can find Micky's mom's place?"

"I'm sure I can. Wow, your parents' house has a lot of windows!" She slid across the seat and took over the steering wheel as Andre got out. She watched him head to the front door under the curved balcony as she shifted into first gear. She expected Isabel's house would be easy to find since Denver was logically laid out. Turning right at the stop sign, she drove Andre's truck back toward the mountains, blue in the distance.

In the Abel's neighborhood, she passed a church with a house attached. She surmised this must be the church Micky attended: red brick with a small dome, and across the street a small Victorian, red brick schoolhouse with an American flag, a tall white cross, and a matching domed roof. She turned the corner, and the brick houses were older, smaller, and far plainer than the Kings' house in Hilltop.

She parked in front of a bungalow with a porch and a picture window on the left side of the door and two windows on the right, like the picture Micky drew in her journal. Peeling paint indicated the house was due for a paint touch-up. The roof shingles were dark green, and a detached gutter dipped down over the tiny red brick porch bordered by a low evergreen hedge. This was the spot where Micky sat out on a cold night waiting for her mother to get out of the shower so she wouldn't be alone with Barf. An older blue Dodge sat in the carport.

Sitting behind the wheel in Andre's truck and gathering up her nerve, Rose wound her watch, looked around for Barf's car, just in case he was here. She'd decided to drop in on Isabel rather than call her to arrange the meeting, just in case Isabel said no. She picked up Micky's notebook, put it back down deciding she wasn't ready to turn it over yet. A door slamming in her face was better than not trying at all, so she slid out of the truck and walked up the driveway past the Dodge and up the two steps to the brick porch. She took a deep breath, and pushed the bell, crossing her fingers hoping Isabel would be okay with a visit. She hoped to learn how Isabel could choose that man over her daughter.

Hearing a rustle inside, Rose examined two strips of peeling paint, then the metal splay of flowers on the aluminum screen door. A tiny woman in a pink terrycloth bathrobe—hair pulled into a neat French twist, red lipstick matching the polish on her nails—opened the door.

"Hi. Avon?"

"No," Rose said, surprised. "No. I'm Rose Worth. Michaela's friend."

The last thing Rose expected was how Isabel's face lit up. A smile washed over her face, and she pushed open the screen door. "Come in, Rose. Come in."

As Rose went inside, her eyes adjusted to the dim light. The room reeked of cigarette smoke. Piles of stuff everywhere, stacks of magazines and little mountains of folded and unfolded laundry beside a standing ironing board. Blocking the light from the picture window, pinch-pleated draperies with orange flower-bursts hung behind the blue sofa. Rose saw the faded recliner chair with lap-table Micky had described, the overflowing ashtray under the glow of the pole-lamp. "Come on into the kitchen. Coffee's on."

Rose followed Isabel across a hallway and through a wooden swinging half-door like in a TV saloon. In the kitchen, she saw the dish rack piled with clean dishes and the sink full of soapy water, and through the window over the sink, sumac with spreading branches and red clusters. Otherwise the back yard was mostly bare dirt except for tufts of crabgrass, dandelions, thistle, and knapweed. A geranium with a bright red flower sat on the sill.

Isabel shoved aside books and papers on the green-plaid Formica tabletop. "I work here sometimes. I do astrology charts." Rose sat down in a chair with a green vinyl seat and shiny chrome legs while Isabel poured coffee from the eight-cup stainless steel percolator on the counter. It crossed Rose's mind this was the kitchen where Isabel called Micky a liar; the kitchen where Micky and Ty planned his draft-dodging trip before Isabel changed his mind.

Isabel set a Pyrex cup decorated with an enameled blue flower in front of Rose and another cup enameled with abstract red birds on the other side of the table beside her pile of papers. Her smile reminded Rose of Micky, the same shape of lips. "Where do you know Micky from? The church?"

"Golconda."

Isabel's smile disappeared. She stared at Rose. Her sweet-sounding voice turned to almost a growl. "When did Mike take her to Golconda?"

"He didn't. He didn't know she was coming."

Isabel squinted at Rose. "Do you need sugar or cream?" she asked stiffly, and Rose accepted a spoon and the sugar bowl. While she added sugar and stirred, Isabel lit a cigarette with a silver lighter and sat down across the table. Her lipstick made a red band around the cigarette's white filter, like the others in the full ashtray on the table in front of her.

"I was just getting acquainted with her," Rose said softly. "I hired her to work at my café."

"Hmm. Micky's friend." Isabel shook her head and held her cigarette to her lips.

"I saw her this morning at the hospital."

"She's going to be moved this week to what used to be a TB sanitarium—now for people with dementia."

Rose frowned. "Sleeping beauty."

"She is!"

"Are they predicting she'll waken?"

"The doctors told to prepare for her to never wake up. I told them I want her to come home. But they tell me she's better off in the sanitarium since I work and she should have someone near at all times."

"Ask Mike to pay for a babysitter!"

Isabel nodded. "Yes. He should."

Rose dipped her cookie into her coffee, took a bite, then a sip.

Isabel tapped her pile of papers. "I've been reading Micky's chart to determine the best environment for her.

A problem I'm seeing is that her fourth house is void, unoccupied, and its ruler is Uranus, which is square Neptune, Saturn, the Sun, and Jupiter. Do you know astrology?"

"No."

"The Fourth House is the house of home."

"Goodness!" Rose had never heard a conversation like this.

"Her Sun is opposed to Jupiter and conjunct Saturn. I guess unhappiness can hit her harder than others. Something jarred her happiness so much she would try to take her own life. Why did her hope disappear?"

Rose shook her head. "I don't believe it did. I think she was getting her hopes back."

"Did she talk to you about something bothering her? Did she complain?" Isabel put a hand over her eyes and took two long, shuddering breaths.

"Micky did not complain to me. She loved music."

"Yes."

"I wonder if music will wake her."

"I didn't think of that. Good idea."

Rose plunged: "She was so excited to meet her father again. Mike went missing for years." She hoped Isabel revealed where he'd been.

"Excited to see him but never wanting to see her mama." Frowning, Isabel picked up her coffee cup.

"I know she ran away from home, Mrs. Abel. I can understand completely how upset you must feel."

"I am in shock. You are right. You may call me Isabel." Isabel's voice was sweet again. It sounded like she was choking back tears.

Rose reached across the table and put her hand over Isabel's.

How many parents go through some sort of chaos with their teen kids? How few cannot make up because their child is unconscious? A flash shot through her mind of Isabel telling Micky she didn't believe what Barf did to her, and she pulled her hand away, feeling idiotically unprepared for this discussion. The truth was she just wanted to meet Isabel to find out what she looked like and how she behaved. She hadn't thought through the visit, preparing to either hand Isabel the journal or find the door slammed in her face.

Rose asked about the bathroom and Isabel directed her through the swinging doors to the hallway. Each of the doors was open to the hallway, so Rose peeked in.

The room that surely must have been Ty's held a three-quarter bed covered by a brown plaid bedspread, with a blond oak bookshelf headboard filled with books, a matching blonde oak bookcase against the opposite wall crammed full. On top of the bookcase were a baseball mitt and a broken tennis racket; on the nightstand, a brown plastic radio and a Westclox alarm clock with the hands stopped at six minutes past seven. A framed painting of a ship with sails puffed with wind hung on one wall, and taped to another wall was a world map.

Isabel's room—still small at about twelve by twelve, and so feminine Rose couldn't imagine a man in that room: ruffled pink curtains, a flowered pink and white bedspread, a large jewelry box (the one with the ballerina?), a vanity table with lipstick tubes and a variety of cologne bottles reflected in the magnifying mirror. Nothing manly in the crowded little room.

Rose's glimpse of Micky's room revealed a single bed with a green bedspread, an old dresser painted an institutional green, and a matching night table. Stark. No trace of Micky, nothing to suggest she ever spent a night here. Rose made up her mind that moment not to give the journal to Isabel, concerned she might dispose of it before Micky got to read it.

She returned to the kitchen, pushing through the swinging door. Isabel had not moved and was rubbing her cigarette out in the ashtray. Rose sat down again in the green chrome chair.

"I like your shade of lipstick. I like your hair, too. What a pretty ponytail. How long is your hair? Can you sit on it?"

"Almost," Rose answered.

"Micky always wanted her hair long. I thought it would be too much trouble. Now seeing her with her hair past her shoulders—" Isabel's voice catches. "She had no good purpose to kill herself."

"It was an accident!"

"The sheriff says so."

"Yes, but Micky—she had a hurt knee. That could make it easy for her to fall and set the pistol off. She liked to shoot, and she's a born singer who just met someone who wants to record her."

Isabel's words rushed. "Yes! She knew so much about music, and not just the silly stuff kids listen to these days. Mopheads. She used to play all my records over and over. Classical—Tchaikovsky, Straus. The soundtracks of *Carousel* and *Oklahoma!* and *Singing in the Rain*. Frank Sinatra. She learned all the words to all the songs overnight. She'd play the records and sing and dance practically the second she learned to walk. I'd think, How could this amazing little girl be the product of me and Mike? I was sure she'd grow up to be a performer. Her True Node is in her 5th House. The entertainment house. And she has Leo on the MC—a creative career."

"It's neat that astrology shows you her talent. It sounds like you gave her lots of music."

"I gave all the records to Goodwill after she ran. She played them so much they really become hers. My mother taught me that letting go is the best way to deal with grief." Her eyes filled with tears. "I'm sorry. I don't mean to get emotional." She pulled another cigarette from the Pall Mall pack and lit it with the silver lighter.

"Any mother whose daughter was unconscious would be emotional," Rose said.

"I know. I know." Isabel bowed her head. "No, no, no." She sat up straighter and looked at Rose. "Too many people are overemotional, and emotionality is one of the roots of all evil. Emotions bring trouble. Fights and tears and being disagreeable. Forgiveness for people who don't deserve it. Forgiveness again and again and again for lies your emotions make you believe."

She slid her chair back and got up to empty the ashtray into the trashcan under the sink, brought the percolator pot back to the table, and refilled their cups, set the percolator back on the counter and replugged it. "I wanted to afford lessons for her, but Micky never had a dance lesson. We were poor, thanks to Michael Abel.

Rarely one cent left over at the end of the month, so I couldn't afford lessons, and the silly school he made her go to opposes dancing. My job doesn't pay that well, and I can only charge so much for charts, or no one will buy them at all."

Rose dipped another cookie into her coffee. "I love her voice."

"The problem is that a performer must be patient and self-disciplined, but every time things didn't go Micky's way, she ran. If Micky had one ounce of patience, she'd realize things always work out in the end." She blew over the surface of the cup against the steam. "I can't believe I said that." She set her cup down. "She must wake up. She cannot have her last heartbeats in the sanitarium."

"She will! She'll wake up. I'm with you, Mrs. Abel. It doesn't make sense that God would give that kind of talent and then end it before most anyone knew about it."

Isabel looked thoughtful. "When Mike called me that day, when he said her name, I was afraid Micky had been found dead by the way his voice sounded. I did not imagine she would be doing this well. I was afraid she was dead."

She slapped her forehead. "Did I say that? No, she isn't doing well. No, she hasn't been doing well. She tried to commit suicide and can't wake up."

"Accident," Rose repeated.

"Did she tell you she ran away all the way to Las Vegas without a car? I don't know how she got there. The hospital called me, and I flew to Las Vegas to bring her home." She dragged off her cigarette. "Strange. I was so worried about her, but I was mad. I got madder and madder, and by the time I arrived, I could hardly talk to her." Isabel frowned with deep wrinkles between her eyebrows. "Not that she would have listened anyway. I was so furious. I didn't speak to her for weeks." The wrinkle between her eyes deepened. "I regret my fury. There's nothing I can do now. I'm sorry. I'm talking and talking."

"Talk all you like." Rose set her coffee cup down.

"I understand everyone needs someone to talk to when they lose someone. I'm there for my astrology clients. What's a little different about me though was I didn't lose her last month to a coma—I lost her two years ago. I went to Las Vegas to find her. Mike could have told me she's been in Golconda all that time. I thought he had sold the cabin to pay his debts. I was shocked when he said he was in Golconda. I believed Micky was in Las Vegas. No stone unturned there."

"No! Oh, no. She came to Golconda a few days before the accident, Mrs. Abel. She'd been living here in Denver."

Isabel looked confused. "Do you mean she just came back to Denver from Las Vegas?"

"No. She didn't go to Las Vegas again like the first time she ran. She's been living in Denver. She came up to Golconda just a week before her accident."

"Nooooo." Isabel's voice came out as a howl. "I looked everywhere for her in Las Vegas. I used up every spare cent to go there."

"Oh, dear."

"Are you sure? Are you sure she was here?" Isabel wiped at her eyes. "No. She couldn't. She'd be all alone.

She would need help, and everyone she knew was part of the church. That's why she went to Las Vegas. Because a couple from the church moved there."

Rose tried to put Isabel's thought processes together. "You mean you are thinking she went to Las Vegas because someone from church moved there?"

"Yes. They moved down there a couple months before Micky ran off. I hardly knew them because I'm personally not involved in the church. Where else would she go?"

Rose decided not to disclose that Micky had arrived in Las Vegas with Lester. She decided not to bring him up at all, and she was certain Isabel was unaware Micky was married. It was up to Micky to tell about herself. It was enough that Rose was telling Isabel Micky's location. "She came to Golconda right after the Fourth. Otherwise, she's been in Denver the whole time."

Isabel pushed back and stood up. "I thought the Las Vegas couple was hiding her. I went there three times. Three times! I accused them of lying to me. I threw tizzies. I'm embarrassed. I made a fool of myself." She grabbed a wet cloth at the sink and began wiping the counter.

It was too complicated, and for a second, Rose again considered giving Micky's journal to her to fill in the blanks. "Actually, she wasn't all alone. She found roommates and she found a job, and she and her roommates explored the city and went to the library and the parks, and they played music, and they encouraged her to go back and finish high school."

"She was a good student! And the choir director was so upset when she disappeared. Madge Davis even came to see me. Micky had everything going for her. Gifted. She had no right to throw her talent away."

"Mrs. Abel. Please believe it was an accident."

"She could see herself dance in the mirror. She was in the church choir. They kept asking her to sing solos. She could hear herself sing. She used to sing with Tyson all the time. She had to know she was talented." Isabel turned on the faucet at the sink and let water run over her hands, rinsed a plate and placed it on the stack-holder, turned off the tap, and pulled the plug to empty the sink. She turned to Rose. "She sang solos at the church. I'm not the only person who thinks she's gifted. Not just mother's prejudice. "

"Excellent singer," Rose said gently.

"I did my best. I raised those kids all on my own. It was not easy."

"I understand." Rose thought about the pranks they pulled on Barf. "Kids can be a handful."

"Thanks to Mike, we were poor. But before she ran, I got a raise and a bonus. We took the bus downtown and went shopping. We went to Neusteters and Denver Dry Goods and May D&F. We still couldn't afford their prices, but we liked holding up the fashions in front of mirrors. At the new Woolco store, I bought her a fashionable dress and a new plaid coat she loved. With Ty gone, I had more money for Micky and me. Lunch out—Cokes and hot dogs downtown at Woolworth's. She bought a Beatles record. I liked feeling rich."

Rose smiled, glad of their special day.

"You are sweet to come, Rose. Besides the choir director, nobody else came to talk to me about her, not even her best friend Tina. I've been alone." She reached up for a carton of cigarettes on the top of the refrigerator. "I hoped Micky and I would be best friends when she grew up. I believed she would realize her mistake and come home." She withdrew a fresh pack and opened it. "I know. I wasn't a perfect mother. But I tried to be."

Rose wanted to ask about Barf/Floyd. She wanted to ask about Ty. She started to ask what mistake Micky made, but Isabel kept talking.

"Life repeats itself. Again, I find my runaway girl in the hospital. Last time we did not talk to each other. This time I do talk to her, but she never answers. I listen so hard for a sign from her." Isabel shook out a fresh cigarette and stood by the sink tapping it on the counter. "What was I supposed to do? Put a net over her? Keep her from running? My life was hard—raising children, going to work, satisfying my astrology customers, keeping a house. She wanted a different mother, one like Tina's mother, the minister's wife. She would say, 'Why can't you be more like Mrs. Long?' And the TV— Mrs. Long let the kids watch TV all the time. I do not favor TV. I believe television influences people. Enables laziness."

"Micky likes how you didn't make her eat Brussels sprouts. She loved the Easter eggs you painted every year."

"She told you that?" Isabel smiled. "I thought she was impatient because painting took so long."

"No, she admired how pretty they came out."

"Well. A little thing she remembered. I hope kids always remember the good things their parents do. You help to reinforce my faith we can make up and become friends when she wakes up, Rose."

"That would be wonderful."

"In astrology, you can see which season people are going through, positive or negative, easy or complex. Unfortunately, I'm better at the astrology of personality and synastry for couples than I am at prediction."

Isabel shuffled through a pile of papers and withdrew one with a circle drawn on it, divided by lines, covered with symbols that she set on the table in front of Rose. "The sky the moment of her birth."

Rose nodded, but the chart did not look at all like a sky. Lines intersected lines, and the symbols, except for the crescent moon, looked nothing like stars or planets.

"Micky has fixed signs on the MC and IC. That means she's stubborn."

"Is that the same MC you said had Leo?"

"Yes. Leo is fixed."

"Is being determined the same as being stubborn?"

Isabel lay the paper on top of her pile. "You got me on that, Rose."

"How do you figure what's on the angles?" Rose asked politely. Angles were apparently the points of a cross.

"From the exact time of birth."

"What if no record of the exact time?"

"We rectify charts by major events in the life. Of course, Micky didn't experience major events because she was so young."

Rose shook her head, stunned. "What would a major event be?"

"Death of a parent. Moving across the country. Moving to another country. A major disease or accident. A divorce. Oh! Even kids react to a divorce. Their ignoramus dad. Of course, I didn't need to rectify her chart because I know the time from her birth certificate." She flipped through the papers. "I rectified Mike's."

"Mine would be rectified, too, because no clue what time I was born." Rose's mind danced over her own past for major events. How her sweetheart dying in Vietnam switched her to a painful universe. She bought Partner, her soul mate. Dad left. Mom died. Major events.

"Look for the time on your birth certificate."

"I was born in the house I live in now. In Golconda."

"Well, you can be sure your mother will remember."

"My mother passed two years ago."

"Oh, no! I'm sorry! Were you close to her?"

"Yes."

"I'm so sorry you lost her." Isabel got up and went to the cupboard and took out a plate. She opened the cookie jar and filled the plate with chocolate cookies. "I made these. You can dip into your coffee. Kind of a mocha flavor."

She patted the pile of papers. "Long ago I did an Golconda chart."

"What time would a place be born?" Silly.

"Public record. For example, the United States began on July Fourth 1776 at 2:20 in Philadelphia."

"How do you know the time?"

"John Hancock wrote it in his diary."

"His diary?"

"It's public," Isabel said. "I learn a lot from my astrology magazines. I can find the article for you if you like."

"No. That's okay."

"The reason I looked for Golconda's founding day was because Mike wanted to invest our inheritance there. Our mothers got killed in a car accident."

Rose thought of them stopped by the side of the road driving back from the funerals with Mike pointing at the sky and Isabel questioning God.

"I couldn't find out when Golconda was recognized as a town, but I was able to do an horary chart for the exact time Mike bought the property. Believe me, I didn't want us going in the dark with the money we inherited. Then I did a synastry chart between Mike's and Golconda's horary chart and mine. Would he listen to me? No. He is not a listening man."

"True." Rose nodded quite sure that Mike wouldn't listen to astrology jargon.

"Would you like to see his chart?"

Rose laughed "I don't think I'd understand it."

"Well, I shouldn't give away information like that anyway. Naughty me," Isabel said.

Rose took a bite of her cookie. "You're a baker, Mrs. Abel. Delicious."

"Another of my alternative lives. I like to bake." Isabel smiled again. "Anyway, be sure to note the time when your baby is born. And if you find out what hour Golconda began, I'd be appreciative." She laughed. "I don't see that skeptical look on my clients' faces. Really. Astrology helps us understand each other so we won't blame people for what they are or aren't." She pointed to what was clearly the moon on Micky's chart, the crescent. "See this? Fast moon with Mercury behind. That indicates the quick mind. But reactive. Impulsive."

Surprised her face gave away skepticism, Rose considered how Micky's journal did not point to a mother who understood her.

Isabel pushed the plate of cookies closer to Rose who helped herself to a couple more.

"Astrology enables analyzing people's birth charts and getting an idea of what to expect from them. Not been much research on suicide yet. It occurs to me she has a stellium of four planets in the 12th house, the house of secrets and sorrows—all opposed to Jupiter. She's a double Libra. She does not like unpleasantness."

"I suppose that is true of just about everyone," Rose said, thinking, What about your chart, Isabel? Why was Micky forced to run when your boyfriend did something to her? Where were you, Isabel Abel? Did you really know her—the girl you drew into symbols inside a circle? The girl who sat up at that cabin writing and trying to understand her life?

"But," Isabel broke into Rose's thoughts. "I think an astrologer can avoid seeing what they don't want to see." She began to cry. She stared across the table at Rose as if she could do something for her, tears rolling down her cheeks. Rose felt as if there was a wall of glass between them and silently watched Isabel, who finally wiped her eyes with the sleeve of her bathrobe. "I'm angry she took her life away from me. I gave her life, and she took it away. She had things to fuss about, but why oh why did she try to end life permanently?"

"Please, please, don't be mad at her." Rose stood. "She said you talked about how many heartbeats a person had. My mom was 43 when she died. It makes me feel better to imagine that Momma used up her heartbeats in what was overall a rewarding life."

Isabel followed Rose through the swinging door and into the living room with the worn blue recliner chair under the pole lamp and the piles and piles of astrology magazines. She touched Rose's arm. "Look at me. Aged ten years since she left. In the mirror I don't know who I am. In astrology, I do."

"I'm sorry," Rose said. Isabel looked beat up. Dark circles around her eyes. Likely speaking the truth when she said she aged. Rose felt she was taking away a handful of grief and longed for her own mother, to talk with her about all of this.

"She had her whole life ahead of her. She had so much to offer."

"You are right." Rose pulled the door open, and light poured in. "She'll wake up. Just have the faith. Micky will wake up."

Isabel blinked and shaded her eyes with her hand. "I'm sorry I've been fussy. I'm so glad you came by. I was upset long before this. Don't blame yourself for my stupid emotions. You come back any time, Rose. Any time at all. If you want your astrological chart done. Or if you have Golconda founding times. Thank you for coming."

Rose pushed open the aluminum screen with the flower scroll and stepped out into the light. The orange truck glowed in the sun in front of the house.

Rose got into the truck and started the engine, then glanced back. The door was closed with no sign that she'd been there. Next door a little girl and boy chased each other around in the front yard. Down the street a shirtless boy rode his bike and let go with his hands. Isabel's house needed paint and repairs, but the other houses were neat bungalows with tidy yards.

A few blocks away, the neighborhood grew commercial: Texaco station, Dave's Liquors, and a strip mall with butcher shop, clothing store, Rexall drug store. Several blocks down the street, the neon sign for "Tubby's" caught her eye. Staring at it, she almost ran a red light. When she slammed on her brakes, the notebook slid off the seat to the floor.

She imagined Isabel sitting on the kitchen floor painting Easter eggs. Sitting at the table after she'd cooked a special meal and the kids throwing food and ruining the dinner while she sat helpless and angry wondering what had gone wrong. Rose did not doubt anything Micky wrote about her mother nor about Barf but did not believe Isabel intended to hurt or destroy her, a relief in an odd way.

Rose had gone to Denver many times for restaurant supplies, but she had never stayed at night, and tonight with Andre, she saw the city spill across the foothills and plains like the night sky sparkling through a hole in a billowy cloud. In bed that night at the Kings after dinner at a fancy restaurant that introduced her to a fancy menu, Rose listened to the city's hum. A still summer night like this in Golconda was abuzz with everything alive and awake with the wind whistling through the trees. In contrast, the Denver summer night was abuzz with motors and sirens and the wail of trains, the dull roar of air conditioners and generators, the creaking of crickets.

As she fell asleep listening, she realized how sounds were unique from place to place. Near Golconda a gunshot would not be unusual; she suspected a gunshot in Andre's parents' neighborhood in Denver would raise attention.

SEPTEMBER 8 TUESDAY

Mike had been out of town for several days, leaving Madeline to manage his clients, so he surprised Rose when he popped into the Opera House as though he thought the café was open late for lunch. Today had been fairly quiet, and outside rainy and cool. The wind rattled the front window. Mike stood by the cash register, red hair slicked down, his plaid shirt tucked into his windowpane leisure pants.

"Sorry, Mike. Closed for the day."

"You shoulda locked up." He leaned on the counter. "Fact is I'm not looking to eat. My wife and kid are coming, so I'm building a house. Fact is we'll be breaking ground next week."

"Wow. Can you complete a home before the snow?"

"You won't know unless you try." He took a step back and turned toward the red rope separating what was once the hotel lobby from the café, then turned back. "Anyways, I'm here because I want to rent a couple rooms from you."

She shook her head. "Why not stay at the cabin?"

"Don't you know? Sales center for Fire Peak Estates now. Besides, currently no plumbing or electricity."

"No vacancies at the new motel?"

"Fact is my wife would like the privacy here."

"Hmm. Where are you staying now, Mike?

"Camping at the office."

"A few vacant houses around town these days."

"Yes, Gloria will be viewing them."

Rose wiped off his prints he left on the glass counter beside the cash register and considered. Quite a long time since anyone stayed upstairs. He put his hand over her hand, stopping her wipe-down. "Rose, I'm going to make you a rich woman. When we start getting folks up here needing nightlife, Rosie's will be the place to go."

Rose pulled her hand away. "Nightlife?" She laughed. "Your imagination cracks me up."

"You've got the space, and you gotta know strip shows are not illegal in this county."

"Strip shows? Uhhh." Rose choked. "Because no one tried to do one. Good grief, Mike."

"Go-go dancers." He shrugged. "They don't got to strip naked."

"Wouldn't women stripping conflict with your passion for religion?"

"Huh? My religion? What the hell?"

"Yes, didn't you send your kids to parochial school?"

He glared at her. "Yeah. You don't know my ex. I protected the kids from Satan." He ran a hand through his red hair and smoothed it down. "C'mon. I've got a cute little boy. You like little kids. You can't tell me otherwise."

He had her. "How long would you want to stay?"

"Depends on how long it takes to find a place to rent. You know the houses around here are shit. Best thing to do is bulldoze 'em or blow 'em up with dynamite."

She agreed. Many of the houses in Golconda were shabby. Of course, people willing to take the money offered by the development project were least invested in their property. What was for rent probably wasn't prime. He ought to be versed in Golconda properties given he owned the real estate office.

"Anyways," he pressed. "The wife needs a vacation. Cooking and cleaning aren't her favorite things to do. Fact is the little guy keeps her busy. Did I show you his picture?" He started feeling for his wallet.

"Yes, you showed me. Several times. And yes, he is cute."

"Twenty-five bucks a day per room. Two rooms. C'mon, Rose." He linked his thumbs into his belt loops; his cowboy boots showed under the flared pant legs of his leisure pants.

"Promise you won't be trouble."

He started out the door, pleased. "No trouble. I like doing business with you, Rosie." He stopped. "Want some advice?"

"I know you'll give me some."

"Stop hanging out with bad company."

He meant Andre. She shook her head, not believing she agreed to renting him rooms. She decided to keep her ears open for word of any new rentals. She locked the door and put up the CLOSED sign.

****

Michaela's car still sat on the vacant lot beside the sheriff's office. Sheriff Runyon had asked no more questions of Andre after he passed a lie detector test, yet Mike continued to spread the word Andre was responsible for Micky's coma. "Even if he didn't shoot her himself, he admits to giving her his gun. He left his gun with a teenager. What sort of nut is he?" Common consensus: Hippies should not be allowed to own guns.

Any time Andre's name came up in the café, there were side glances at Rose. The voices hushed or someone immediately changed the subject to the Fire Peak development.

"Progress. Like Mike said. American progress."

"Logically obvious why a ski resort wasn't developed here years ago. Undependable snow."

"But they can make snow!"

"At least our property values are rising."

"The Fire Peak Development offered me thirty grand. Can you believe it? Last year we'd be lucky to get seven."

"When prices shoot up, higher property taxes."

"Higher taxes ain't bad if we're getting something for them. Better sewer system. Better school."

"How about paved streets?"

"I don't want paving. I love Golconda as it has always been."

"Always been? Back when the mines were open?"

"Get over it. Nothing stays the same."

"Them speculators sure make me uneasy."

"Ah, hell, Golconda's always been a speculator's place. What was the gold rush for in the first damn place?'

"How many people been getting welfare? That will change."

"Our kids keep leaving. Where the hell could they work if not for this project?"

"Some kids will go. Some kids will stay. That's life."

"Golconda used to be rich; got poor, and now we're gonna be rich again."

Listening to them, Rose considered how some people valued stability and things staying the same, and some people valued opportunity and what might come. Actually, neither was guaranteed.

Over at Zimmer's Tavern, conversations under the influence of liquor become more spirited. The stay-the-same tended to be more rowdy, louder, and drunker than those who were eager about the opportunity Mike and his Fire Peak Development team were bringing to Golconda.

SEPTEMBER 12 SATURDAY

A few days after Mike had moved in, she was installing new syrup into the soft drink machine, and she felt a tap on her shoulder. "Do you know where Mike Abel is?"

She spun, expecting one of the speculators or investors. The tapper was not a member of the Fire Peak Development team. In fact, Rose was startled to see a young man who very much resembled Micky.

She set the syrup jug down. "My gosh. are you Ty?"

"Yes, I am. And you're Rosie, right?"

"Wow. How neat to see you."

"Yeah! Madeline told me to check over here because you were renting Dad a room."

"He's not upstairs right now. He's probably out at the sales office."

"Where's that?"

"Your old cabin."

"A sales office? What kind of sales?"

"Cabin sites—and also construction of cabins. A townhouse development is supposed to be built in the spring."

"Bummer! I loved camping at that place!"

"Ski Fire Peak!"

"I've never skied. But I guess Dad started thinking about this project a while back."

"Yes." Rose nodded, touched his sleeve. "I am so sorry about your sister."

"Did you see her when she was here this summer?"

Evidently Isabel didn't tell him Rose had visited her. "I did," she said. "I hired her."

He pulled off his glasses and wiped them on his shirt, held them up, looked through them, and put them back on. "Tough visiting her at the sanitarium."

"Any response? Anything new?"

"No. It's like she's sound asleep."

Ty had grown up. The last time Rose saw him, he was a shrimpy kid. Now he was anything but shrimpy. Tall and muscular, wearing a tie-dyed tee-shirt and a blue kerchief tied around his head, he was growing a mustache, and she was glad for his sake no earring in his one obviously pierced ear since his father would not like it and would give him hell.

"After I close up," she said, thinking of Micky's notebook, "could you come by my house? I'll be back home by three. I have something of Micky's."

He looked at his watch. "I'll go out to the cabin and see if I find Dad, and then I'll come by. How do I find your house?"

She gave directions—a couple of blocks up the hill behind the Opera House—the blue cottage with the adjoining pasture and stable.

"Okay, I'll catch ya later."

Jake, who took Rose to the movies several times before Andre moved in, was now having lunch with Dean who owned the movie theater. "Ooooh," Jake teased. "Your boyfriend's out of town, and now you're flirting with a stranger."

"Ha ha," Rose refilled his Coke.

"You free now?" Jake asked.

"*Easy Rider*," Al announced.

"Not what you think," Rose said. "More coffee, Al?"

"Hippie man is no good for you."

"Chocolate pie today. What do you think?"

"I think you ought to give the suspect hippie the cold shoulder."

"I think you need to mind your own business," Rose said coldly and put down their check on the table.

****

"Dad wasn't out at the cabin. Locked, but I could see into the windows. Pretty much the same with the old furniture and stuff." Ty sat in a cushy blue chair under an impressionist painting of a wild horse Rose bought in Golconda's junk store.

She brought him iced tea and slices of lemon and sat down across from him in her rocker. He pulled a Marlboro from its red box; she pushed the Folger's can filled with sand over the coffee table toward him.

"Across the creek, there's a new place," Ty said. "A round house. Is that going to be Dad's new house?"

"Oh! No."

"Be a surprise if Dad was building a round house. Then again, I don't know him very well anymore. If I ever did."

"Same old Mike to me. A new wife and child though. I haven't met them yet."

"Yes. Madeline told me." Ty squeezed a lemon slice, so the juice dripped into the tea. "When you said you had something of Micky's, I thought of the sapphire ring Mom said she took with her when she ran."

"Oh! Gosh, I don't know where the ring is. I assume it must have gone to the hospital with her."

"She's not wearing it."

"Have you asked the clerk at the sanitarium? Places like that always have to take care of the stuff people bring with them."

"I don't know if Mom asked them or not. Of course, Micky could have lost it or sold it before any of this happened. Did you notice her wearing it?"

"I don't recall. How is she? Any changes?" Rose hadn't been back since her visit with Isabel.

"I was holding her hand, and I swear she knew me. Her fingers started moving while I sang to her, and she was completely still when I stopped. I started singing again, and her fingers moved again."

"Wow! That sounds super hopeful. Good!"

"I wish I knew what happened."

"Early in the morning the day she was hurt, we heard the sound of a gunshot."

Ty looked startled.

"Two shots," Rose said. "I was staying at my friend Andre's house. The round house you saw. Friday afternoon we checked on Micky at the cabin, played some games and practiced shooting with Andre's pistol."

Ty leaned forward, listening.

"Our visit concluded on a high note because we informed Micky that your dad still owned the cabin and she'd very likely see him next day. She was beyond excited. A total delight to see joy explode. We went home, expecting Micky would have her reunion with your dad Saturday. We were curious about it, for sure. Sunday morning, we awoke to the gunshots. We were forgetful and left Andre's Ruger at the cabin. And the accident happened up the trail. We don't know how."

Rose got up and went to the tall bookcase and took Micky's black notebook down from the top shelf.

"Andre took breakfast over to her that morning, but she wasn't at the cabin."

"So she was staying out there."

"Yes. She thought someone else owned the cabin so needed to scram out of there. But when I said 'Michael Abel,' she fell to her knees saying, 'Thank you, thank you, thank you, God.' I'll bet that as much as anything on earth, she wanted your dad back."

"I know the feeling," Ty said.

"Andre thought the gunshots sounded like his Ruger and didn't find his gun in his truck that morning, He headed over to the cabin. Micky was gone, so he checked around for it and figured she was safekeeping it somewhere and would be back by the time he came back down Fire Peak. He took a run up the trail you and

Micky made. Near the top of Fire Peak, he found her unconscious and bleeding and carried her down. Her car was parked at the cabin, so he drove her to the doctor in town."

"Wow. Micky had a car?"

"Her husband bought the car for her."

Ty jumped up. "Husband?"

"Yes, she got married."

"Omigod! Mom doesn't know that, or she would have told me." He sank back down into the cushy blue chair. "Probably she would."

Rose cradled the notebook. "Andre gave this to me to keep for her, and I've had it ever since." She handed the notebook to him and dropped into the rocking chair facing him. "I am ashamed that I read it."

He looked mystified. "What is it?"

"Her diary."

"Wow. Crazy. Wow. Married. Who?"

"His name is Wally. She wrote a letter to you. You can find it where the ribbon is. Are you staying at the new motel, or were you planning to stay with your dad?"

"I didn't plan to stay at all. I was going to see Dad and head back."

"Please stay here," Rose said quickly. "I've got an extra bedroom. Please stay. I'd love to talk with you— catch up on your life."

He hesitated. "I don't want to be in the way, Rose."

"Not at all. You still need to find your dad. He has to be around somewhere."

"Well, if you're sure," he conceded and opened the notebook while Rose took his glass to the kitchen and refilled his tea.

"Make yourself at home, Ty. I'm going out to take care of my horse. Partner needs some exercise."

Feeling another wave of guilt for having read it and knowing too much about their little family, she headed outside to where Partner was standing by the fence waiting for her. She put his bridle on, and to warm up, led him around the corral. She mounted him, and off they went, a four-beat gait down the street. They turned on the road that led to the trail that can be taken to the rocky path that ended on the hidden springs. A brisk alpine wind said end of summer. The beat of Partner's hooves on the road echoed in the woosh of falling leaves. They reached the high meadow and left the trail. Partner broke into a cantor so now it sounded like three beats. His ears leaning forward, Partner trotted and snorted happily.

The black spiral notebook lay on the coffee table next to an overflowing ashtray. Ty stood at the window, tears streaming down his face. He had skimmed and read, skimmed and read, and being inside Micky's mind made him remember too many things he would just as soon forget.

He said, "Don't mind how I'm acting. I appreciate you kept her diary. I'm with you. I also read the whole thing." He automatically shook out another cigarette. Smoking was how he grounded himself when distressed. He held his lighter to his cigarette, consciously watching the flame at the end. Micky was frozen, no way to make her sing. A wave of guilt swept him for not keeping in touch with his little sister and another wave because she carried his secret like a hidden weight in her heart, and a third for betraying her privacy and reading her secrets.

"It will be okay," Rose said. "Come to the kitchen."

She diced tomatoes and green peppers; Ty drank more iced tea and ate a stack of homemade crackers and slices of cheddar. Hungry—not a bite since he left Denver.

"Do you know where your dad was all those years? When he stopped coming to Golconda, we figured his project fell through and he got tired of the mountain life and just didn't come up anymore."

"Nope." He took off his glasses and cleaned them on the corner of his shirt. "Mom said it was Dad's business to tell me, not hers. A couple years ago, she sent his address to me and said I ought to write to him. The address was in Carson City, Nevada. I wrote to him and asked him why he deserted us." Ty put his glasses back on. "I never heard back from him though. For all I know, it was the wrong address."

"When did you come home, Ty?"

"A couple weeks now."

"It must feel strange."

"Yeah. For real." He dragged on his Marlboro; smoke came out with his words. "Mom suggested I come to Golconda and ask Dad for a job. Given how things are, I had some misgivings. Mom started talking about finding out if he would remember he was my father, so I got curious. Not that I necessarily would want to work with him, but in person, how will he react if I ask him for a job? Ask him if he remembers me?"

He tamped out his cigarette and pulled a fresh one from the package. "The drive up here gave me a lot of time to think about what to say to him. Now I'm not so sure what I'll say. I was pissed at him while I was driving up—but that's not even close to what I'm feeling now after reading her diary. Mad at Mom, too."

Rose spoke softly. "Micky was thrilled beyond thrilled that she was going to see your dad. I have never seen someone so happy. Dancing on air. Bowing to the earth."

She poured two glasses of wine, and Ty carried the glasses to the old-fashioned dining room with wainscoting and dark plum wallpaper, centered by a mahogany table with scratches and deep notches to mark its age. She brought out the salad and soup and a plateful of sliced whole wheat bread, and Ty sat in the chair under a framed print of what could be interpreted as either a sunset or a sunrise with a golden and pink illumination over a mountaintop.

"So, Dad is selling lots out at the cabin? What's all that about?"

"The ski area at Fire Peak is a major part."

"Downhill skiing on that mountain. Wow. Is there enough snow every year?"

Rose outlined the development plans—the ski area, building the condos, selling cabin sites—complete with a cabin if the buyer wanted one.

"What a project!"

"Truly."

"I should had gone up the trail.'

"You can go up tomorrow. If it's still there what with all the bulldozers."

SEPTEMBER 13 SUNDAY

At dawn without much sleep, Rose got up and dressed in jeans, boots, and a deerskin suede jacket, and left Ty sleeping as she headed out to the corral and bridled Partner. In the early morning, Night Street was silent except for the sound of Partner's hooves clopping rhythmically down the road kicking up a little dust. Night Street hosted all Golconda's businesses: red brick, two-story buildings, their old facades chipped, ancient advertisements painted on walls of reddish brick.

Above Delmar's grocery store on the second story below the unscreened windows, flower boxes held zinnias, all dead brown since Golconda got its first freeze. Partner paused at the hardware store, and Rose could see through the dusty window everything piled and crammed together in some order only the owner understood. Shopping there seemed almost like a treasure hunt.

The window on the door of the old assay office still wore fancy gold script. The modern plate glass window Mike installed on his real estate office seemed out of place. The western clothing store that used to occupy the building displayed cowboy hats in the window for most of her life.

The land on the east side of Night Street sloped downward; the west side sloped up. On the hill behind the real estate office stood the school—red brick with peeling white frames around the windows and a play-yard with a tall, rusty slide, and swings with wooden seats hanging from long chains. Across the street from the school, two little red brick churches with pointy steeples faced each other like identical twins. The Catholic on the west side and the Protestant on the east, host to the Baptists, the Methodists, the Lutherans, and all the traveling ministries.

Rose rode Partner out to the edge of town where the new concrete block motel and its giant blinking Vacancy sign stood. Beside the motel was the new gas station with shiny pumps and signage tall enough to be seen from the highway. It had a self-serve policy, but Rose had never filled up there. She would always be loyal to Burt.

White, green, turquoise, and purple houses dotted the yellow, rolling meadows and hillsides like giant flowers. Unbelievable that once upon a time, many thousands lived here. Piles of weathered, grayed boards marked the spot where someone's house or shack used to stand. Rose's blue house stood way up on the hill beside Partner's pine log stable. The air this morning, fresh and cold, an early shine on everything. Railroad tracks clung to the mountains, but it had been years since they carried the precious metals to the mill.

Partner nibbled on the long grasses. Abandoned mines everywhere—a whole landscape turned inside out for silver and gold. Compared to how long it had been since these mountains first formed, the time it took for the miners to fracture them was an eye-blink in eternity.

She did not want to be gone long since Ty was there, so she and Partner turned and trotted back. As they approached the Opera House, Mike called, "Hey!"

Surprised, she reined Partner to a stop. Mike was getting something out of his long, black car parked in front.

"Gloria," Mike shouted over his shoulder through the open door to the lobby. "Come out here. I want you to meet our hostess."

A small woman with skinny legs and a big fluff of stiff, platinum blond hair appeared with a little redhead boy about two years old in her arms. She set him down and smiled at Rose. "Rosie, this is my wife, Gloria. I picked her up at Stapleton yesterday." Ahh, where he's been, to the airport in Denver. Rose leaned down to shake hands with her, and Gloria's flowery perfume wafted through the air. Her hand was soft as if it never sank into a sink full of dishes. Her sapphire ring caught the sunlight.

"Elegant ring," Rose said.

Gloria smiled. "Mike gave it to me."

Rose gave Mike a sharp look. "Seems you like sapphires." She did not take her eyes off him.

"Yeah, sapphires. Pretty stones." Was he uneasy about the ring? Perhaps he just needed to adjust the top button of his shirt, which he was fiddling with. "This here is my little son."

He bent down and lifted up the child who immediately began to squirm and want down. The little boy was chubby and cute and faintly resembled Ty with vivid blue eyes. How interesting, Rose thought, to finally meet Mike's wife.

She waved and trotted off. As she passed by the lot next to Sheriff Runyon's office where the Falcon was still parked, she could not help but think Mike must had taken the ring off Micky's finger and given it to Gloria.

The sun was up and bright now, the breeze steady and cool, and she wondered if in the developed future she would still be able to ride her horse through the center of town at dawn on Sunday mornings. She liked watching the silent and still Golconda come to life. As she and Partner headed up Snow Street, disappointment. Ty's blue Dodge was no longer parked in front of her house. Where did he go?

Inside, he had made the bed smooth and tight, Army-style. She wished she didn't leave this morning before he got up, wished that she hadn't assumed he'd still be sleeping when she returned. No breakfast, for goodness sake.

She prepared a cup of coffee on the stove, and from the bookcase, she pulled out her postcard album and sat down on the rug to insert the latest card from her father. On top of the little round table next to her was a framed photograph of her mother in a somber dark suit. Every week, Rose received a postcard from her father in Alaska—all those weeks and weeks, 52 weeks every year for the last ten years. Her letters to him and his postcards to her made up their conversation. On a postcard featuring the headwaters of the Racing River,

Pops had written: "When a man's got a foot in two countries at once, he has to choose. Whoever wants two ends up with nothing."

"A statement to ponder," she said aloud and put the album away, then carried her coffee and the *Denver Post* out to the front porch. Just as she started to read a headline about the release of a brand-new car called a Pinto, the breeze picked up and blew the newspaper across the porch. Rose jumped up and chased the pages and gathered them together. As she folded, she read that the hostages from one of the recent hijackings had been released. Three hijackings in the last couple weeks. The hijackings made it scary to think about flying up to Alaska to visit Pops.

Too many disturbing thoughts passed through her mind, so she took the folded newspaper inside, zipped up her jacket and headed out again, this time on foot. Church services were concluding; soon everyone would be out and about around Golconda.

There used to be houses all along Snow Street, from her house all the way downtown. That was back when the mines were active and population in Golconda substantial. Nothing like abandoned houses constantly crumbling and crashing down to rubble. Mostly between Rose's house and downtown were tall yellow grasses—since the first freeze, the fireweed and fairy trumpet vanished. The old union hall still stood on the corner of Snow and Night Street, but union meetings were long gone. Since the mines closed, no need. Golconda survived because it was the hub for the surrounding ranches with its two churches, the shops, and the school.

The wind kicked up dust on the road and made the long, yellow grass shimmer. The wires on the poles alongside the road swayed. A peregrine falcon flew across the sky with a chipmunk dangling from its beak.

By the time she got to Night Street, she was thinking about how needy the town looked with dusty streets and falling-down buildings, the old water system that could hardly handle the people who were already living in Golconda, the rusting playground. She supposed Mike and the investors surely knew how unpredictable the weather was and were making sure to include snow-making equipment. She listened to the final hymn at the Protestant church, and dozens of people flowed out to the street from both churches. Delmar and Madeline came out of the Protestant church, just as Andre's orange pickup truck came into sight.

"Hey!" she called, feeling her heart lift as he pulled to stop beside her. "I thought you were going to be gone all weekend."

Jori slid out the passenger side wearing pink sunglasses and holding the still-bandaged doll she'd named Michaela. "I'm stahving to death," she said in her high little voice.

"She was still sleeping this morning when we took off," Andre said. "She just woke up."

"We can make brunch," Rose said happily. She held hands with Andre, walking toward the Opera House Café. Andre started telling Rose about how Jori watched a cool new kids' program called *Sesame Street,* and he wondered if Golconda would be able to pick it up.

They passed Mike's long, black Cadillac parked in front of the cafe.

The doors to the café and lobby were side by side facing the street, but inside only a red velvet rope separated the two rooms. Rose tended to use the back stairs from the kitchen rather than the wide staircase where a strip of worn, plush red carpeting protected the imported mahogany.

In the kitchen, Andre squeezed oranges for juice; Jori stood on a stool helping Rose scramble eggs and butter toast. Mike and Gloria's little boy appeared, and Rose made a quick mental note to be sure to go up and lock the door at the top. It could be dangerous if the little guy came running down when the café was busy and the grill hot.

Jori stopped spreading grape jam on a slice of toast and stared at him. She was about twice his size. She still wore her pink, plastic sunglasses. He wore shorts with a diaper sticking up in the back. Jori grabbed his hand and led him out front to a table, and in seconds the two of them were playing under and around the empty tables.

Andre poured orange juice into four glasses. "Crazy you gave Mike the rooms upstairs."

"Easy money." Rose laughed.

"You want to ride out to my place with me and Jori?"

"I want to, but I need to shower and check on Partner. Plus, I want to see if Ty's come back."

After they cleaned up, she took the little boy's hand and led him up the back stairs to Gloria and Mike. Jori's bandaged doll named Michaela lay on the first step, so she picked it up. At the top of the stairs, she let the little boy into the hall and locked the door behind him. Downstairs, Jori popped back in through the café front door and dashed up to Rose to get her doll.

"Why still the bandages?" Rose asked handing it to her.

"She can't get better until the stars stop falling out of the sky." Jori held the doll in her arms like a baby, but it was a preteen doll wearing under the bandages a pink and white striped dress and a pearl necklace.

"Stars falling out of the sky?"

"I saw one zooping down like a gween ball, but my dolly Mikawa sees twillions and willions." Strange, Rose thought and walked Jori outside to the truck.

When she came back through the front door of her café, she found Mike and Gloria and the little redhead kid sitting at a front table.

"Not open today, Mike. Day off."

"How's about you give us a cup of coffee and some toast? You could do that for us, eh, Rosie?"

"Brunch at the Fire Peak Inn at the new motel." She glanced at her watch. "Or at eleven, a burger at Zimmer's."

"Aw, c'mon, Rose."

Gloria smiled. Unlike the women in Golconda, she wore much jewelry and steamed with cologne. She held the little boy on her lap and rubbed his hair with her hand. He squirmed. "You're a little button, aren't you?"

"C'mon, Rosie. You can make an exception this time. See how the little guy's hungry? If you're anything like your mother, you wouldn't let a little boy go hungry."

"I already gave him breakfast, Mike. Are you implying you didn't miss him?" She retrieved a candy bar from the shelf inside the glass case under the cash register. "Here's dessert for the little guy." She hesitated to ask him if he knew Ty came to Golconda.

"Oooh, a Milky Way," Gloria said. "You'll love this, Button."

Mike stretched out and rocked back the chair. Rose stood with her hands on her hips waiting for them to leave. "All closed up, you guys."

Mike slowly tipped his chair forward. "She's not going to feed us, babe. What can I tell you about Rocky Mountain hospitality?"

"I close the café on Sundays, and for the rare times I rent out rooms, I don't include meals."

"Oh, sorry," Gloria said. As she pushed the little boy off her lap, Rose spied the ring on her finger, the points of the star pointing to the surrounding diamonds.

"Now, Rose. Don't give Gloria a bad impression of her new home."

"I'm sure you understand how someone needs a day off," Rose said to Gloria, who nodded and got up.

Mike stood, after all. "Why don't you got those beds made upstairs while we're off somewhere finding something to eat, Rosie? It doesn't bother us if you go in our room, does it, Gloria?"

"Oh, no." She scurried toward the door where the little boy was trying to get out, her bracelets jangling.

"Maid service is a lot extra, Mike."

"Oh, we have plenty of money," Gloria said. "Don't we, Mike?"

"C'mon, Gloria. Fact is Rosie's in a bad mood today. Probably because of her boyfriend's new girlfriend."

Rose squinted at him but held her tongue instead of saying maid service was a million dollars in gold and that Jori's mother was not Andre's girlfriend. She locked the café door behind them and climbed the back stairs. In the back hall running perpendicular to the main hall, she removed some linens and the carpet sweeper from the hall closet. She piled the fresh linens on the marble top of the table in the hallway next to the suite and left the sweeper beside the door. No harm in cleaning up after themselves. If they want maid service, they could move to the motel across town. She did not go into the rooms.

She hoped to see Ty's car either parked somewhere in town or parked again in front of her house, so she hurried down Night Street. No stores open but people out enjoying the September sunshine. On warm Sundays, walking through Golconda could take an hour with all the possible conversations. Today, some people stood in a group outside the churches, and a few elderly sat on the sidewalk benches, chatting.

Rose caught up with Carmen, her best friend since forever.

"Is it true Mike and his wife are staying with you?"

"For now."

"I didn't expect Mike's wife would be so citified. Are those eyelashes false?"

"I don't know." Rose laughed.

"They sure look it. And that bubble hair. Whooee." Carmen was Golconda's hairdresser. "Where are you hurrying off to?"

"Mike's son is in town. You remember him? As a little kid, he used to come up to camp with Mike? I got to catch him." She walked faster, leaving Carmen, and darted up the street toward her house. "See ya later!" Carmen called.

Nope, Ty's car still was not here.

She took her shower and dressed and was getting ready to head out to Andre's, figuring Ty must have gone back to Denver, when he knocked on the door.

"Hey Ty!" She ushered him in. "I bet you're hungry."

"Very."

"I'm going to be heading out to Andre's in a bit. First, let me feed you."

She filled a plate with a ham sandwich and handful of chips. "Ty, I want to talk to you about Andre before you hear what people are saying. Rumors about him are nothing new."

"Sure."

"When he started building the round house, people made comments like 'I hear communists build round houses.' 'A house was meant to have corners.' or 'That hippie longhair is going to turn Golconda into a haven for drug addicts,' or "I bet he has ties to the USSR. He'll spread propaganda.' Now the rumors changed. They're saying: 'I bet that hippie shot her.'"

Ty held a potato chip midair.

"Andre did forget his pistol, Ty. Nothing can change that fact. But I guarantee you Andre did not shoot her. Quite the opposite. He tried to save her life. If not for him, chances are high she would not be alive today."

"Micky called him her angel. Thank Andre for what he's done, Rose."

Rose smiled. "Ah, yes. Her angels. Did you go up the trail, Ty?

"I did. I know where he found her. I could see partially the shape of her body in red on a boulder near the tree with our initials."

Rose shivered.

"I just saw your dad. I met his wife and little boy."
"For real?"
"In fact, I just sent them off to get brunch."

It occurred to her if she hadn't read the notebook, she would not have ended up in the middle of another family's problems. Ty would not be here now because she would not have invited him to stay with her.

The deep frown between his eyebrows made him resemble his mother. She didn't want to see Mike again, but when Ty asked her to accompany him to the Opera House, she relented. "They're probably finished with brunch. I can go with you."

Walking down Snow Street, Ty kicked a rock, sending up dust. "Dad used to always say, 'Son, make a lot of money.' Didn't figure I could afford to go to college. So, I got my first real job on a garbage truck and figured I'd think over what to do next. The Army made up my mind."

They walked by the piles of old, gray boards and the long grasses hiding the places where people used to live. He kicked another stone, and it flew down Snow

Street. "Did Micky shoot herself because of Wally or Dad or Mom? Or Barf? Or those assholes? Or me?"

His voice sounded tortured. Rose stepped in front of him and stopped. "Ty, I believe it was an accident. And if it weren't? If she meant for it to happen?—she lost a baby. Ty, look at me. Remember. Grieving. She also lost Chaz."

"That speed freak was no fucking kind of guy for her either. Conscientious objector. Oh, sure."

"She cared about him, Ty. She lost his baby and couldn't even tell him."

"Her blood doesn't belong on that rock." He broke into a run.

"Ty!" He kept running, and she kept walking, slow and steady behind him.

When Rose reached Night Street, Delmar cornered her in front of his store. "You okay, Rose?"

"Yes. Why?"

"Some weird guy come running by."

"He's Mike Abel's son."

"Oh. Yeah? Huh. Hum. Damn. I forgot his older boy. All grown up. Wasn't bothering you, was he?"

"Oh, no. No, not at all." Rose squinted down the street.

"Mike's got a room with you, right? What did you do to scare his pup, Rose?"

"Me scare him? C'mon, Delmar."

Delmar laughed, and his face turned rosy; his wrinkles deepened. "To be serious here, I want to say . . . I got nothing against Andre, Rose, even with the rumors going around. But he's talking out against the development, and ironically, all the while he's building his own commercial studio. He's not going to provide jobs in Golconda. But Mike—you know, he has a lot to offer. True, Mike's pissed off a lot of people. Not everybody wants all these changes. Like Dwight. His boy got beat up bad over there in 'Nam, and Mike implied Dwight wasn't a patriot when Dwight said his boy wouldn't like coming back to a resort instead of the town he left."

"Think Dwight Junior will recognize your store? You've been making some pretty bold changes yourself, Delmar."

"Got to keep up with the times. You sure Mike's boy's not bothering you?"

"No bother at all, sweetie," she lied. "No bother at all."

She found Ty sitting erect on one of the old velvet chairs in the lobby smoking a cigarette.

He immediately stood. "Sorry I ran off, Rose."

"I assumed you needed exercise. I wasn't up to bounding along with you. Lazy in my old age, I guess."

Ty half-smiled. "Reading Micky's diary made her so alive to me. Can you believe? Mom never wrote me that she ran. In her letters, she rarely talked about Micky. She just wrote tales about stuff happening at the auto parts shop and astrology. I was kind of pissed Mick never wrote me, so I quit writing her."

Rose motioned. "Your dad's car, Ty. Might as well go to it, eh? Shall we see if he's upstairs?"

Ty smashed out his cigarette in the floor ashtray and followed Rose up the mahogany staircase that once was entirely elegant, but now the plush carpet threadbare. As they arrived in the main hall, the linens still sat on the table. The transom window above one of the doors was open, and the child said, "No, no, no," in a voice sounding like Alvin the chipmunk.

Ty knocked on the door, and Gloria opened it. Her sweet cologne overcame the scent of lavender furniture polish. Open-eyed, her long lashes touched her eyebrows. "This is your dad's wife, Ty," Rose said, and the blank look left Gloria's face.

"Oh! Mikey, come here." Instead of Mike, the tot crawled on his knees toward the door.

"Mikey, this is your big brother." Gloria pulled him to his feet. "Show your brother how you can how-do-you-do."

Mikey gazed up at Ty and opened and closed his fingers like a wave. Ty's hand automatically touched the pocket holding his cigarettes.

"Oh, Mike!" Gloria jangled away, leaving Ty and Rose at the door with the little boy staring up at them and opening and closing his little hand.

Wearing a plush white bathrobe, the red hair around his ears damp and smoothed down, Mike looked Ty up and down. "My God! Caught me off guard here. Well, hell. Gloria, this is my other boy. My God! Come in, Tyson. Come in."

Rose nudged silent Ty into the room.

Gloria picked up little Mikey. "Oh! Exciting to meet you! I'm your stepmother!" Ty nodded but did not speak.

In his loud voice, Mike made introductions all over again. "Ty, meet Gloria and baby Mikey."

"Maybe Mikey and I ought to go somewhere so you men can be alone."

"The school playground?" Rose suggested, and Mike said, "Why don't you take her over there, Rosie?"

Ty spoke for the first time: "You can't miss it. Go to the real estate office and up the hill behind it. You can't miss it—right beside the red brick school. Rose is staying with me."

"I'm lousy at directions." Gloria's voice sounded little-girl, but she put a sweater on Mikey and led him out the door saying, "Does my little button want to go to the playground?" and her little button squeaked, "No, no, no," all the way down the hall.

Unmade bed, toys strewn across the floor—a homey atmosphere for what Rose expected would be a tense conversation. Beside the door was a red velvet settee, and Rose pulled Ty down beside her. A little puff of dust flew up, and Rose felt embarrassed she hadn't vacuumed the furniture.

Ty pulled out another cigarette and tapped it on the wooden arm of the settee. "Mind if I smoke?"

"Nope. Nope. Not at all. Picked up a bad habit from your mother, I see." Mike stood in front of the two of them as if he didn't quite know what to do. It was the first time Rose had seen him flustered. He went over to the dresser and got an ashtray for Ty.

"Sit down, Mike," Rose said. He pulled the dressing table chair over and straddled it.

"So, so, so." Mike smiled a toothy smile. "Long time no see."

"You said it."

Rose realized Ty did not seem at all nervous. In fact, he looked cool, calm, and collected sitting erect on the settee.

"You're looking good, son. Real good. Guess the Army treated you okay. I was in the Navy myself, you know."

"I know."

"And your mother grew up in an Air Force town. And your grandfather was in the Army for World War I. Did you know that?"

"I don't know anything about my grandfather."

"Well, he was. He was." Mike sat there in his white bathrobe, overflowing the chair, nodding and nodding, rocking the whole upper part of his body into his nod.

"So, tell me about him." Ty stared piercingly at Mike. "How did he die? Did he kill himself?"

Mike stopped nodding and snapped up straight. He leaned forward, with his hands on his knees on either side of the chair. Ty did not blink. He sat on the settee next to Rose, perfectly still with the ashtray balanced on his knee. "Did he?" he persisted.

"Where'd you hear that? From your mother?"

"No. Like I said, I don't know anything about him."

"My father was the best man I've ever known. He was in World War I. Not an officer but a regular enlisted man. He experienced hell in that war and lost an arm and his hearing in one ear. When the Depression set in and times got tough, there wasn't work anywhere, and so he hooked up with some vets to go to Washington, DC, to ask the government to give them their bonus." He gazed at the window, and Rose followed his gaze, glad at least that she did remember to wash the windows.

"I remember how down at the rail yard, we all sneaked into a boxcar with a bunch of other families. A cattle car. I remember the flies and the crying kids." He looked at Ty. "I also remember people pulling out their harmonicas and guitars. We'd sing the tunes. Ho de ho deo do ho. Minnie the Moocher a red hot hoochie coocher." He laughed.

Both Ty and Rose sat quite still on the settee, surprised Mike was telling a true story instead of a joke.

"You kids don't know that song. Yeah, yeah, yeah. Well. We finally got to DC and set us up a camp. What a raggletaggle bunch, all right. The women would wash things out in the river and lay them out on the banks to dry. Those ladies made soap out of lard. The smell of lard never rinsed out of your clothes, which kept the flies hanging around you. Our little town we set up out of crates and tarpaper and broken-down cars."

"Wow," Rose said.

"One afternoon, a parade of soldiers appeared. The vets and us kids lined up on the street cheering for them. But those soldiers started wheeling into us—like we were enemies. Hitting people, knocking them down with their bayonets." Mike shook his head.

"The soldiers on horseback put on gas masks. World War I was the first time of using gas, and man, were we scared. The soldiers started throwing canisters. I ran like Jesse Owens to the bridge. My collar up over my nose. Next thing comes the tanks. Man, you wouldn't believe the noise. Sirens. Horses tramping and snorting and whinnying. People yelling, screaming. Total zoo. The soldiers come and start tromping down the gardens and doused our whole camp with gas. Man, the fire was terrible. The flames shot sky high, and on the river, you could see rich people's yachts! We got herded like animals over the bridge and to the highway to Baltimore, our tarpaper and crate village burning behind us."

"Wow." Rose never expected a story like this from Mike.

"My father ended up working on a bridge project in the Florida Keys. Me and Mother stayed in Georgia. A hurricane struck the Keys, and my dad was never found. So you asking if he killed himself was a rude damn thing to say."

"Sorry," Ty said under his breath.

"Me and Mother got on another boxcar headed west. Clovis turned out to be the place of deliverance my mother (bless her soul) prayed for. I swore the day would come when I wasn't going to be poor. Like my father said, what happened to us over in Washington DC was a war on the poor. I swore I'd fix my life so nobody could ever treat me like I was nothing but a bum."

He adjusted his robe, pulling it closer together.

"My mother got married again—to the other grandfather you never met. He taught me what to strive for before he keeled over from a heart attack." Mike stopped and stared hard at Ty. "So there. Now you know a little something more about your family."

Ty stared back at Mike. "Thanks for telling me, Dad."

He picked up his lit cigarette from the ash tray. "Seems to me I don't have much family. The grandfathers I never met died; the grandmothers who had the car accident, I met at their funerals. You took off. Now my sister is in a coma. Mom blames you. What kind of family is this?"

Mike stood up. Looking down on Ty, he said in a loud voice: "You got a new mother and new brother! Your sister comes into my office with wild hair. Her dirty hippie dress. I couldn't believe she was my own kid. I felt like giving her a hard spanking right there. Right where everyone could see I don't condone a girl looking like a tramp. The good Lord knew what she'd been doing with herself. Your mother tells me she was missing for two damn years. Two years! How do you think she was getting by all by herself all that time? Her eyes all bright, too. Comes to me all doped up looking like that. I figured she was looking for a handout so she could buy herself more dope. I wasn't going to be a part of that. No siree."

Ty sucked in his breath and let it out slowly, slowly like smoke. Rose knew he was struggling to keep himself calm; she struggled for calm herself.

"Where were you, Dad?" Ty demanded. "Where were you those two years Micky was gone? Where were you all years before? You weren't protesting in Washington. You weren't in a hurricane. Where were you? Why did you disappear on us?"

Mike looked as if he was not used to someone being direct with him. "What'd your mother tell you?" he asked and sat himself down again on the chair.

"One." Ty put up his forefinger. "Riding a camel in Arabia." Middle finger. "Two. Big game hunting in Africa." Ring finger. "Three. King of Timbuktu. Four." Pinky. "You became a priest. Which was it, Dad?"

Mike roared laughing. "Hah, Isabel, Isabel. Hah. hah. She can always come up with something. Hahah." Ty did not laugh. He stared icily until finally Mike stopped. "Your mother's nuts."

"You were the last person to see Micky before she was shot."

"How do you know that?" Mike sputtered. "She just popped in on me from nowhere. Caught me off guard."

Mike got up and walked over to the dresser for his pipe and lighter lying on top. "The hippie comes by and tells me, and next thing ya know, I'm cruising down to Denver to the hospital, and then I changed my mind. No insurance on that girl. I'm not going to be stuck with some huge bill. Who said I was last to see her? It was the drugged-up hippie who said he found her. Big mountain like that. How did he happen to find her so quick? Sorry, Rose. But you got to face the truth."

Rose shook her head, but Mike pushed: "Andre was responsible."

"He saved her." Rose stood up.

"Oh, excuse me. Don't mean to offend you because I know you been chasing after him. But I'm telling it like it is."

"Bullshit, Dad."

"He shot her and had Rose here is his alibi."

"Bullshit, Dad. And I've got proof. So drop it."

"Proof? What kind of proof?"

Ty got up and stood in front of Mike who was tamping down tobacco in his pipe. "Let's back up a little, Dad. I asked you if your father killed himself. And you say he was a good man and tell me what happened to him. And I thank you for filling me in after all this time. But now I'm hearing you say Rose here was up to no good—and I'm hearing you say Micky was trouble."

"No, no, no. I'm just saying that hippie led her astray. Next thing he's going to lead you astray, too, Rosie."

Rose held her breath. "You are saying Micky knew Andre before he knew me? You are wrong, Mike Abel."

"Tell me, Dad. Before that happened in Washington, did your father take off when you were a kid?"

"No, he didn't take off. Son, I don't know what you're trying to pull here, but I don't like it."

"You want me to spell it out for you? I'm asking you where the fuck you were for all those fucking years."

Mike stared at Ty, put his pipe to his mouth and clicked a flame from his lighter. "I don't answer to young whippersnappers."

"You haven't seen me in all these years, and you call me a name?"

"Look." Mike tucked his robe around him; his bare feet planted. "Now look, son. We haven't seen each other in a long time. There's no call for us to get testy with each other. We just got to get reacquainted."

"Sure, Dad. There were a lot of years unaccounted for. Let's get reacquainted. Since we're trading stories, now, for your information, Mom had a boyfriend, and this boyfriend really liked kids. You know what I'm saying, Dad? I mean he *really* liked kids."

"So he liked kids, and you think I don't like kids. I hung in there for a long time. Don't forgot how you used to come visit me all the time before you go thinking he's the better man."

"I mean he *really* liked kids. In fact, he liked kids so much Micky and I tried to get rid of him, but Mom liked him more than she liked us."

"I don't want to hear about your mother's love life. None of my business. I put that behind me a long time ago. I got pissed once—once. And swore never again. I've held my vow."

"Is that the time Mom got a black eye, Dad?"

"I don't know. Let's don't go down a track like that. Look, I've got a pretty new wife, and you've got a pretty stepmother and a cute little brother."

"Bet you wouldn't want Gloria to find a boyfriend who really liked kids."

"Stop it, Tyson. I love my kid. Isn't he cute? You saw him. Your brother."

"Was I a cute little guy, too, Dad? Mom's boyfriend thought so. He also thought Micky was a cute little girl."

Mike dropped down in the old red velvet chair by the window. "You were both cute kids. Hell, I didn't take off because I didn't like you. Is that what you think?"

"That is what I think. Because you left us with this other guy who really liked kids. And one day I was hinting to you me and Micky ought to live with you because the guy was a pervert—and then you were gone, Dad. You disappeared."

"I don't remember a conversation like that, Ty."

"Yeah, gone. Just like that. You were gone. And time goes by and time goes by, and one day when I'm far, far away, I got a letter from Mom with your address. I wrote you, but you didn't write back."

"Hell of a feisty letter, son. Sure I wrote you. I wrote you back."

"I don't believe you. I didn't receive it."

Ty paced back and forth in front of Mike, his hands in his pockets. Rose found it almost hypnotic to watch him. For once, Mike didn't say anything. Ty stopped pacing and stopped in front of Mike. "How about being straight with me one fucking time? How about that?"

"Your heeby-jeeby mother didn't want me in the picture, Ty."

"A little bitty woman like her? Chases off a big man like you? Get off it, Dad. I can handle the truth."

Mike remained silent. To Rose, the room seemed full of dust. In the corner was a cobweb she'd missed, suspended from the ceiling.

Ty stood still, staring down—glaring down—at Mike, and finally Mike said, "Son, some things are better forgotten."

"What kind of things? What things are better forgotten?"

"I did some time," Mike mumbled.

"It has been some time?" It was all Ty could do to keep from shouting.

In a loud voice, Mike said, "Goddammit, son. I said I *did* some time! *Did* some time!"

Ty sank down on the settee. "Did some time? You mean like jail?"

"Yeah, something like that," Mike said. "So the cat's out of the bag." He looked hard at Rose. "I appreciate it if you don't go spreading a rumor about me around town, Rosie." She gazed back at him. His face and neck were blotchy red.

"I won't say anything if you stop accusing Andre."

Stunned, Ty had never imagined this. Mike got up, gracefully holding his bathrobe closed and said, "I'm getting dressed." He walked into the bathroom and closed the door behind him with a little bang.

"You hear that?" Ty said to Rose. "Wow. Wonder what he did." Ty stared at the closed bathroom door. "Jail. Wow. What would he go to jail for? What crime did he do?"

"Hmmm." The room felt hot, stifling. "Hey, let's go downstairs, Ty. I need something to drink."

"So do I." Ty gave one last look at the closed bathroom door and followed Rose down the back stairs to the kitchen where she went to the Pepsi machine and filled them each a large glass.

Through the front door came Gloria and little Mikey. Gloria waved. "It was so nice to meet you!" she called, and Ty bowed slightly. She carried Mikey up the stairs, her bracelets jingling.

"I don't know what to do now," Ty said. "Jail. Wow."

"I didn't expect that," Rose said.

"I wonder what he did."

"Me, too."

"If we had known that was why he was missing, it might had been easier. We could had at least kept in touch."

"At the same time, though . . ." Rose began, thinking that she would not use Mike's truth against him.

"Maybe everyone knew but me and Micky. Weird to think of it. Mom had to know."

"Who is everyone, Ty?"

"The church? Well, he never attended it after he left the neighborhood. Guess they wouldn't have known about his crime."

Carrying their full glasses, they left the Opera House. Outside, the breeze sent golden aspen leaves flying from the trees; otherwise, the street was quiet with no one close by. Rose wanted to check on Partner, so they strolled up the hill toward her house.

"I guess it was a reasonable excuse for him being out of touch," Ty said.

"I was waiting for a story of adventure. Mike's always got a tale to tell. Now you know your mom's reason for not telling."

"Kind of. But I'm pissed. She seemed to take pleasure in telling us how bad Dad was. I look forward to asking her."

They walked past Sheriff Runyon's office, and Rose pointed to the Falcon in the vacant lot.

"Micky's car."

Ty strode through the tall weeds to the Falcon. "So . . . the car Wally bought for her."

He tried the driver's door. Locked. The passenger front door. Locked. The back passenger side door to his surprise opened.

He pulled up the lock button on the front door and leaned inside. "Looks to be one of the first Falcons made. I can imagine her lying on the front seat watching the stars her first night." The glovebox, empty. He ran his hands under the front seat. A surprise: A folded piece of notebook paper. Written in blue ink, huge letters said:

If you are one of the remodelers, do not read this. Just give to Michael Abel.

"Looks like a letter to Dad."
"Wow."
"Shall I read this letter? Or take it back to him?"
"Whatever you think best, Ty," Rose said, wanting him to unfold and read right now.
"Let's go back."
"Are you sure you want me with you?"
"Yes." Ty stared at the large brownish bloodstain on the back seat and closed the Falcon doors.
The afternoon sunlight—brilliant in the deep blue sky. Quivering aspen trees shone bright gold, and the rocky top of Fire Peak stood naked, with a tiny cap of snow. The breeze carried the autumn chill, and Ty zipped up his jacket.
They turned back.
Rose unlocked the Opera House door, and they left their glasses in the kitchen sink.
Upstairs, Ty knocked on the door. Gloria appeared with a finger to her lips. "Shhh. I just put Mikey down for his nap in the room across the hall."
"I have a letter for Dad," Ty said in a low voice, and Gloria held the door open wide so they could come back inside. Mike had the *Rocky Mountain News* turned

to the sports page on the table beside him, and he was evidently surprised they had returned.

"I went by Micky's car, and I found this." Ty held up the letter.

"What?"

"A letter to you from Micky."

Mike reached for the paper, but Ty held back. "If anything, you owe it to me to read this out loud."

Mike looked uncomfortable. "I don't actually read out loud that well," he admitted.

"Oh, God, Dad."

"I'm serious," Mike said. "True, Gloria?"

Gloria, standing near him, nodded. "Yes, true. His reading out loud is not good."

"What is this?" Ty said. "The Day of Confession?"

Mike frowned. "How about if you or Rosie reads?"

"That will work." Afraid his voice might choke, Ty handed the letter to Rose, who accepted, surprised.

Gloria pulled the dressing table chair over next to Mike and sat down, and Ty and Rose in unison sank down on the red velvet settee. Rose unfolded the notebook paper covered with Micky's tiny blue script and took a deep breath.

Daddy, this is to you.

I drove into town as soon as the sun came up. I sat on the hood of my Falcon in front of your office in the morning chill and waited for you. I was afraid to leave for even one second in case you came and I missed you. My heart beat so hard it felt like someone was playing the drums inside my chest.

Madeline arrived and asked me if I wanted to wait inside, but I said no. I wanted to see you the very minute you drove up.

Eight years.

I did not expect you to drive up in a black car like the car I rode in when we buried my baby. Yes, I had a baby, Daddy. My baby was born dead, so you were not a grandfather. My baby's real grandparents and her real father were not at her funeral because none of you ever knew she was born.

And if you had known, would you have come, Daddy? Would you have driven to the cemetery in your funeral car? Would you have stood beside me and held my hand while they put her little casket into the ground?

I want you to know I am not crying while I write this. I am sitting at the table in the cabin you built, and there are no tears here. My head feels swollen and heavy, but I am not crying.

What did you think when I jumped off the hood of my car and ran to you?

Did you think, "Who is that disgusting looking girl?"

How long did it take you to recognize me, Daddy? Why did I have to say my name twice before you knew it was me?

You shook your head and said, "Oh. Oh. Michaela." You got frown lines in your forehead, and you didn't look happy at all to see me.

You said, "How are you?" You said that like you were meeting me for the first time. I tried to wrap my

*arms around you, but you stepped back and shook my
hand. Your hand was cool and dry.*

"Long time no see," you said.

*Yes, Daddy. A long, long time no see. You sort of
smiled, and you said, "Well, hey. Let's go in for a cup of
coffee. Talk a bit."*

*Madeline sat at the front desk, smiling so big, I
could see the lipstick on her teeth.*

*"Madeline," you said. "Do you remember my
daughter?"*

*"My daughter," you said. I was washed in joy
because you claimed me. "My daughter" sounded
beautiful.*

*"Bring us some coffee, Madeline," you said, and I
didn't tell you that I don't like coffee. I followed you into
your office. You sat down behind your wooden desk,
and I sat on one of the office chairs in front of it. You
selected a large brown envelope from a stack of mail,
and said, "I've got my work cut out for me this week."
Madeline brought in two matching turquoise coffee
mugs and handed one to me. The coffee was pale brown
and milky.*

*I held out my hand so you could see my sapphire
ring. "I still wear it, Daddy." In a voice like you thought
I stole it, you said: "Where did you get that?"*

*The sunlight poured through the window, and the
shine of the star in the center of the ring made me think
of the firmament of your soul. You looked as if you had
never seen it—yet the last time I saw you, on my tenth
birthday, you gave me the ring.*

*"How's your mother doing?" you asked. "Must be a
year, year and a half since I last talked to her."*

How in the world would I know how Mama is?

"Weren't you in some kind of trouble?"

You lit up your pipe, and I sat in the hard plastic chair watching you and taking tiny sips of the bitter milky coffee.

"Ah, yeah. You ran away from home." You blew out your words on a grey stream of smoke. "Tramp."

Yes, Daddy. I did run. And yes, I am a tramp. Solotramp.

You said, "How about that Ty, huh? All grown up in the Army. Got a letter from him a while back. Showing his oats."

How come you got a letter from Ty? How did Ty know where you were when I looked and looked and couldn't find you?

Secrets and lies. Lies and secrets.

Who can bear to live in this kind of world?

I asked where you've been, and you said you served your time like a man. What does that mean?

Remember when you and Ty and I used to shoot tin cans set up on the rocks? You said I shoot good as a man. You and Ty would shoot ducks, shoot them like they were no more alive than soup cans. Poor ugly ducks.

Ugly ducklings turned into swans only in stories. In real life the hunter gets them every time. And they don't go to hell, Daddy, or heaven, either one. They just lie on the snow while the sun comes up and the sun goes down, and eventually they dry up, and turned to dust, they blow off on the wind.

Picture an ugly duckling, Daddy, with a bullet through her heart.

Hope you are pleased to have your sapphire ring back, Mr. Michael Isaac Abel.

GODISNOWHERE,

MIA

Gloria was crying. "Is this the same ring you gave to your daughter, Mike?" She yanked off the sapphire ring. "I know it is. First, I trusted you. Then I find out you'd been in prison. 'Just a mistake about money,' you said. And then—stupid me—you gave me this ring— 'trouble with jewelry,' you said, and I packed up Mikey and came to Golconda with you." She stood up, gave him one last withering look, threw the ring over her shoulder as she spun out of the room and shut the door hard behind her.

Rose folded the letter and lay it on the round marble-topped table next to the settee. Her mouth was dry. She needed to leave. Oppressive. Ty got up, too, and arms crossed, looked down at Mike. The ring lay in the middle of a fading lily on the Victorian needlepoint carpet. Ty stooped, picked it up, and stared for a moment at the intersecting rays of the star. Instead of handing the ring to Mike, he put it in his pocket. "Goodbye, Dad."

Mike looked as if he'd been hit with a ton of mine tailings.

"Goodbye, Mike," Rose said.

"The letter sounds like a suicide note," Mike said.

"I disagree." Rose turned the old porcelain doorknob. Ty followed her down the wide front staircase past the red velvet rope, and through the heavy front door to the street. "Let's go to my place."

September's late afternoon sun hovered close to the mountains, and the breeze grew cooler.

"I guess Micky meant nowhere." Ty sounded despondent.

Rose shook her head. "No. She loved it here, Ty."

"I wonder how many heartbeats she has."

At that moment, Andre and Jori pulled up in the orange truck. "Hi, Wosie!" Jori held up her bandaged doll to the truck's window and waved its arm up and down, and Andre called, "Hey! Wanna ride?"

Rose and Ty climbed over the rear gate into the bed of the truck. Andre shifted gears and glided past Micky's Falcon and a crumbling old chimney where a bluebird perched. The last sun rays were brilliant over the red brick buildings in downtown Golconda, and the painted wooden houses dotting the foothills glowed.

Andre parked in front of Rose's cottage. Jori jumped down and darted toward the pasture. "I just wuv Pawtna," she shouted.

Andre came around and flipped down the back gate. "Hey, Ty. I hear you're a singer."

Ty climbed down, and face to face with Andre, saluted him. "I hear you're an angel."

"Sometimes he is." Rose's eyes locked with Andre's, and she felt a sudden surge of joy, like a beautiful song pouring through her veins. How weird that a person can feel angry and sad and at the same time so gratified.

Ty pulled the sapphire out of his pocket. "I've decided to bury this ring up the Fire Peak trail."

"It'll be dark soon," Andre said. The sky flushed pale orange along the mountains as the day began to disappear. "Did you want to bury it now?"

Ty gazed toward Fire Peak remembering how he and Micky created the trail, a big project for a couple of kids, clearing stones and vegetation, deciding upon the easiest way up the mountain.

He could dig a hole next to the bristlecone pine where he carved her initials on the narrow trunk: MIA. The best things and the worst things happen in the same place—on their trail.

"Well—keep in mind that it won't be long before a ski trail likely runs across the spot," Rose said. "Tonight though, how about we cook some brats and make music?"

"At my place," Andre reminded her.

"I'd like to see your round house and your studio." Ty followed Rose and Andre through the tall, waving grass to the corral where Jori offered Partner an oatmeal-molasses-carrot cookie.

Rose stroked Partner's forehead. "One thing I've noticed about life," she said, "we can be either be driven by our fears—you know—worry, expecting the worst, being paranoid." Partner raised his head, and Rose looked at the men. "Or we can choose to live for our joys."

Andre nodded. "Best way."

Jori held out another cookie to Partner. "Music is joy," she said. "Wight, Wosie?"

"Right!" Ty and Andre agreed at once.

"You are joy, Jori," Andre added. "And Rose is joy."

"And Pawtner's joy, too!"

Ty planted the ring back in his pocket, intending to bury it under the bristlecone pine with Micky's notebook at sunrise.

PART FOUR

MAY 17, 1971 MONDAY

An abstract eternity passed through her mind like endless numbers—101010101010101—like endless beats—brmm brmm brmm brmmm—brmm brmm brmm brmmm.

Changes: brmma bbbboom brmmm

Then brmm bababa boom Ssssh hmmmm brmm hum.

Scales of melody flowed over the hum. Notes sequenced. Boom crash boooom

hummmmmm.

Do re mi do re mi mi mi do re do re mi mi mi

"Look." She heard a whisper. Her eyes opened, and the world was new.

She tried to say, "Where am I?" but out came the tiniest high-pitched sound—fa chummmma shhhhhhuuu. She pushed forward to sit up but fell back onto the pillows. No strength.

At that moment a man with glasses came through the door. The woman who was standing beside Micky's bed held a finger over her mouth, whispered, "Shhh," and pointed at Micky.

Micky blinked her eyes. She frowned. She looked around the room. Where was she? Who were these people?

No memory of anyone nor any place. Her mind—a tabula rasa.

Days passed, and she recognized objects. First she remembered their sound, then their function: the toothbrush against her teeth, the pencil scratching against paper; she heard the names in her mind and spat out the words: spoon, toothbrush, comb, paper, pen. Her voice was soft and tinny, a baby voice. The man with glasses whose name was Ty told her she sang like a four-year-old child. He sang with her:
"Wink!" said the mother / "I wink!" said the one
So they winked and they blinked / In the sand in the sun.
Songs tumbled through her mind. Every song she'd learned came to life. Sounds poured through her mind. The words floated out, and she sang, tapping her fingers in time to her heartbeat—I see the stars / I hear the rolling thunder
She sang and sang and sang, stopping to listen to what was playing in her mind, capturing the tune and the words.
Hope I die before I get old /
Songs filled her mind, and her voice would not stop.
Rekindle flames you think are dead /
"Honey," a woman in white said, "you can't sing now. Other patients are trying to sleep. It's not that we don't like your voice. Your voice is real pretty. But they got to sleep to get well."

JUNE 2, 1971 WEDNESDAY

Released from the sanitarium, Micky rode in the old Dodge with Isabel. She liked how you could change the radio stations by pushing the buttons. Inside the house, Isabel asked: "What looks familiar to you?"

Micky scanned the living room. Orange flowers on the draperies. Piles of astrology magazines. She didn't know what to say. Then she pointed at the pen on Isabel's lap board. "Pen," she said.

"I'm sorry I got rid of all your stuff," Isabel said, "because perhaps they could remind you so you could remember."

"What stuff?"

"Nothing special, just old books and toys. Your Puss'n'Boots lamp, for example. Your Poppy doll." Isabel showed Mickey to the green bedroom. "Does it look familiar to you?" Micky shook her head no. Nothing was familiar except the tools—you sleep on a bed, and you put clothes in the drawers or on hangers.

"My wish has come true—I get to be friends with my daughter." Isabel hugged Micky and kissed her cheek, and Micky hugged her back.

Micky found it neat her middle name was Isabel. But Isabel said her initials MIA meant "missing in action," and her mistake in naming Micky was what caused her to get lost.

"I got lost?"

"Yes, you lost your way."

Ty said, "When you ran away."

Micky filed those facts into a folder in her brain. They seemed abstract to her. She shrugged.

Ty said, "Hey, call her Mom, okay?"

Mom didn't sound as pretty as Isabel, and Micky made up her mind that she would not change her middle name to Mom, just because Isabel Abel changed her name to Mom.

Mom told Micky she used to call her "Mama."

"How did I spell it?" Micky filed that fact away in her brain.

JUNE 6, 1971 SUNDAY

Ty showed Micky a picture of Dad in the Golconda newsletter he'd brought down, about the 'man who is changing Golconda.' "This is our father, Micky. Call him Dad. You know what a father is, right? Like Andre is to Jori?" Andre, Rose, and Jori had visited a couple times; Andre said he hoped her voice would keep developing.

"We have a man like him?"

"It's biological. Every person has a mother and a father."

Ty told Mom he was not going to tell her about sexual reproduction, and Mom agreed. "No, Micky's like a little kid."

Dad came to Mom's house that afternoon, and Micky shook his hand and did not let go since Jori was often holding Andre's hand, and she wanted to treat Dad like a father. His hand was big and soft. She held it to her face. It felt natural. "Micky, come take these beverages to the table," Mom said, so Micky let go. It fascinated her how Dad and Ty moved their arms in the same motions, that their voices including their laughs sounded alike.

Dad sat at the table with them for Duffys and snickerdoodles. "I wanted to see how Micky's doing."

"We have a telephone. You could have visited her in the hospital and the sanitarium, Mikey."

"I just don't like the atmosphere of those places. It's not like I could do anything for her. She wouldn't know if I came or not." He looked at Micky. "You know me now?"

"You're Dad, my father."

"Wow." Mom said. "The whole family together."

"The last time we all sat down together was when you guys had the major argument about buying the land in Golconda. You got the apartment near downtown that day, Dad." Ty looked at Micky to see if she remembered.

She filed the facts away in her brain.

Dad finished his root beer, and Micky hugged him goodbye.

Later Ty told Micky Dad had another kid. "His name's Mikey."

"Mom calls Dad Mikey, Ty."

"Yeah, like you, Michaela, he's named after Dad."

"But you aren't."

"I'm named after Mom's brother Tyson who died when he was three years old."

"Sad," Micky said. "Died is forever."

"Not necessarily. Mom believes that Tyson's soul and my soul are the same soul."

Micky filed that fact away. "What is a soul?" she asked.

"The part of us that lives forever."

"Where is it?"

"Our church said that the soul dies, too, but will get resurrected on Judgment Day." Ty tapped his forehead between his eyebrows. "I think our soul is here."

"John the Baptist died twice."

"What?"

Micky shrugged. "Words just pop out of me."

"Did you learn that in church?"

"In the black book."

"What black book?"

Micky shrugged.

"You mean the Bible?"

"Yes. The big black Bible."

Micky loved how Ty would answer all her questions patiently. Plus, he would sing with her and taught her everything she wondered about, including the rules of baseball and then croquet in the back yard, and yesterday he drove her to the library to get some books. She checked out ten! First Ty read to her, and then she read *Jemima Duck* and planned to read *Miss Moppet* next. Ty also checked her out a biology book from the Sears Golden Science Library.

JUNE 10, 1971 THURSDAY

Micky Michaela Isabel Kaela Mick Abel's Diary

I Me You Slow Fast Words Singer Buzzing Puzzling
Abandoned Jaywalking Backpacking Subjectively
Changeability Accomplishment Characteristics = 15
Heavyheartedness Photosynthesizing Greatgrandchildren
Irreconcilabilities Uncharacteristically
Incomprehensibilities Counterrevolutionaries
Overintellectualization Semiuncharacteristically = 24

I don't remember if the i and u can go together. Could that be allowed?

I'm stuck. What has 25 letters? It would be fun if they arranged the dictionary by number of letters instead of the alphabet.

Writing is something I know how to do. Like singing. When a song has to come out, my voice can

find the notes. I feel a persistent pressure of words
pushing to come out of my mind. I can't write fast
enough to grab them. I wonder how they will all come
together in sentences. I wonder what I will discover
from writing down the words demanding to come out.

Solotramp
I walk before you
I walk in the night
I walk beside you
I walk by myself
I eat while you eat
I eat with you
But I am alone.

I walk behind you walk every day.
I sit beside you
the movie plays
I make my bet
you make yours
But we are alone

Every day my mind dreams
Every night I build castles
Every day I walk with the masses
All the time I breathe alone
I am a solotramp
oh yes a solotramp.
alone

like you alone.
Like you. Alone.

I hear the music as I write the words. When I sing it, I hear Ty's voice blending with mine, but it doesn't sound like Ty. Weird. Maybe instead of Ty, I am hearing a famous singer. Mom always has on KBVL. But the voice doesn't sound like anyone who sings on that station either.

Mom told me I used to sing at church. Could the voice I'm hearing be someone from church whose voice my brain recalls? That makes sense. I bet that's where I heard the voice before.

'Great is thy faithfulness!' That song has Father in it. Father means Dad. I'll ask Mom to take me to church to sing.

I'm crazy wild to hear another voice in my head besides just mine. I asked Ty if he hears other voices when he sings, and he looked at me like I was nuts and said, "No! Are you kidding?"

"I was just wondering," I said. "Because I do."

"Imagining singing along with the original singer. Your musical ear."

I like that. My musical ear.

JUNE 13, 1971 SUNDAY

Perfect weather, high 70s and sunny. Rose and Andre sat on the sofa in Isabel's living room, the curtains open behind them, Isabel's pile of astrology magazines a sliding heap on the floor between the couch and her chair, the window cranked open to bring in the breeze.

Whenever Mom was gone, Micky opened all the curtains in the house to let the light in.

Andre was telling Ty and Micky about a riot at Red Rocks Thursday night. Micky put her hands over Jori's ears. A riot sounded scary! "For sure this will affect what bands get booked now," he said. "Helicopters hovering. People getting gassed! Oh man, what a scene. The cops couldn't stop them from playing—they rocked." He frowned. "Similar to the gassing at the Pop Festival."

The words "pop festival" caught Micky's attention. "The tear gas went upwind, so people started freaking. Zephyr was playing 'Saint James Infirmary Blues' and called the crowd to come onto the field."

Micky sang. "I tried so hard to keep from crying."

"I like you to sing, Micky" said Jori, who recently finished kindergarten in Golconda. Micky scooped Jori off her lap and rushed down the hall to her tiny bedroom, now occupied by a miniature stereo system and a new pile of library books. She opened her diary notebook to where she wrote 'Solotramp' and grabbed the Abilene guitar Ty bought for her. She felt shaky and nervous to sing the song she just wrote in front of all of them, but she pulled a dining chair across the room and sat down and strummed an A major chord. Shy, she played the leading chords and began to sing: "I walk every day / I walk before you."

Micky kept her eyes on the guitar strings and tapped the floor with her bare foot. When she finished, they all clapped, and Andre said, "Your voice is back. I need to record you."

"Record me? Wow!"

"You can sleep over!" Jori shouted, and the next thing, Micky was packing to go up the mountain.

Sitting in Ty's new (used) 1966 Galaxy, following Andre's truck, Jori sat between Micky and Ty looking for signs with the next letter of the alphabet for the traveling game. They drove through the city and up the mountains where signs became rare, and Jori taught Micky the children's song 'Hushabye.'

Finally, they pulled up to a tall, round house, and Micky had a strong sense of déjà vu.

"Have I been here before?"

"Silly wabbit," Jori said.

AUGUST 13, 1971 FRIDAY

After many days of practice, Micky watched Cerebral Detail's first two sets at the Krazy Katz Bar, sitting alone at the end of the bar with a Pepsi. Then Kev the keyboardist announced: "For our final set, Mick Abel will be singing tonight!" Derek began a "Solotramp" riff on his guitar, and Micky climbed the three steps to the stage. The audience applauded as Kev sat down at his keyboard and Nels joined with his sax. Standing at the microphone, Micky took the deepest breath of her life.

The patrons danced. She loved it. She danced and sang with all her spirit. Toward the finale of their last song of the set, she noticed a cute guy and a girl staring at her weirdly from the dance floor. They disappeared into the crowd of dancers in moments, but she didn't forget about them because when she looked at them, she had a strange, sparky feeling that stayed with her.

AUGUST 14, 1971 SATURDAY

Rose drove her truck down to Isabel's house with all the ingredients for a picnic in the park before Micky's second performance. They made turkey sandwiches in the kitchen while Isabel worked on a chart in the living room.

"I think the audience liked me."

"I'm absolutely sure they did! A treat to hear you sing."

Feeling on top of the world, Micky removed peanut butter cookies from the cookie jar and piled them on a sheet of waxed paper, folded the paper around them, and lay the package in Rose's picnic basket and slipped the sandwiches into waxed paper bags.

"At the end, I saw this really cute guy and really cute girl, standing on the dance floor staring at me like——- weird—just so intense! They made me feel all sparky."

"Sparky? Well, you can be sure they loved your voice."

"The sparky feeling. Like déjà vu."

"Ahh. Could be you know them, right?"

"Maybe. Maybe they'll be there tonight, and you'll see them. Ty told me Tina used to be my best friend and lived in the house next to the church we went to. He said they got transferred to another church, so she doesn't know I'm back. Could the girl last night be Tina?"

"Sure! Be so fun if you reunited. Do you have a picture of her?"

"No. I don't have any pictures. Lately it's like everything's déjà vu. I read the first page of a book, and all of a sudden, I get the feeling that I've read it before."

"And you likely did!" Rose snapped the picnic basket shut and looked at her new watch Andre had given her for her birthday. After she'd put it on admiring how pretty it was, he told her that in the jewelry store where he'd bought it, he'd seen something else he liked. He grabbed a harmonica out of his pocket and began playing "Here Comes the Bride", and next thing Rose was wearing a pear halo engagement ring, and they were planning their wedding. It sparkled on her left hand as she grabbed the picnic basket.

Coming through the swinging half doors, Rose asked Isabel, "Are you sure you don't want to go to the park with us?"

Isabel pulled out her pen she had tucked behind her ear. "My client is coming at five. She's concerned that Mars is retrograde and opposes Venus all week. Mars and Venus duplicate this transit in her natal chart."

Rose looked doubtful. "Why the concern?"

"Like gender oppose gender. Clashes. Be assertive or be cooperative."

"Can't we be both at the same time?" Rose asked. "That is, cooperate assertively?"

"Good point." Isabel laughed. "Maybe you'll be an astrologer someday, too, Rose. Or a counselor."

"Your cookies are yummy, Mom," Micky said, wiping crumbs off her mouth with the back of her hand. "Will you be coming to the Krazy Katz Bar tonight?"

"No, a place for young people." Isabel shook her head. "I wouldn't fit in. Be careful!"

Ty parked his Galaxy behind Andre's truck. A block away, a red neon sign flashed *Krazy Katz*. "Nels added sax to 'Solotramp'," Micky told them as they all walked to the bar.

Rose and Andre took a booth while Ty and Micky fetched ice water for Rose (who said she would prefer a gin fizz, but you could get only 3.2 beer here), a pitcher for Ty and Andre, and a Pepsi for herself. She kept walking back and forth from the table to the stage where the lead player and soundman were setting up. Pacing and pacing—so nervous. Andre reassured her that happens to performers a lot and not to worry.

"Drink water," he said. "Stretch."

Micky substituted ice water for Pepsi. Hard to sit down and sit still. In the restroom, she took off the green band from her ponytail and pulled her hair over her shoulder to brush it smooth. She heard Kev introduce the band as Derek opened with a slow vamp on his guitar; Nels flowed in on the sax.

As Cerebral Detail played the first set, the club filled. The dance floor rocked during their second set. Micky kept sitting down, getting up, pacing through the crowd into the hallway and back to the table. Just before she was scheduled to go onstage, the cute guy and cute girl came through the door and took the last two stools at the bar. Micky slid into the booth next to Rose and pointed them out. "Is that girl Tina?"

"No," Ty said. "Tina was tall like you, Mick. I've never seen her before."

Beside the mural of a green-eyed guy with big teeth, the cute guy let the cute short girl climb on his back and write on the ceiling. People's signatures covered the ceiling. Micky squinted but could not make out the letters.

The band members took position on the stage, Micky behind the standing microphone, Derek thumbed down the strings on his Gibson; Gerry plucked a bass note, and Rob hit an electrifying snare—'Solotramp' began, and Micky's nervousness vanished. It felt fabulous to sing with the band. She sang from her heart.

The last verse began when the cute guy lurched across the dance floor through the dancers and ran up the three steps to the stage. He took hold of her mike stem and leaned in close to her and sang into her microphone: "Every day my mind dreams."

Cerebral Detail looked extremely surprised but played on.

Micky kept singing and stared into his face, trying to recognize him. His voice sounded just like she'd heard in her head when she wrote down the words in her diary.

"I'm alone like you, alone, alone _____" The final chord, and the drum rolled.

Derek shouted: "Mick Abel—and . . . her . . . her harmonist." The cute guy leapt off the stage and barreled through the crowd across the room. He grabbed the cute girl's hand and pulled her out the door, leaving their beers and half a pack of Marlboros on the bar along with his Zippo lighter.

Kev announced, "Time of the Season!" and morphed into the song on his keyboard. Micky gripped the mic, took a deep breath, and breathed "Ahhh." Her heart pounded. That was the weirdest moment ever. Sparky. After the band had finished for the night, they asked Micky who "her harmonist" was.

"I'm not sure."

"How does he know the song?"

"I'm not sure."

"You said you wrote it."

"I did."

"Andre wants to record it. Are you sure you wrote it yourself?"

She had to tell them briefly about her coma and her loss of memory. "I wrote all the words down in my notebook. And while I was writing them down, I could hear a guy's voice in my head. That boy has the voice."

"Sounds like you remembered 'Solotramp', not originated it," Kev said. "We'll have to keep an eye out for him—we'll need his permission to record."

When Rose, Andre, Ty, and Micky went to the White Spot for dessert, Micky got a chocolate sundae. "Who could that cute guy be? If I didn't write the song myself, how did I learn 'Solotramp' from him?!"

Rose cleared her throat, took a sip of her cola, and cleared her throat again. "Micky," she said. "I have a confession."

"Oh, no," Ty said, like he was reading her intention. Rose's face flushed, and she pulled her ponytail over her shoulder and twisted it. "I have a confession," she said again, and flushing red down her throat said, "Micky, I read your journal."

"You did?" Micky stared at Rose.

"Oh! I gave it to her to read," Andre said.

"I read it, too." Ty stamped out his cigarette although he'd just taken a couple puffs. They all appeared troubled.

Micky tried to think of what she had written in the new notebook that was serving as her journal. "How did you get it, Andre? I haven't missed it at all. Do you mean you borrowed it when I was asleep?"

Ty reached out and motioned her to look at him. She saw whiskers on his face and the specks of yellow in the blue of his eyes. "Andre found you shot, Micky."

She let go her spoon, and it clattered to the table. "Shot?"

"Oh, dear." Rose said. "You didn't know."

"I should have told you," Ty said.

"Oh! Is that why I was in a coma?"

"Yes."

"Who shot me?"

"Well—the sheriff said—"

"That you did," Ty said. "You shot yourself."

Micky took a sharp breath. "I tried to kill myself?"

"I personally don't think so," Rose said. "It was an accident."

Micky crossed her chest with one arm over her scar. "Oh! Is that what this scar is?"

"Yes. Did you wonder about it?" Ty asked.

She shook her head no. She had not thought about her scar at all. Like a birthmark, she just took it for granted.

Rose took a long breath. "In your journal, you wrote about Chaz. Chaz would be the cute boy who sang with you tonight. You wrote in your journal about how you and he wrote 'Solotramp' together. I should have told you when you first sang it to us."

Micky was a hundred percent bewildered. "How could I? How could I write it with him? I don't even know him. How could I say he wrote it with me? What are you talking about? He didn't write that down in my diary!"

"Oh! Oh! No. No. Not your new journal. The diary you kept before your shooting."

"Oh! Oh. Wow." She felt stupid. "You're saying that I knew him before my coma." She picked up her spoon and stuck it into the whipped cream layer on the sundae and tasted it, wondering why she had never asked anyone how she got into the coma.

"I'm curious why he didn't stay to the end to talk to you," Ty said. "In your journal, you wrote that Chaz died, Mick.

"An angel?" Mick looked at him hopefully. "Why I felt sparky when I saw him? Because he is an angel?"

Ty shrugged, and she gazed at the spiral of chocolate she swirled into the ice cream.

"Do dead people really show up on earth as angels?" Rose asked

"I think he's alive," Andre said.

"We saw him. We heard him." Ty emptied the cream pitcher into his coffee. "He must be alive."

"Okay. I kept a journal. In my pre-coma days." Micky tasted the mixed-up ice cream. "Did I write that I was going to do myself in?"

"No," Rose said. "Not exactly."

"Do you still have it?"

"I buried it," Ty said. "On Fire Peak. But I think a ski slope is going in there."

"Why didn't you given it back to me to help me remember, Ty?"

"I don't know if you would want to read it," Rose said gently. "In it, you talk about 'ungood memories.' You prayed for God to take your memory."

"God. 'Majestic in holiness, awesome in glorious deeds, doing wonders?'"

"Wow," Ty said. "You're reading the Bible?"

"It just popped out of my mouth. Is that a song?"

"It's a Bible verse from Exodus, Micky," Ty said. "Remember? Reciting verses in church and school?"

She frowned. "What if I remembered 'Solotramp' but didn't write it?"

"Either way, we'll need to get his permission if he's alive."

"You wrote it together, I'm sure," Rose said.

"So weird. I prayed to lose my memory, but now I realize that when you lose your memory, every memory is a good one."

"I don't know about that." Rose touched Micky's wrist. "But I do truly, truly apologize for intruding on your privacy."

"I didn't think of it as an intrusion," Andre said. "Rather an emergency. I gave it to you in case Micky had written something that would help her."

"Who else would shoot me? Do I have an enemy?"

"Nah," Ty said. "No one would want to kill you!"

"Tina? Miasma?"

"What?" Andre asked.

"Miasma. Tina. Miasma."

"Miasma means stinky," Rose said.

"I couldn't believe your friendship was over just like that," Ty said. "You and Tina were always together. Then your fight."

"Why did we fight?"

"When you ran away, you stayed at Freddie's house. Freddie was Tina's boyfriend."

"Because of that, my best friend called me stinky and broke up with me?"

"Maybe you were a little stinky after spending a night outside and sleeping in a boy's closet," Rose suggested.

"By the way, I hear that Freddie was drafted," Ty announced.

"Miasma," Micky said. "Stinky." She filed both the definition and the event into her brain.

"I buried your journal at our favorite place where we carved our initials into a bristlecone tree after we finished making the trail," Ty said. "Do you remember?"

Micky gazed at Ty trying hard to visualize the past.

"Ahh. It was you two who made the trail," Andre said.

"Remember, Mick?" Ty asked. "The bristlecone?"

A timeline flashed through her mind, like all the days of her life zipping by without a second to grab an idea, nor a second to reflect. Her brain was a muddle.

She shook her head. "I don't remember. I wrote about my life. I need to read it."

"I will find it," Ty vowed.

"Memories are important." Micky crossed her arms over her scar.

"Some are, for sure," Andre said. "Others, not."

"A clash?" she asked. "Mars versus Venus?"

"More like good versus un-good," Ty said.

SEPTEMBER 2, 1971 THURSDAY

Micky practiced Thursday afternoon with the Cerebral Detail who asked her if she found out anything about Chaz. "You must have sung with him a lot."

"I guess."

"Okay, okay. A memory thing?"

"You guys are so understanding," she said, laughing. It was embarrassing not be able to remember. She couldn't tell them he died and was now an angel. That could raise more questions she didn't know the answer to.

"Man, it's hot, almost like the middle of July!" Kev the keyboardist dropped her off in front of Mom's house.

"Time for me to start learning to drive! I depend on you too much!"

"No problem."

Ty's Galaxy was parked in the driveway behind Mom's old Dodge. Micky admired the Galaxy's pale blue color and soft blue carpeting and the push-button radio. It would be fun to learn to drive his car.

In the living room, Ty was sitting on the couch reading the new *Popular Science* article "Rain Made to

Order" about massively seeding the clouds in drought areas. In the kitchen, Mom played the radio loud while she boiled spaghetti and stirred a red mushroom sauce. After Ty took Mom and Micky to an Italian restaurant, Mom began studying sauces, so lately pasta was often on the menu. Micky was hungry—she'd been singing her heart out all day.

"Will you teach me to drive, Ty?"

He looked up startled. "Your Falcon?"

Micky was confused. "Your Galaxy?"

"I mean your car."

"My car? Wait a minute. What car?"

"In Golconda. Sorry! I should have showed the Falcon to you when we were up at Andre's studio."

"Do I know how to drive?"

"You drove your Falcon to Golconda."

"I did? Wow! I already know how to drive? My own car? Far out! I know how to drive!" She wanted to jump for joy. "Do I have a license?"

"No."

"You mean I was bad. Driving without a license."

"Yes, you're bad." Ty laughed. "You had a permit."

Micky looked at Ty seriously. "You can't believe how freaky it is to realize I used to have a such a different life."

"I can imagine." He frowned and indicated Mom in the kitchen with his head. "Don't say anything to Mom about the car, okay? She doesn't know you can drive."

Micky was shocked. A pleasant shock. Everything good was happening for her. Chaz the angel came to answer her question about the voice in her head, and now she would be driving like a normal woman. Maybe

I tried to kill myself, but I didn't die, she thought. I get to sing with a band, and we going to make a recording—especially 'Solotramp' if Chaz visits me again. The good life!

She set plates and silverware on the round table in the dining room and cracked out the ice from the metal ice tray in the freezer and filled three glasses with water. Ty examined Mom's large plate of spaghetti covered by a thick red sauce. "Meatballs?"

"No, Ty, I want you to taste the fresh tomatoes I cooked for five hours."

"Looks super. I'm going to buy you a TV set, Mom. You can watch a cooking show."

"Thank you but no. I have five cookbooks." Mom removed the garlic bread wrapped in aluminum foil from the oven and sat down. She pulled open the foil and the scent of garlic came out in the steam.

"You can keep up on the news, Mom."

"Today I learned that King Curtis got murdered," Micky said, grabbing spaghetti with tongs to put on her plate. "He was the leader of the Kingpins. Cerebral Detail gave me a 45 of Kingpin's instrumental of "Billie Joe" so that I can practice singing with the music."

"How was he murdered?" Ty asked.

"Stabbed by drug dealers."

"Murder is not a dinner table topic," Mom said. "Is there TV in Golconda?"

"One channel," Ty said. "If you don't own a TV, you can watch at Golconda's one and only bar."

"I'd like a TV, Ty," Micky said. "I can put it in my bedroom."

"You need to graduate high school, Micky."

"I'm going for the G.E.D., Mom."

"I approve of that, but I do not approve of the TV."

"It's the 1970s, Mom!" Ty said. "Everyone owns one."

Mom passed the bread wrapped in aluminum foil. "How many years has mankind lived without it? The existence of the TV may seem long to you, but it's a fraction of time since TV was invented. Its value has not been tested."

"Here we go again," Ty said. "If they showed an astrology program, I bet you'd have bought a TV long ago."

"If TV's so darn good, why aren't there astrology programs?"

"Age of Aquarius," Ty sang. "You accepted radio, Mom. We are now in the electronic age."

Micky turned her fork to wrap the spaghetti. "Did I always love spaghetti?"

"We used to buy the canned version," Ty said. "Now Mom is opting for more variety in life." He laughed. "Piquant, Mom!"

Mom carried her plate to the counter and grated parmesan cheese onto it. "The people at work are helpful on auto parts, but aside from that, their whole conversation is about TV. They're furious about the TV football blackout, and their rage makes work unpleasant." She sat back down. "Otherwise, they're always talking about Geraldine, who I do not know."

"If you had a TV, you'd understand. Look. We want you to be up on the trends, Mom. You're so secluded."

"I know many, many people better than most people do," she said. "The easiest thing to see in a chart is the pattern, and the pattern shows how some people go deep with a few refined interests while others have many shallow interests. My planets are all wedged in the first and twelfth houses. This means I go deep into people's interests."

"What about us, Mom?" Micky asked. "Are we deep or shallow?"

"You lean toward the deep, both of you. Basket-shaped charts. The handle is the opposite side from the cluster. That means if we had TV, you two wouldn't do anything else but watch it."

Ty started laughing.

Micky asked: "Does astrology tell if someone shot me or if I shot myself?"

Startled, Mom said, "It was an accident, Michaela."

Micky pressed. "How did you see the accident in my chart, Mom?"

"In synastry of your chart and the chart of the event, there are 6 planets in the 12th house, including Mars, Uranus, and Pluto. That morning you got shot, Pluto opposed Neptune, Mars, and Mercury and squared Jupiter. Do you want to study astrology, Micky?"

"Maybe I do."

"Think about it: an accident can be as small as knocking over a glass to accidentally setting off a bomb. Why I prefer natal charts to event charts. I like telling people how they can improve their relationships. Harmful events can be be minimal or deadly."

"How would you improve your relationship with Dad, Mom?" Ty asked.

"That relationship doesn't matter anymore, Ty. I got you two, and nothing else matters." She pushed her plate away and lit a Pall Mall.

"At least That Man Floyd isn't hanging around," Ty said.

"That Man," Micky repeated. "Barf. Barf."

SEPTEMBER 4, 1971 SATURDAY

"Our Fire Peak trail has really been destroyed," Ty said, holding Micky's black spiral notebook. "That's where the ski lift is going to be installed."

The chopped-down trees and relocated boulders left no bearings, but he kept looking, and at last, behind a gigantic rock pile, he spied the bristlecone pine, its bare branches poking into the sky; leaning downhill on the other side, soft brushy fronds. Close up, he saw his handiwork carved into the narrow trunk: TEA & MIA. Digging down in the soft dirt about a foot, he found the notebook that he'd wrapped in plastic before burying it.

"What right do I have to keep your memories from you? You have a right to them."

Micky's heart started beating furiously.

"Just because you have your diary doesn't mean you have to read it right now," he said.

"But what are we without memories?"

"I don't know. I do know I like you just fine without them. Consider: you don't have to have memories to have a complete astrological chart."
"Do I need a memory to go to heaven?"
"I highly doubt it," Ty said.

SEPTEMBER 5, 1971 SUNDAY

Ow! What an icky déjà vu feeling! Micky read the first two pages of her journal. Made her gag. If ever a girl is treated like that, she needs to run. She understood why nobody was in any hurry to give her back that memory!

"I did the right thing leaving Wally," she said aloud.

She couldn't read any more and stuck that creepy old notebook in the closet on the top shelf. She knew she should keep reading to find out more about Chaz the angel, but she was afraid of another ungood memory. Was it important for her to know how he died? Maybe if someone killed him, then that same person shot her.

But why?

'Solotramp' is not that happy of a song, she thought. All of us are solotramps because what goes on inside us is alone because our memories are solitary. She resolved to look through the journal for Chaz, but not just now. An image of Wally and his bouffant hairdo had started coming into her mind.

SEPTEMBER 12, 1971 SUNDAY

No evidence of the angel Chaz at the gigs this weekend. But Micky got a shiver every time she thought of him coming on stage to sing 'Solotramp' with her. "At least he has a good voice," Kev from Cerebral Detail said. "Otherwise he coulda ruined our rep. Now we gotta find him so we don't get sued for stealing his song." The only song left to mix for their album was 'Solotramp.'

"At least you have proof you wrote it, too," Kev said. "So cool if it's a big hit."

"I'm glad I understand it was his voice in my mind when I was writing it down."

"Audio memory," Kev said.

Micky and Ty took a walk through Mom's neighborhood and into the area where the basement house used to be and new houses were under construction. She told Ty, "I did the right thing to leave Wally."

"Wild you saw that blazing arrow with the word GO," he said.

"I am thinking I could not have been sad enough to shoot myself. I was free because I escaped from him. I think I need to add a line to 'Solotramp' about freedom. Owing no one, owned by no one."

"I like that idea," Ty said.

"I figured I remember songs because I hear them here." She tapped her temples on both sides of her face. "I can write down my thoughts that talk to me in my head."

"Soon you'll remember everything."

"I remember the minister's voice." Her voice became loud and gravelly. "'God knows all things and never changes.'"

Ty laughed. "You've got his voice down well, Mick."

"From the time I woke up in the sanitarium, everyone has been sweet to me. Everybody. Except in some of the books I've read, all people are good. But when I start reading my old journal, I get a different opinion. So I can't read any more."

"Do you remember anything about that guy Nathan?"

"Nathan?"

"The guy Chaz drank the yagé with. Who gave him the *Don Juan* book."

"I don't remember Nathan."

"Oh, you haven't read that much of your journal yet. He's the guy who moved into Chaz and Floss's apartment when they moved in with you."

"Did Nathan kill Chaz?"

Ty started. "What?! What are you remembering?"

"I'm not remembering. Why did you ask about him?"

"I was thinking if we could find him that he might have an idea on how to find Chaz so he can sign off on 'Solotramp.'"

She laughed.

"Are you going to keep reading now that you know what an ungood memory is?" he asked.

"I guess I have to read that creepy old notebook, but it's hard! Besides him tying me up, do I want to remember even small stuff like Wally reading over my shoulder when I write? Now I am wondering about the value of memories. Good versus ungood. Remember you said I already have plenty on my plate."

"Definitely. With the band and studying for the GED, you do! Who needs bad memories!"

That evening, she handed him a sheet of paper with her questions for the day.

-Did I write down where Chaz and I lived?
-Can you make an angel come to you?
-Is there a way I can just read the Chaz part?
-Could Nathan be my enemy?
-Did Chaz ever go to Golconda with me?

"No," Ty said. "You did not write down exactly where you lived, but we can drive over to where I'm thinking it was." He wrote "no" beside her other questions. "I don't know about angels. You wrote about Chaz throughout your journal. No reason to think Nathan would be your enemy. No, Chaz never went to

Golconda, but you were planning to go the next weekend after the Pop Festival."

"Where there were riots. Andre told me about them. Good thing we didn't go to it after all, right?"

SEPTEMBER 18, 1971 SATURDAY

Snowflakes! More and more snowflakes! Micky and Ty had planned to take off at noon for Rose and Andre's wedding scheduled for late afternoon in Golconda. Now it seemed doubtful. As Micky put away her studies for her G.E.D, she heard a crash: a giant limb from the maple couldn't take the weight of snow. Outside appeared treacherous, no evidence that Ty had already shoveled, but she put on her coat and hat and gloves and headed outside. The branch spanned the front yard, so she decided to drag it to the trash area on the side of the carport. She yanked the limb a few inches walking backward and pulling, but a torrent of snow blew into her face and blinded her. She changed course, dragging the branch with her hands behind, letting the wind push her along. Suddenly the weight got lighter. She assumed Ty had come to help.

When she glanced back, she dropped her end of the branch.

Chaz.

Chaz gave the branch a push, and she picked up her end again, the snow battering her face. "We need to talk, Mick." Chaz fixed the branch securely on his shoulder, and she managed to lift her end on her shoulder, too. They carried the limb over the snow-covered driveway Ty shoveled an hour ago and around the cars to the side of the carport by the trash bin.

"That was hard. So cool you helped me!" She liked the way his hair curled out from his cap and the little goatee on his chin and the startling flash of his eyes. He was wearing a blue parka and black gloves. "I was astounded you came on stage to sing with me! My angel!"

He looked embarrassed. "I can't explain it."

"I felt all sparky."

"Really," he said.

The snow fell in immense wet flakes.

"Thank you for coming. I can't wait for 'Solotramp' to be finished." She shook the snow off her muffler, and they moved under the carport out of the snow. "I've added a couple more lines about freedom."

"How will we decide who gets our baby and when?"

"It belongs to both of us no matter what."

"Oh!" Chaz said. "The baby?"

Micky laughed. "Our song."

"What about the baby?"

Her heart started pounding. No one had mentioned a baby to her. "I don't know."

"Mick, I'm sorry I lied to you. I'm sorry I OD'd. I can't tell you how sorry. Honest to God. But even if I was bad, don't the child and I have a right to meet each other?"

Micky felt sucked back into being lost, just when she was feeling normal. OD'd? She tried to think what that meant. She gazed down at her boots, planted into the snow. "I don't know what to say."

He sounded like he might cry. "I understand you're mad at me. But I want to see our child."

"I don't know." She felt overwhelmed with idiocy.

Chaz said he lied. Not good. And made no sense she had a baby with him. Her husband was Wally. Did she leave a baby with Wally? If Wally has her baby, will he let her see it? Where would a baby go? She hated feeling so confused. She had to read the stupid thing.

"Please. Let me know." Chaz handed her an envelope. "Think about it. Here's my address. I'm sorry, so sorry."

As quickly as he appeared, Chaz swept the snow off his van's windshield with his sleeve, then jumped in. Micky stood there staring, and he clunked down the street and disappeared into the storm. The snow—a barrage of huge white flakes, the path made from dragging the maple limb already disappearing.

Utterly baffled, Micky headed back into the house and kicked off her boots, getting snow all over the rug by the front door. She brushed the snow off her coat. As she hung it in the closet, the phone rang. She heard Mom's voice: "Hi Rose. I'm concerned—"

"Rose wants to talk to you, Micky. No wedding, Ty!" Mom carried her empty coffee mug through the swinging doors to the kitchen. In the hallway, Micky picked up the receiver lying on the phone shelf.

"Hey, Micky. Just wanted to tell you we have to postpone the wedding because of the weather."

"Ahh, too bad. Did your Pops make it?"

"He did. All the way from Alaska! I picked him up last night at Stapleton, so we're all staying with the Kings—Andre's parents."

"Oh, wow, Rose. I just saw him."

"Saw who?"

"My angel. Chaz. He helped me move a branch that broke off our maple."

"Really?"

"Rose, he asked me about a baby."

"Oh! Omigod." Then Rose was silent. Micky listened for her voice. She breathed fast like when she was pulling the maple branch.

"No one has told you! Oh, my. Oh, dear Micky."

"What?"

"Nobody's told you anything!"

"Where is the baby?" Silence again.

"Rose?" Micky pulled the telephone cord under her bedroom door and sat down on the end of her bed holding the receiver to her ear. "Rose? Are you there?"

"You lost her."

"Lost her? What?"

"She was born . . . Oh, lord, Micky. Stillborn."

Micky caught her breath, feeling an instant stab in her heart. "The baby—ungood memory."

"No. No, Micky. Just sad."

"Whose baby?"

"Yours and Chaz's."

"Is that what I wrote?" She held the beige receiver to her ear, eyes shut.

"Yes. Are you okay?"

Micky stretched the cord straight and watched it spring back to coil.

"Did I care?"

"Of course you did!"

"Life without a past. Bizarre. I don't remember the baby."

"Or Chaz."

"I don't remember him from before, but I remember him from the stage."

"New memories now."

"Only an angel would arrive at exactly the time to help with the branch. He wanted to know about the baby. He gave me an envelope." She slipped her finger under the flap, withdrew a piece of paper, and read aloud. *"Please can we talk? I miss you. Love you. Miss you. Love you.—C-"*

Chaz's address was printed tidily under his message.

"Wow."

"The baby, Rose. Does Mom know?"

"I'm not sure. I think not. But Ty does."

"I guess never mind I am sick to my core to read about being tied up, I will read the creepy journal." She stuck her finger through the coil until all she could see was the very tip of her fingernail sticking out of the smooth beige wire.

"I expect it will be hard, sweetie."

"I wish I were with you now."

"Me, too."

"If I had not written it all down, I wouldn't know of Wally, and then he wouldn't exist. Because none of you know him. And we'd never know how Chaz knew 'Solotramp.'"

"Yes. If I didn't read it, I would know nothing about you. And if I didn't give your journal to Ty, he wouldn't know about any of this either."

"Why didn't you guys tell me?"

"Un-good memories, how you prayed to lose your memory."

"Unless I read it, anything people tell me now would be my truth."

"A good reason perhaps to keep a diary."

"Or not to." Micky uncoiled her finger. "Is the road bad to Golconda?"

"Electricity is out, but now that the phone's back on, I'm going to call up a couple people to spread the word that the wedding is delayed."

"Delayed to when?"

"We'll get it figured out. If you need to talk, you can find me at 222-2161. Love you, girl."

"Love you back." Micky hung up the phone.

Ty lay across his bed in his room reading *Dune*, and Mom—still dressed in her pink robe since Turner's Auto Supply closed because of the storm—read a new astrology magazine. Fortunately, she'd bought a carton of Pall Malls before the storm and stored it on top of the refrigerator.

So. No wedding this afternoon. Micky plumped up the two pillows on her bed. She got the notebook out of the closet. Black spiral, narrow-lined. Nothing eye-catching, just an ordinary notebook. She settled on the bed, opened it, and reread the first three paragraphs, then pushed off the sick feeling. Suddenly she could hear Wally's voice—Texas accent, soft, persuasive, adamant.

She lay down with the notebook on her chest, her hands crossed over it. "I want my memories of Chaz to return," she said.

She lay still, trying to roam her mind for memory of him. She could hear Wally's voice: "Jealousy arouses a husband's fury, and he will show no mercy when he takes revenge."

She sat up and flung the notebook across the room. "I never want memories of Wally." She got out her new notebook and began writing:

Dear Chaz, my angel,
The baby was stillborn.
I feel excited and anxious and fearful at once.
I have so many questions. I want to talk to you. Since you have an address, does that mean you are alive?
MIA

Then she went to Ty's room. "Too bad about the wedding," he said.

"Another question. Why didn't you tell me I lost my baby?"

Ty took a long breath. "I didn't want Mom to know."

SEPTEMBER 20, 1971 MONDAY

Outside snow melted rapidly over the green grass. A few trees were beginning to turn autumn color, but broken branches were everywhere. The weather was crazy—over 90 degrees a week ago and then snowing a foot yesterday. Today: blue sky, the street a broad wet puddle. Micky got up early this morning, and propped up the pillows with a board across her lap (like Mom's) to study math for the G.E.D. Just as she was getting ready to walk to the post office to mail her note to Chaz since Mom was out of stamps, the doorbell rang. She opened the front door.

Chaz stood there. "Do you want to talk?"

"Do you want to come in?"

"Do you want to go for a ride?'

Micky slid on her boots, grabbed her purse, and put on her coat.

Outside was chilly, but the sun dazzled, making her wish she had sunglasses. Small broken branches littered the drifts of melting snow in the yard. Chaz flipped his cigarette into the melting snow and opened the passenger door of his van. "Hop in."

He started it up, but they just sat there on the green bench seat looking at each other. "I was going to mail this to you today," Micky said and gave him the letter.

He opened the envelope and unfolded the note; she watched his face.

"Our baby was stillborn?"

"Yes."

"What happened?"

"I don't know. "

"Girl or boy?"

"I don't know."

"How could you not know?"

"I've been recovering from being shot," she said.

"Shot? Bullshit!" Chaz looked stunned. "Shot? What? Who shot you?"

"They say I shot myself."

"Shot yourself? What!?"

"First I was in the hospital and then the sanatorium."

"Shot yourself? You never owned a gun! You wanted to die saving someone's life! What?"

"Mom and Rose and Ty think it was an accident, but the Golconda sheriff decided I tried to kill myself." She put her hand over her scar. "I don't believe I tried suicide. But I don't know."

"I looked for you in Golconda, Mick. Remember? We were planning to drive up to Golconda the weekend after the concert."

"We were? What concert?"

"Pop Festival, remember?"

"But you died, right? So we didn't experience the riots."

"I died? What? What do you mean?"

"Wally said you died. I wrote it down."

"Wally!"

"My husband Wally. He took pictures of me, and I left him."

"What the hell? When were you married to that dickhead?"

"I don't know. But July 5, 1970, is the date that I left him."

"And I went to the hospital June 1969."

"What was wrong with you? Why did you go to the hospital?"

"Why don't you remember?"

"Because I got shot."

"Crap! I was in the frigging hospital until October! Wally, that is, Dr. Wally White the veterinarian, gave me and Nathan a bottle of what he told us was yagé, and I ended up in the psych ward, aka, the Zoo."

"What is yagé ?"

"A hallucinogenic plant, remember? Why can't you remember anything?"

"Because I was shot." Micky felt frustrated. "When I woke up from my coma, I didn't remember anything."

"You don't remember me?"

She shook her head. "No. But I remember your voice. When I was writing down the words to 'Solotramp', I could hear your voice in my head."

"And you don't remember our baby."

"I wrote in my diary after I ran away from Wally July 5, 1970. But it makes me feel crummy to read it. Rose said I wrote about you and the baby. Rose read my diary, so she knows everything."

"Who the hell is Rose?"

"My friend from Golconda. And Ty read it, too."

"Your brother in the Army, right?"

"Yes. Then he buried it. But then he dug it up and gave it back to me. After I read the first two pages, I couldn't read any more. I know I should. But I wrote ungood memories."

"You do remember Wally though?"

"Well. I remember his voice. "Jealousy arouses a husband's fury, and he will show no mercy when he takes revenge." She imitated his tone and accent.

"What if he shot you?"

She shrugged. "The sheriff is sure I shot me. But I think that since I escaped from Wally, I would not have tried to kill myself because I was happy to be a solotramp."

"Fucking scary, Mick!"

"I know."

"Okay. Well, the first thing I did that October day I was released from the Zoo was find your mother's number in the phone book. Isabel Abel."

"Yes, that used to be Mom's name."

"She sounded grumpy and said that you most certainly did not live there and hung up. But me and Floss drove over here to the house anyway. Our baby was due in October. No answer to the doorbell, no car in the carport, so with Floss keeping an eye out, I peeked in a window with no curtains. A single bed covered by a green bedspread and a green dresser. The room reminded me of the Zoo."

"My room looks better now."

"Boss told me you disappeared without a word—you didn't even pick up your paycheck."

"Boss?"

"Your boss!" Chaz imitated Boss's voice: "I'm going out of bizness. Yup, I know I'm gonna lose the biz."

"Oh!" Micky said and changed her voice to a growly tone. "Use this on the grill. Scrub, girl, scrub."

"Now, get this: Floss happened to see Wally's car in a shopping center in front of the vet clinic with his name on a sign hanging in front. Crazy. It was Wally. A veterinarian! Not a bone doctor! But he operated on your knee!"

"I have a scar on my knee."

"Yes, I bet you do. So, me and Floss dropped in on him, and he said he hadn't seen you." Now Micky felt confused again. "Floss?"

"C'mon, Mick. My sister!"

"Please could you do her voice? I have noticed that sound helps me remember."

"Where's my keys? I can never find my keys," Chaz said imitating Floss's voice. "Does anyone have my keys?"

Micky closed her eyes and leaned back on the seat. "Okay, okay. Ba boom. Ba boom." She tapped on her thigh. "Ch chu. Ch chu."

Chaz stared at her.

"Percussive," Micky said. "Ch chu. Ch chu. Ba boom ba boom."

"Okay," he said. "The Percussive Girls."

"Floss. Little Floss."

"She's in barber school now."

"Floss was with you at Krazy Katz. Right?"

"For the embarrassing night when I jumped on stage with you."

"The band was glad you have a good voice, Chaz. When did you and Floss see Wally?"

"Soon after I got released from the Zoo. Early October. 1969. Wally asked how the yagé went. Told him it took me to a place I've never been. Lord, have I got a story! Never again for me. He said, 'I thought it was a dumb idea. But you young people have to try everything once. Nature of the beast.' I said, 'Then why'd you give it to me?' And he said, 'Desperation is the raw material of finding the shaman." I asked him if he knew it was going to turn out the way it did, and he said that Burroughs made quite it clear in his book, yagé was a not a predictable trip. I made him write down the name of Burrough's book. Told him we were next going to look for you in Golconda where your dad had a cabin. Then me and Floss drove up there to look for you."

Micky stared at him. Confusion felt like a spinning washer. "Then Ty was wrong. You have gone to Golconda."

"How would Ty know?"

"Oh, you're right. He read what I wrote about you in my diary. Are you dead? My angel?"

"What!?"

"Wally told me you died."

"He lied! He told me and Floss that you were most likely in a JD reformatory."

"For what?"

"For being a runaway, I guess. Hah. He said you used to cheat at canasta. Meaning that he was really accusing me of cheating since you and I were always partners."

Micky stared at Chaz. "Was I a cheater?"

"In a way, I guess you are. You married Wally. That's cheating on me, right?"

"He told me you were dead. Wow. You're really alive. Ow. I guess I must have cheated."

"Really! We asked a bunch of people in Golconda if they'd seen you, and a guy with a long beard said they'd remember a pregnant girl because it was a rare sight in a dying town." He pointed up the street. "Is that the church you went to?

Micky nodded. She hadn't been back because neither Mom not Ty were fond of joining her.

"Then we visited that church."

"Ty says I used to sing there a lot."

"Oh man. A memorable experience for sure! The minister's sermon was about the first king of Israel, Saul, and how God ordered him to destroy Amalek." Chaz's voice changed to the preacher's voice: "'Do not spare them, but kill both man and woman, child and infant, ox and sheep, camel and donkey.' Then he started banging his fist on his podium and shouting that Saul was wicked because he did not kill all the people or the animals in Amalek. He screamed that God said, 'Rebellion is the sin of witchcraft."

"'And stubbornness is iniquity and idolatry,'" came out of Micky's mouth. The sound of the pastor's voice, the sound, so familiar, so intense. She clenched her fists.

"That pastor's memorable—for sure. I wondered why God couldn't kill them all himself and why he would make the commandment "Thou shall not kill" but order people to kill. What the hell did this pastor have to do with being an enemy of Amelek?"

Micky said: "We must do the will of God."

Chaz laughed. "Yup, that's what he said. Then the choir sang 'Power in the Blood.'"

Micky sang: "Would you be whiter much whiter than snow / There's power in the blood power in the blood."

"Yeah," Chaz said. "You remember that!"

"I guess because of the sound." Micky unclenched her fists and folded her hands in her lap.

"After the service, we asked most everyone there if they'd seen you." Chaz made his voice sound like an old woman's: 'She's gone missing, don't you know? We miss her singing.' Where exactly were you, Micky?"

"I don't know. I think with Wally. Wally told me you died."

Chaz punched his palm with his fist. "Did he also tell you he gave me and Nathan the yagé?"

"I don't know."

"He gave us two bottles of the tea—one for me and one for Nathan."

"Nathan is your friend?"

"Haven't seen him in ages. But yeah. Last time I saw him, he said he was flying to Mexico."

"Not an enemy?"

"No! Why?"

"He wouldn't try to kill you or shoot me?"

"No! He let you borrow his guitar!"

"Oh."

"Wally used to stop by sometimes while you were at work and smoke a joint with me, and the day before I OD'd, he came by and asked if I ever tried yagé . He told me he met Don Juan in Texas, and Don Juan was using yagé along with peyote back when Castaneda was his apprentice."

"Who is Don Juan? Who is Castaneda?"

"Remember the book?"

Micky shook her head.

Chaz sighed. "Don Juan was a Yaqui shaman."

"What's that?"

"Wise man."

"Do wise men take drugs?"

"Wally told me and Nathan that shamans always take challenges, and all shamans take yagé tea. I remember me and Nathan dancing around singing Ayahuasca."

"Ayahuasca. Ayahuasca. I remember." Chaz and another boy dancing around a kitchen passed through her mind. "Nathan? He came out okay?"

"Yes. Difference is that I did speed also."

"Speed?"

"Yes!" Chaz said abruptly. "You begged me all the time to stop."

"Speed?"

"Meth." He took a deep breath to calm down. "This crazy hunch came over me that Wally gave me the tea so he could get me out of the way to get close to you. I remember how he used to look at you, Mick, when we were sitting at the table playing cards. Maybe the tea wasn't identical in the two bottles. He could have given me something different from what he gave Nathan. Nathan had no problem, but off I went in an ambulance. Maybe he was hoping it would kill me. Then again, I did shoot some meth."

"You're alive, right?"

"Of course I'm alive! I thought you were pissed at me because of the drugs, and that's why we couldn't find you. And Floss said you figured out that we're not from Chicago but from Colorado Springs."

"You aren't dead."

"No, baby. I am happy to see you, Mick." He covered her folded hands with his hand. "How long did you live with Wally?"

"Not sure."

"Are you divorced now?"

"No. I don't think so." She did not want to remember Wally. Blank space. He tied me up and took pictures of me, she thought. I don't want to remember.

"You have so much to tell me, Micky. Where have you been? How'd you hook up with the band? How long you been with them? What do you remember?"

"I just started with Cerebral Detail, Chaz. You came my first and second night. Then I looked for you the next weekend, but you didn't come back."

"Had to work. I have two jobs, the hospital and the restaurant. When were you shot?"

"After I escaped from Wally. Did you wake up with your memory in the Zoo hospital?"

"Guess so," Chaz said. "I remembered you."

She got the sparky feeling again.

"Do you remember when Wally did the surgery on your knee?"

"No. But now I understand why I have a scar."

He put his hand on her knee. "A miracle has landed in my life," he said. "You."

"I'm sorry about the baby."

"So am I." Chaz wiped at his eyes. "In fact, I'm fucking crushed. I had expectations. Ya know? Do you know where our baby's buried?"

"No."

"I'm going to ask you to read your diary. Or ask Ty questions, okay? Like was the baby a boy or a girl."

"Okay," she said.

"Like when did you get married to Wally."

"Okay," she said.

"Like why did you quit your job."

"Okay."

"Like how did you get a gun." She nodded.

"Did you really love me? If you can forget me, does that mean you never loved me?"

"You make me feel sparky. I remember your voice."

"And 'Solotramp.' You remember."

"I remember songs the easiest," she said.

"Let me kiss you and see if you remember that," Chaz said.

She felt suddenly shy but lifted her face toward him and automatically closed her eyes.

The kiss was light, like a brush of silk on cotton.

OCTOBER 3, 1971 SUNDAY

Dad came into Mom's house carrying a white box with a bakery cake, a carton of chocolate ice cream, a wrapped package with a pink bow, and a card. Ty and Micky had gone to see the *Summer of '42*, and Mom said to Dad: "Do you remember that year?"

She put away her astrology board on the end table next to her chair.

"You still doing that mumbo jumbo bullshit?"

Mom laughed. "How about you, jailbird? Are you still thieving?"

"You are a pistol." He stood looking down at her.

She laughed again and got up and took the bakery box to the kitchen. "I'll put on the birthday candles. Oh—look at the pink rosettes. Aren't they pretty?"

He followed her through the swinging doors. "1942?—boot camp, then the South Dakota. '42—Tonga. Going through the Panama Canal, you could hear these miserable grinding sounds." He stopped and shook his head. "Well—temporarily defeated by a coral pinnacle, so back to Pearl Harbor."

He looked hard at Mom. "Letters from you—I liked them."

"You were my mission, Mikey."

"In '42 you were waiting for me."

"I should have known better."

"That you would love almost everything I do?"

Mom laughed again and lit a Pall Mall, and the kids came through the door.

Dad joined them for cake and ice cream and sang Happy Birthday, and just as he was leaving, he gave Micky a card and little white box. When she hugged him, he hugged her back; then was gone, cruising up the mountains to Golconda.

Micky set up the TV Ty gave her on top of her chest of drawers, then opened Dad's card. On the cover, a birthday cake and white streamers. Inside, he wrote:

Dear Micky—
Got it rong in your letter to me cuz I am a man that likes things in his one hands you throw me off when u came into my office, I not re ject u.
Happy Bithday Baby Love Dad

His card confused her. She opened the little box. The diamonds around the star sapphire caught light and shimmered. The ring fit the middle finger of her right hand perfectly.

When she showed it to Ty, he said: "Do you remember he gave this first to you when you were ten? I buried it with your journal, and when I dug it up, I gave it back to Dad to give back to you."

"What letter is Dad referring to?" She showed him Dad's birthday card.

"You don't remember writing Dad a letter, do you?"

"No."

"It's stashed up at the cabin. You want to see the cabin, don't you?"

"I do."

"Have you read your journal yet?"

"A little. I have some questions though, Ty."

"Sure."

"Do you know Wally?"

"No."

"How did I meet him?"

"Hitchhiking. Give me your journal, okay? Then I can look up the answers for you if I don't remember exactly."

Micky opened her closet door and took down the black spiral notebook.

"You still don't remember the day you were shot, right?"

"Not sure I want that memory. Do we need to love the hard-to-love, Ty?"

Ty shrugged. "Most people are at least a little hard to love."

OCTOBER 9, 1971 SATURDAY

Micky watched Rose slip into her white gown. "This was Momma's," she said. Carmen coiled Rose's long, dark hair on top of her head and pinned on her veil. They were in the bedroom Micky once slept in at Andre's house.

"Look, Rosie." Carmen stood Rose before the full-length mirror.

"I look like a bride." Rose kept staring at herself. "No. Who do I look like? Snow White?"

Rose and Carmen giggled like little kids, and Micky joined in. Rose grabbed Carmen's hands, and they spun around in front of the mirror, Rose's dress swirling white satin and lace.

"Oh!" Carmen said. "You need to put on the blue garter." She let go and opened a brown paper bag lying on the bed.

Rose slid the garter up her leg. "Can you believe it? This solotramp is getting married."

"I totally believe it," Micky said.

Gathered outside over fallen gold leaves, Golconda residents and Andre's family and friends and musicians waited for the wedding to begin in the woodland of autumn aspen and red scrub oak beneath Fire Peak, now a bit stripped of forest because of the new ski trail and lift. Rose's father wore a blue bolo tie with a turquoise setting. Jori stood next to him, a blue ribbon in her wild blond hair, a lacy blue dress. Her bandaged Michaela doll watched the ceremony from the tree limb where Jori placed her.

Andre and Rose repeated the wedding words of the Justice of the Peace: "To love and to cherish, until parted by death."

Jori held Andre's hand and beamed, and Rose knelt so she and Jori were face to face. "I will cherish you forever, Miss Jori King," she said, and fastened a locket around the smiling child's neck. Andre raised Jori in one arm and swept his other around Rose, and Rose flung her arms around both of them.

Standing in front of the recording studio with a view of the new corral and Partner and Jori's Michaela doll and all the guests, Micky raised her voice to read the lyrics of the song she was writing.

> Above anything scary
> beyond any barrier
> I love you beyond agony
> I love you beyond memory
>
>
> You are my story beyond chapter
> Beyond tears, touch, and laughter
> You are the breath for my soul
> We are the breath for our whole.

Fidelity to destiny
A journey to eternity
I love you to the end of time
I love you beyond the end of time

Love you love you love you till the end of time
Love you love you love you beyond the end of
time

Micky and Ty left the wedding reception to visit the cabin. They came to the log crossing the icy creek, and Micky stopped. The sound of the creek was so familiar. She stared at the water running over rocks below.

Ty bounded across, but Micky found it hard to put her foot onto the log. She stood looking across the creek to the yellow grasses and down to the wavy water. Ty bounded back. "You okay?"

"I don't know why I feel uneasy about crossing on the log, but I don't want to wade in these pretty shoes."

"Maybe because of your memory of falling out of the raft?"

"I fell out of a raft? When?"

"You were about six. Mom and Dad were getting divorced. Dad took us rafting. Fast, high water, nothing like how calm it is today. We hit a wave and tipped. Out you went, and Dad grabbed your foot and pulled you back in. You were way freaked out. Here. I'll walk you across."

Ty walked behind her with his hands on her shoulders, and she cautiously stepped along the log. Then they entered the meadow, yellow grass with patches of snow. The shooting target and all the cans were gone. Now a new pole spanned an electrical wire to the cabin's roof. A colorful red and blue sign hung above the cabin door: SALES OFFICE.

"Divide and populate." Ty laughed and told Micky that when the office was ready—electricity and the phone—he would be selling five-acre lots and premade cabins—dividing and populating the 200 new acres Dad owned. The afternoon sun shone on the white trunks of the aspen trees, and Ty opened the door for her. Old green velvet sofa, black and white striped mattress, painted scratched buffet. A folding table being used as desk and a two-drawer metal file cabinet. Flyswatter.

Micky lifted the rusty cast iron pot on the woodstove. "I'm sure I never lit this stove. I ate peanut butter sandwiches and fruit."

"You remember," Ty said.

"I read it in my diary." She put the heavy pot back on the woodstove.

Sitting down on the old bed, she bounced a little on the black and white mattress. "Sounds like Mr. Squeak," she said, surprising herself with a brief flash of being in bed with Chaz. Ty opened the top door of the scratched wooden buffet and took out a brown office envelope. "This is the last letter you wrote, Micky," he said. "To Dad."

Her heart leaped and snapped into beating faster, her hands trembling. She unclasped the envelope and pulled out the paper.

Her own handwriting on the page in blue ink.

A gigantic pang. All the longing to see missing Daddy stabbed her, the total of every moment burned and scraped every part of her: Every second of longing compressed into enormous weight.

Slam of disappointment. The man she thought was her Daddy turned into a mistaken identity, made-up Daddy.

"Mick, are you okay?"

"Micky?"

She pressed her forehead with her fingers, pushing feelings out of her mind. The feelings hurt so much, waves of hurt in her head. Her head felt giant.

Every moment she ever missed Daddy poured through her and ran her over flat.

Pelted by a swarm of unrelated memories:

o Walking behind Wally into a church, a jabbing in her heart, her mind empty.

o The baby kicks her rib. She holds very still wanting to feel the kick again.

o Shop window: a family in a garden. A mom and a dad and a boy and a girl, just like the Abels once upon a time.

o Chaz touches her cheek. He says, "Mick, I love you."

o A preacher waves his arms and pounds his fist on the altar. He points at Micky. She comes out of the choir to sing solo.

o "In the sweet by and by / We shall meet on that beautiful shore." The sound of the choir behind her.

o The hymn "In the sweet by and by" so horrible the queen had the composer hanged.

Real memories? flashes of dreams?

Submerged, her whole life rushed by in unconnected gushes.

"I had a life," she said.

Flash: A girl with black hair standing on her horse's back riding around the perimeter of the ring. Rosie. Rodeo.

Flash: Micky falls branch by branch from a cherry tree behind the church, a gash in her knee, blood pouring down her leg.

Flash: A wild gray kitty in the sumac nurses three brand new kittens, the purr so loud it sounds like Daddy's snore.

Flash: Rocking in the wide, grey rocking chair with Tina, holding a bowl of popcorn; two cowboys get shot on TV.

Tina—where? Tina.

A record turning on Mom's record player, the needle playing nothing, click click click.

Flash. Icy water covers her head. She chokes, coughs.

An inundation of images:

Roller skating with Tina past blooming white roses and orange poppies.

Baby doll with curled eyelashes and two teeth.

Drawing in chalk four-square on the driveway.

Tina laughing and laughing.

Getting under desks at school, waiting for the atom bomb to drop.

Canasta with Chaz and Floss and Wally.

Lester points a gun at her.

A bottle of whiskey on the table beside the bed, Wally's hand on her leg.

Her sapphire ring. Dancer in jewelry box.

Mom frowns, looks like a bulldog, turns away.

Holding Chaz all night in Mr. Squeak.

Flood waters pounding against the house.

Deluge of memories.

She kept putting her hands over her scar, protecting her heart. " "Maybe I did try to kill myself." She didn't cry. Ty sat beside her on the bed, laying his hand against her back. She took the longest, most shuddering breath.

"I remember going to see Daddy at the real estate office. After all those years, I got to see Daddy. And he didn't love me. I was anyone on the street."

"Ditto," Ty said. "I 100% identify with you."

"Pain is a root: always there," she said.

"I'm sure that's true."

She reread her words in the letter. As she folded the letter back up, her star sapphire on her right hand caught her eye.

Daddy wrote a message to her on her birthday card. He said he didn't mean to make her feel rejected. Now Daddy was Dad. She liked Dad fine. She took another long breath and got her voice. "It's okay, Ty. I'm okay. You love me."

She put the letter back in the envelope, and Ty put it back into the buffet. "Dad said it was a suicide note. But I think you were brave to tell him exactly what you thought."

Called toward the sunlight and the wooden porch where she wrote most of her un-good journal, she got off the bed, and Ty followed her outside. The blue spruce stood like a stately guard with nicks in its trunk.

"You used to throw your knife at this tree, Ty."

"Yeah, right here." Ty touched the spot he used to aim for, and she visualized how Ty would grip the knife between his fingers and fling it time after time, aiming for the same spot and usually hitting right on—thunk. He would let her pull out the knife to give back to him, but never let her try throwing. The handle was made of stacked leather and a deer antler, looked like ivory.

"Do you still have the knife?"

"No. Baggage claim at the airport in Berlin, bag never showed."

"Your knife is still somewhere in the world. Somehow it will come back to you."

"You optimist. Sure, it'll turn up—with a lot of magic."

"You were magic with carving, Ty, right? Where is that stump you carved the scary, hunched-up crow on? You did that, right? Right? How neat to be able to remember it!"

"Hmm. Wonder where that piece of art is," Ty said, looking around.

Leaning against the spruce, Micky found herself pummeled by more memories.

Running out of Daddy's office feeling two inches tall and shrinking. Driving the Falcon back to the cabin to pack up her stuff. No knowing where to go, what to do. Empty, emptied.

Everything she believed and everything she hoped—just a puff of air. She wished she could turn into a falcon and fly away.

She sat on the cabin's porch with her notebook and pen.

Chickadees whistled to each other and hopped from branch to branch; a peregrine falcon soared across the sky, and she imagined it coming down, swooping her up and taking her away.

Two choices: Run again godknowswhere—or stay in Golconda and work for Rose and face Daddy any time their paths crossed. Where could she go? The exact same situation as the moment she left Wally, before it dawned on her to go to the cabin, she thought.

She could camp in her car until she could afford a place. Never mind Daddy. Despite facing his judgment on the streets or in the café.

She closed her eyes, concentrating every fiber of her being on remembering. It felt like her head was swelling. No body. A giant head filling and swirling.

The gun on the table inside the door.
Exploding with happiness. Going to see Daddy.
Loading it, reloading it.
Setting up the cans to shoot down.
Daddy will be impressed.

The taste of the orange juice. The clouds above the mountain like an orange flame. Daddy is a stranger.

How to survive? Must leave the cabin, but where?

Her knee throbs. Why did God let her be so hurt all the time? Is Daddy right? She is no more than a tramp? Paying for her sins? How do other evil people get away with so much?

Why must everyone she loves leave?

She takes her letter to Daddy and folds it into thirds. She anchors on the porch by the door with a piece of quartz on top so it can't blow away. She pulls the sapphire ring from her finger and sets it on top of the quartz rock. "Enjoy your ring, Mr. Abel."

Then she wraps her food up in a blanket and takes the hard climb with a bum knee up the trail on Fire Peak to figure things out. A slow hike up to the bristlecone where the trail ends. She sets up camp, figuring she needs to be closer to God. If there is a God, where else would He show up but in that beautiful, awe-inspiring spot?

She'd left her notebook behind. Now she has nothing to write in. If her knee wasn't hurting so much after the climb, she could run down and get it. She thinks: Oh well, if Daddy finds it and reads it before I get back, then maybe he'll know I am a real, live girl with a mind and a heart and a soul. And maybe he will love me again. Maybe he'll even give me back the ring.

Simple camp. Past the end of the trail at the top of the mountain in the flat clearing on top, she brushes dirt and leaves together with her hands until she make a soft spot. Although she misses her notebook, she is used to being a solotramp. That means she can be completely alone.

Something so cool about being far from anyone at the top of your favorite mountain.

Blasting out your voice. Singing every song you know. On the north side of Fire Peak, when you're bellowing toward a slew of mountains, your voice echoes like your soul talking back.

So many mountain songs to sing. "Comin' 'Round the Mountain" put her in a better mood. She got silly with new lyrics: not only driving six white horses but wearing blue pajamas and riding in a Falcon and eating all the fudge up.

She snaps her fingers through "Ain't No Mountain High Enough" wishing she could get up and dance with Tina the way they used to do. She sings "Climb Every Mountain" from the Sound of Music at least a dozen times on the north side, loving to hear the echo. "Go Tell It on the Mountain" makes her think of singing with Tina. She tells herself: "Every mountain, Micky." Her voice burgeons, echoes back.

She feels her soul like an invisible core.

God speaks to her through music. Tune, harmony, rhythm, beat, the mountain echo.

She eats all the oranges, and when it gets dark, she stares into the stars and thanks God for the beautiful spot where she lies under her blanket with a shirt rolled into a pillow.

Memory stopped. Mind vacant. She strained with her mind. "Ty, I don't remember anything after camping up there."

"Let's go up." Ty couldn't find the artistic stump, so he closed up the cabin, and they hiked up the mountainside. There it was—the only leftover from their old trail—the twisty bristlecone standing in a boulder field, its top branches looking like bare pointy sticks, its green bottom limbs carrying latticed cones with prickles.

Micky traced the sharp angles of the letters carved into the small trunk. M I A. "Amazing you cut so delicately with your big hands."

"I am an artist with a knife," Ty said.

At her feet: the freshly shoveled outline of Ty's burial spot for her notebook and ring.

"Where did Andre find me?"

"The boulder isn't here now, but it was right over there." Ty pointed.

She dropped the icky journal of un-good memories into the hole and brushed dirt over it with her hands and then stamped on the spot.

She spied a red pipe coming out of a wood-shingled roof below. "What's that?"

"Dad's cabin," Ty said.

"You're kidding. I thought it was further away."

"Nope, that's it."

"Amazing how everything changes from a different perspective," she said. "I thought the trail took us far away from the cabin—so many turns we created up and around the mountain. But it's not that far."

"As the crow flies," Ty said.

They hiked to the top, to the flat place where she had camped that night, and Ty said, "And now the major question. Did you carry the gun up?"

She sat down in her camp and closed her eyes. Nothing happened. "I don't know. Black hole in my brain when it comes to that. I only remember it on the table in the cabin."

"Hearing a gunshot might bring the memory back."

She nodded—but not sure she wanted to remember how she got shot.

Did she take the gun with the intention of killing herself? Did someone (maybe Wally but not Nathan?) stop by the cabin and grab the gun and follow her up? Some extremely unlikely complete stranger? She wanted to know, yet not. She did not like the idea of a shooter on the mountain. The letter was written by a totally sad girl, she thought. Would she have tried to kill herself?

A massive load of disappointment tumbled over her.

She didn't fight it this time but let herself be smacked by a ton of bad, dark feelings. Heavy, dark, beyond sad.

Amazingly, in moments, the ton began to disperse, and she remembered eating oranges in her camp and closing her eyes to the kaleidoscope of sparkling stars, pulling her blanket up to her cheek.

Ty touched her shoulder, and disappointment vanished, weight dissolved.

"Who you love goes away but returns," she said, putting her hand over his. "Sometimes what you think is good is bad, and what you think is bad is good."

"Paradox," Ty said.

"Paradox," she repeated.

Ty and Micky's shadows grew long and distorted over their pathway down Fire Peak. Faint music from the reception flowed across the creek. On the hillside, tents were set up for everyone from out of town to camp, no matter the October chill, predicted to be 34 tonight.

The last rays of sun disappeared behind the mountains. Darker second by second. The sound of the music guided them to the creek.

Micky felt the rhythm of her life's own beat. She danced across the log with the chorus of the creek and sweet guitars—melody flowing through the trees, bass humming, drumbeat thumping. Solo but not alone. Empty of worry, filled with joy.

OCTOBER 10, 1971

Mick Abel
10/10/71

Last night at the wedding, I sang with the band, and Kev did a thumb's up that went right into my forehead! Right where Wally always poked!

My memory of my last camping trip exploded in my mind.

I did take Andre's gun up the trail with me. I left a note so he could find me.

I'd been asleep for awhile under that starry sky when I woke up to Wally shining a flashlight into my face.

"It's time to come home, Michaela."

My first thought was, Wow, am I dreaming this? A bizarre extension of my non-good memories?

I sat up. "No."

"Yes." He stood up still aiming the flashlight at my face and held his hand down to help me up.

"How did you find me here?"

"You know I always know where you are. Come on. Time to come home."

I stood. My knee twinged. On higher ground, I looked him straight in the eye before he aimed the light at my face again. I closed my eyes and pictured where I'd placed Andre's gun on the nearby boulder. I edged in that direction.

"You know you belong at home. God wants you to be a good wife."

"No. I don't have to experience travail with you." I kept edging toward the boulder.

"You need to do as your husband says."

"I would purposely make your life utterly unhappy, and I don't want that on my life record."

I grabbed Andre's gun, cocked it, and started limping down the trail just as the sun started to glimmer in the distance. He lunged after me. I pointed it at my head and said: "I will kill me rather than go back with you and ruin your life, Wally. You can hit me and hit me and hit me, but I'll do the killing for you. I will save your life by ending mine."

The mischief Ty and I did on Barf would be extremely minor compared to what Wally would encounter if he forced me to stay. At my little campground that night, my bad side of my brain filled with ideas of tortuous tricks.

Maybe I shot me. Maybe he shot me. Maybe it was an accident with a struggle over the gun. I don't recall hearing the shot. At least he didn't take me home with him, and at least I didn't shoot myself in the head.

It will be okay. Everything will be okay.

THE END

ABOUT THE AUTHOR

A Colorado native who has lived in six other states, Eleanor Addy Binning's MFA is from the American University, and she teaches college composition and research for MSUDenver. Latest hobby: making high-protein crackers from flax, seeds, and mushrooms. She likes to create beats behind her poems, and she loves photographing flowers and sunsets. Her creative bucket list is long and detailed. Her illustrated book of toxic love poems is titled DRAMA.

ACKNOWLEDGEMENTS

Greatest thanks to everyone who has read, commented on, and put up with me over the long process of writing SOLOTRAMP. I love and appreciate you so much!